Broken Chords

Rachel Lynne

Seven Oaks Press

Forgiveness is the fragrance that the violet sheds on the heel that has crushed it.

-Mark Twain

Contents

No Wake Zone

Prologue

INSTRUMENT CASES AND AMPLIFIERS stacked to the ceiling divided the room into narrow aisles. A single bulb in the hallway barely penetrated the gloom, casting the space into pockets of light and shadow.

Outside, the wind whistled and howled, and rain battered the hull, muting all sound. At the beginning of one aisle, a drum kit was partially unpacked. Cymbals and drumsticks sat next to a keyboard stand; the snare and kickdrum were still encased in their canvas shrouds. Two guitar stands and a foot pedal board sat nearby.

Farther into the room lay a body, sprawled amidst colorful bits of wood, lengths of wire, and steel strings. A pool of blood was forming under his head, creeping across the floor as the ship pitched and rolled with the storm. A torn piece of paper was clutched in his hand.

A shout disturbed the silence, followed by the slam of a metal door.

Between the Devil and the Deep Blue Sea

Tina

FOUR MORE STEPS. THAT'S all it'd take to get me through the door. I took two of them and then chickened out and reversed course for the third time. I gave myself a mental shake and an order to suck it up, Buttercup: I had to go in, no choice.

I snorted. Well, no real choice. If I didn't reconcile with my father then my best friend and nominal boss, Ivy Michaels, would not let me buy into her café, and to be a full partner in the Cosmic Café I'd meet the devil himself; an aging rock legend should be a piece of cake in that competition.

It'd been over ten years since I'd willingly been in the same room with my dad. I hadn't been able to avoid him at my mother's funeral, but even then, our conversation had been minimal. After that, the only way I'd seen him was on the cover of tabloids.

I'd been happy to see he'd gotten sober, but that change wasn't enough to lure me back into a relationship and I was fine with that; despite the opinions of Ivy and the shrink she'd made me visit.

I huffed. What neither of them seemed to understand was that my father's sobriety or lack thereof was not the main reason I'd cut ties with him. My avoidance of my dad centered around the company he kept; specifically, the predator known as Richard Warner.

My stomach heaved at the thought of the man. Up until now, I hadn't thought-The invitation had been last minute, and Ivy had pushed me to accept it before I could talk myself out of it.

Last minute shopping, packing, and getting coverage for my shifts at the Cosmic Café ... only now, with the ship making its way out of the harbor, was it hitting me that Warner was probably on the cruise; all my life, where ever my dad went, Warner was never far behind. Why would this be any different?

I swallowed hard and backed away from the lounge doors. How would I avoid him? My hands began to shake ... I couldn't do this!

I paced the hallway and contemplated alternatives, but I knew there weren't any, not really. If I didn't buy into the café, Ivy would have to find another investor because the loan she'd gotten from her godfather had been called in. I cursed James Brogan and his legal troubles for starting all of this!

Of course, ranting at fate wasn't going to help. What I needed was Dutch courage, just a shot or two of bourbon-heck, I'd settle for a glass of Pinot to calm my nerves, but my drinking was what had gotten me into the current mess ... I rolled my eyes, just thinking about Ivy and the whole Christmas disaster.

I mean, so we'd been suspected of murdering the neighbor. We'd solved the case, and everything was fine. I didn't know why Ivy was in such a snit almost three months later-

"Ma'am, this is a restricted area at this time, can I help you?"

I jumped and spun around to find a giant of a guy frowning at me. He wasn't dressed in the ship's officer uniform; those white shirts and shorts combo cracked me up, but even in his sport coat and chinos I could tell he was official, he had law enforcement written all over him. I gulped and pinned a smile to my face. "Uh, hey how ya doin?"

He smiled, but it didn't reach his eyes. "Ma'am. This area requires a pass."

Crap, I'll bet he was talking about the lanyard that was sent with the cruise tickets ... I dug in my bag, but I was pretty sure it was sitting on the dresser in my cabin. Double crap ... I met his eyes and tried to look cute.

My gaze skittered away because he wasn't buying it. I noticed his name tag, Tyson Penshaw, Chief of Security. I shook my head. Just my luck to run into Dudley Do-right.

"Uh, it's uh, I didn't realize that I needed, and it didn't go with this dress so-"

"Ma'am," he placed his hand at my elbow and started to nudge me towards the atrium. "You'll need a pass -"

"Kristina?" Chief Dudley and I both turned to see a tall woman with short, spiky orange hair striding toward us. She held a clipboard and was dressed in leather pants and a white t-shirt; gotta be with my dad's band, though I couldn't place her.

"It is Kristina Crawford, right?" She smiled and offered her hand. "I'm Nikki Hardy, Assistant Road Manager for Eclipse." She pointed at my dress. "Love the outfit!"

Oooh, I didn't know her, but she'd admired my lime green mini dress and vintage white go-go boots and seemed intent on rescuing me ... I'd take it.

"Thanks, Chief, I'll take it from here."

Dudley dropped my elbow but didn't back off. "She doesn't have a pass, all entry to band areas are restricted to pass holders-"

"I know, I set up that policy." She smiled but it was one of those firm, no-nonsense, back-off kinda smiles; I was really liking her now.

The security chief scowled. "If you compromise once-"

"Normally, I'd agree with you, Mr. Penshaw, but you know Chad Crawford, lead singer for the rock band Eclipse? The band you're trying to protect?"

The security chief nodded.

"Well, this is his daughter, whom he hasn't seen in ages and is anxiously awaiting the arrival of so if you don't mind, we'll just make an exception this once," it was her turn to guide me by the elbow, "have a great day, Chief, come along Ms. Crawford, we'll get you another lanyard."

Giving a little wave to the chief, I matched my steps to Nikki Hardy's and then slowed as I realized she was leading me through the Alchemy Lounge doors I'd been trying to avoid when this whole mess started- crap, out of the frying pan and all that ...

"Uh, so ..." I stopped on the threshold of the door she was holding open. "Uh, so how long have you been with Eclipse? It's pretty cool, you being the road man-"

"Go on, Kristina, he won't bite."

Okay, she'd seen right through me, maybe I needed to revise that liking her thing.

I fidgeted with the hem of my dress then realized I was probably flashing someone and smoothed the fabric back in place, not that it covered much more than the tops of my thighs; oh fudge, why had I worn it? I stood out like a sore-

"Hey, take a deep breath."

I blinked and met her gaze. Her eyes were a vivid aquamarine, probably colored contacts, and they were radiating warmth and concern which was nice but also a bit weird; it was like she knew me. "Have we met before?"

I bit my lip. That had come out a bit more blunt and sharp than I'd intended, even for me.

She smiled and shook her head. "No, but your dad and I are friends" she shrugged. "He talks about you a lot." She took my hand and gave it a slight squeeze. "Just relax, no pressure, breath in, that's it, now let it out, all the negative energy is flowing out with that breath, you are lighter ..."

Her voice was soft, really gentle like a warm breeze. I kept eye contact with her and found myself doing just what she said. In and then out ... "Wow, how did you do that?" I shook my head and smiled. "I feel ... well ..." I shrugged.

"Lighter?" Nikki laughed and gave my hand a final squeeze. "It's nothing, just a bit of relaxation technique. In my line of work that skill comes in handy."

I frowned and then it clicked. "Oh, you mean stage fright?" I snorted when she nodded. "Chad Crawford has never been afraid of the spotlight in his life! He owns whatever stage he's on."

Nikki laughed. "Oh yes, no argument there." She tipped her head towards the front of the lounge where a group of men were talking; my dad included. "Chad doesn't have stage fright, but we all have our moments, and Cliff is a bit neurotic."

I laughed because the bass player for Eclipse was just what she'd said, my mom had always said he was high strung. I grinned at Nikki and let her nudge me into resuming the trek toward my dad. "I won't tell him you said that."

She grinned. "He wouldn't deny it!" She kept me chatting until we were within earshot of my dad. "Chad? Look who's here!"

My heart kinda rose in my throat as my dad turned and rushed toward us.

"Kristina Carol! You came-"

His arms were wide, and I cringed, knowing he was gonna hug me. I'd missed him, I could admit that, but I wasn't quite ready for warm and fuzzy. I stepped back and nodded. "Uh, I go by Tina now, Chad."

The smile dropped from his face. "Uh, of course, I shoulda known." He glanced at Nikki then lowered his arms, shoving his hands into the front pockets of his ridiculously tight jeans.

"How could you?"

He sighed and looked at the far wall. His jaw was set, and a nerve ticked in his cheek. I could all but hear his teeth grinding. I was regretting my tone, it'd upset him and now we stood in awkward silence; oh yeah, this was gonna be the cruise from hell, and worse, I had to do it sober.

Nikki cleared her throat. "So, is this your first cruise?"

I took back the not liking her thing. "Uh, it's my first rock and roll themed cruise but my best friend, Ivy, and I did four days to the Bahamas."

Nikki's eyes widened. "Nice, the Bahamas are awesome, aren't they Chad?" He grunted something as Nikki plowed on, bless her heart. "The Firestorm Tour did two nights there last year."

I nodded but the chit chat went in one ear and out the other. I was busy watching my dad. He kept glancing at Nikki, and she'd give him this little head nod, kind of encouraging him or something; it was weird and familiar in a motherly ..., no! It made me think of a long-married couple kind of thing; Nikki knew my dad far better than in a road manager way.

Huh, wasn't sure how I felt about that. Nikki Hardy was probably ten years older than me? Maybe a little more. If I had to guess, she was forty, forty-one ish.

I did some mental math. Not cradle robbing exactly and he certainly didn't look his age. I snorted. Chad Crawford wasn't gonna disappoint his legion of female fans any time soon. He still had the long hair, golden brown to match his perpetual tan, barely any lines around his mossy green eyes, and his penchant for painted on faded blue jeans and form-fitting t-shirts proved his devotion to clean living ... hey, that was probably a safe topic.

I waited until Nikki ran out of breath. "So, Chad," he flinched, and I guessed it was because I was using his first name. I felt bad about that too, but I was only able to take one step at a time; meeting at all was the first one. "You're looking good, keepin' the groupies happy."

Nikki laughed and my dad's lips twitched for a minute before he joined in. "Smart mouth. It's dedication to exercise and clean living."

I nodded. "So, it wasn't just a passing fad ..." His sobriety was just as notorious as his addictions; the car wreck that had killed Kev Lerner, Eclipse's drummer, had sent shock waves through the music scene. A tragedy all around, but the fact that Chad had been driving fueled the media frenzy to unbearable heights.

I had already cut ties with him by that point, but it was impossible not to hear about it on every TV station and magazine cover. The speculation had been that he'd be charged with vehicular manslaughter, but surprisingly, my dad had been legally sober at the time and the wreck was blamed on weather conditions; it'd been snowing heavily, an infrequent event even in the Georgia mountains.

His eyes clouded a bit, but he gave a half-hearted smile. "Nope, going on ten years clean, made it past fifty."

I snorted. "Uh, past fifty-four old man, you'll hit the big five-five this year."

He mock-shuddered. "Why ya gotta remind me, kid"

I smirked. "You fishin' for compliments?"

He snorted and shook his head. "Nah, jokes about age are just that; doesn't bother me to hit another birthday." He raised his eyebrows and cocked his head to the side. "Better than the alternative, don't ya think?"

What I thought was gonna remain a mystery because a commotion at the back of the room drew our attention. "Ah, what now?" Chad made a disgusted sound and threw up his hands and Nikki started cursing under her breath.

I followed their gazes and gasped as my nightmare came true; Richard Warner was on the ship. My fingers curled into fists as a rock formed in my gut. Could this cruise get any worse?

Warner was drunk, high, or both. He ambled across the stage, getting in the way of the techs and roadies trying to set up. I searched for an excuse to leave and prayed he'd stay on the other side of the room.

"Nikki, I thought you'd-"

"I tried, Chad! I personally escorted him to his cabin, but he wasn't happy about being on the lower deck."

Nikki rolled her eyes and began telling my dad how Warner had pitched a fit after finding out he wasn't staying on the private floors like the band members.

My father snorted. "What more does he want? It's a free vacation for him and it isn't like anyone expects him to actually work!" He snarled. "I still don't understand why Rob included him."

My eyes widened. Never before had my dad taken that tone or even uttered an impatient word about Warner; maybe there was trouble in paradise? One could hope-

"You idiot! I'm gonna break your neck if -"

A crash on the stage, followed by curses and threats drew my gaze back towards the stage in time to see a guy about my age with his hands around Warner's throat.

Two roadies and Benny T, the new drummer for Eclipse were righting the equipment that Richard had knocked over but, in a testament to Warner's popularity or lack thereof, no one seemed in any hurry to pull the angry guy off of Warner.

Nikki huffed. “I better break that up. That kid has murder in his eyes.”

My dad snorted. “If the fool had knocked over my bass, I’d look like that too!”

Nikki laughed and was about to walk over when one of the roadies stepped in and shoved Warner down the stage steps.

Nikki and my dad sighed in relief but my heart started pounding because Warner now had my dad in his sights. He was stumbling his way across the room, all the while griping to my dad.

I caught a few slurred complaints about his room but most of what he was ramblin’ about was unclear and I didn’t care. I just wanted far away from him.

I started to back away, no matter what Ivy or the shrink she’d made me talk to had to say, I was not dealing with my father and the walking waste of oxygen he called a personal assistant.

Chad turned and gave me an anxious look. “You’re not leaving? We’re almost done setting up. I thought we could have dinner before the meet and greet-”

“Well, lookee here! It’s my baby girl ...”

My mouth went dry as the drunken fool closed in on me. I spun around and rushed to the exit, ignoring my dad's calls to wait. My hands connected with the door lever.

Feeling like the hounds of hell were nipping my heels, I rushed through the door and straight into a wall of warm muscle.

"Ooomph,"

"Whoa, where's the fire?"

I tried to stop, but momentum was not my friend and my sudden reverse didn't suit my high-heeled boots. My ankle twisted as one boot lost its heel.

My savior clasped my upper arms, steadying me as I leaned over, unzipping my vintage treasures. "Crap, they're ruined!" I slid them off and looked up. The thanks died on my lips. "Ian?"

"Tina?"

I closed my eyes and gulped. Really, what gods had I ticked off? Not only did I get close quarters with my estranged father, but the universe had seen fit to put my biggest fear and loathing in the form of Ricky Warner into the mix and now, now I got to run into my ex, who I had never wanted to be an ex, lover.

I forced a smile I was far from feeling. "Ian, um, what a surprise!"

A lopsided grin stretched across his handsome face. "Surprise is an understatement." He shook his head, "What are the odds?"

I snorted. The way my luck was running, I wouldn't even hazard a guess. Wishing the deck would split apart and devour me, I tried for casual and uninterested. "So, yeah, incredible, running into you, literally!"

He smiled, flashing the dimple that I adored. "How long has it been? A year, year and a half?"

Two years, four months, six days, and a handful of hours ... but who was counting?

My hands started to shake. I couldn't do this. The shock of the slime ball Warner and now Ian ... I forced words past the lump that was starting to clog my throat. "Uh yeah ... look, it was nice seeing you again, but I've got to-"

"Ian, are you not going to introduce me?

My gaze flew to the short brunette with bright red stiletto nails clinging to Ian's arm like a limpet. My eyebrows rose. Oh yes? Did I also get an ex-lover's girlfriend? Why yes, it appeared that I was to have that privilege. How did that saying about karma go?

"Uh ...Tina this is, uh ..."

The woman huffed and nudged Ian aside as she thrust her hand towards me. "I'm Doctor Judith Fogarty, Ian's fiancée, and you are?"

Her words slammed into me like a sledgehammer. My stomach rolled and my heart started pounding again; I didn't need this! My face felt hot, and I fidgeted under the woman's stare. "Uh, I'm uh ..." I forced my brain to function even though most of it was in shock. "Tina, um Tina Crawford."

I glanced at Ian. He was staring at his fiancée. I frowned; Ian's mouth was hanging open as if he was shocked, and he was glaring at her. I heard him say something to her then he turned to me and flashed a tense smile. "Uh, we aren't, there's been no discussion about getting married."

The doctor huffed and glared at Ian. I shook my head, whatever was going on with Ian and his whatever she was, it was no concern of mine. That ship had sailed regardless of my heart's continued ache... I bit my lip and tried to force down the tears that were threatening to fall.

Too many emotions, too many old memories, and too many tangled cords of broken relationships were tugging at me and all I wanted to do was escape; To curl into a fetal position, preferably with a bottle of bourbon, and block out the whole terrible, no good, very bad day.

I stammered congratulations and turned, rushing toward a flight of steps that led somewhere; didn't matter, anywhere was better than where I was.

"Tina!"

Ian's hand closed around my arm. I paused on the second step and closed my eyes, begging for some kind of divine assistance because if I didn't get out of there I was going to lose complete control of my emotions. I tugged and Ian released my arm. I half turned but avoided his eyes. "I've got to go, Ian but it uh, it was nice seeing you." I set my bare foot on the next step. "Enjoy your cruise!"

He huffed. "Wait, please!"

The please got me. I turned and met his eyes for an instant before lowering my gaze to study the multicolored swirls on the carpet.

"Thanks, I won't keep you." He nodded back towards the lounge. "I gotta get in there, my band is playing this cruise, but maybe we could get together later? Drinks? Or Dinner?"

Small favors. A gig meant he'd be busy for a good portion of the nine days at sea. I glanced at him. "Uh, we'll see. I'm here with my dad and we haven't seen each other in about ten years so ..."

Ian's eyebrows rose. "Wow, I uh, you never mentioned your father when we were ... I mean," he shrugged. "Guess I thought he was dead. But that's great you two are getting together, bring him to a show, I'd love to meet him."

I smiled and started back up the steps. "We'll see. He's actually working on this cruise too, so our time together will be limited." I pointed towards the Alchemy Lounge and told a little white lie. "Think we're getting an early dinner before he has to be back in there ..."

Ian frowned. "Your dad works for the cruise line? Or is he with one of the bands? What's his name, maybe I know him!"

"My dad is Chad Crawford. I'll see ya around, Ian." I raced up the steps, ignoring his shocked questions.

I fell into the first empty deck chair I found and leaned over with my head between my knees. I wasn't hyper-ventilating, but it was a near miss.

God! Why had I told Ian who my dad was? It came out before I had really thought about it because all I could concentrate on was Ian had a fiancée and Richard Warner was on-board, and how the hell was I going to make it through the next week without a drink?

But Ian was like a dog with a bone, and he would surely worry me to death until I explained how we'd dated for over a year and I had failed to mention my connection to one of his all-time favorite bands.

This was ridiculous; I needed a drink! Ivy and that shrink were unreasonable, no one could be expected to absorb the kind of emotional body blows I'd suffered in the last couple of hours without support.

I was weak, I freely admitted it, but one drink wouldn't hurt, and Ivy would never know.

I scooped up my ruined boots and made a beeline for the Tiki bar.

Wide Berth

Ian

TINA DISAPPEARED UP THE stairs, leaving me with my mouth hanging open. Chad Crawford! How? I shook my head. We'd dated for two years, and she'd never said- I snorted.

Why was I shocked that she'd kept something so big to herself? The whole time we were together I only met one of her friends and that was by accident.

We were never a normal, just hanging out in pajamas on a Sunday afternoon kind of couple. Time spent with her was always an event.

She'd plan moonlight picnics on the Tybee Pier, "kidnap" me for long drives in her convertible or wake me up far too early to catch the sunrise over the marsh ... Tina never let me share her life, just postcard moments in it.

If there was more than a party girl to her personality I had never been allowed to see it and, in the end, that was the reason I'd broken up with her.

I gritted my teeth and my hand curled into a fist as the old frustrations rose; I didn't need this, my life was on a different path, not that I was completely happy with parts of the pavement.

I shook off the emotions of the past and turned to go back to the lounge for my first meeting with my idols, and my gaze landed on Judith.

Man, for a broad so smart, she was making stupid decisions, with sticking around after saying that crock of crap to Tina being a huge one.

The feelings Tina had stirred up carried over and I admit I took my frustration out on Judith, not that the whole situation with her wasn't already pushing my buttons. "Fiancé? How dare you?"

Judith had the grace to blush but that didn't ease my temper. "We were never that serious and whatever we were ended two months ago!" I shook my head, knowing my dad was at least partly behind Judith taking the cruise.

"Ian, I was trying to assist you in fending off that-"

"What the ...?" I frowned. "Assist me with what?" I shook my head and started towards the lounge entrance.

"If you would let me explain-"

"I don't have time, Judith, I have a meeting."

I heard her footsteps behind me, but I didn't slow my pace.

"Ian, please. I realize that my comments could be presumptuous-"

"Presumptuous?" I spun around and glared at her. "It's a lie!" I resumed walking.

"I was only trying to help you disentangle from that, that groupie!"

That stopped me in my tracks. For one thing, I didn't think Judith Fogarty knew the word groupie, for another, she was referring to Tina Crawford and I couldn't let that go.

"Judith, I don't need your help with anything, and Tina Crawford is in no way, shape, or form a groupie, she is an old and dear friend. Now, I have to get in there so please, just stop."

Her lips pinched into a tight line. "Very well, shall we meet for dinner?"

I rolled my eyes. "Judith ...," I was rarely at a loss for words but this time, with this woman ... there was no easy way to say the truth she refused to see. "I am on this cruise to work and to be blunt, I didn't invite you to accompany me-"

I held my hand up as she started to interrupt. "Look, I can guess who is responsible for you tagging along, and I promise he'll be getting a phone call the first chance I get, but you ..." I sighed. "We are not a couple, you get that, right?"

Her lips were pursed, and her expression reminded me of an angry four-year-old; kind of pouty and pissed.

"Judith?" She finally raised her eyes to meet mine. "Are we clear?"

A reluctant nod was all I was going to get. "Good. Now if you'll excuse me?" I pulled the door open and started through when her voice rang out.

"Ian, might we at least meet for dinner and discuss this?"

I snorted and shook my head. Had to hand it to her, the woman did not give up easily. "Your time would be better spent seeing if they have a cabin for you."

I ignored her huff and headed across the floor to join my bandmates. I had no doubt my phone would blow up with messages from my dad very soon, but right now I was going to meet Chad Crawford, Drew Alton, and Cliff Harris original members of Eclipse.

I could guess what Judith wanted to talk about and why my dad had encouraged her to show up as my "plus one"; he'd hoped she could convince me to accept the teaching job he'd lined up at the college.

My fractured and recently stitched-up relationship with my dad was going to suffer both from my rejecting Judith but also my reluctance to accept the job, but it couldn't be helped.

A massive heart attack had sent me rushing home from California. My fears over losing my dad had caused me to rashly accept his idea that I return to my classical music roots. I'd tried to embrace the new career. I'd tried to keep the peace, even dated Judith at his suggestion. But, in the end, rock and roll ran in my veins and when the offer to open for Eclipse had come, I'd dropped everything and made it happen.

That my band had even been considered was due to my old friend and former bandmate, Benny T being the current drummer for Eclipse. My dad had been disappointed but surprisingly accepting of my decision to take the gig; I should have known he had something up his sleeve.

I sighed and slowed my pace, observing the activity on the stage while I tried to get my focus back on what was important. I couldn't allow Judith's presence or my dad's machinations distract me, the stakes were too high.

Loud voices drew my attention. Jason Young, my bass player, and Cole Edwards, a killer drummer we'd found to replace Benny T, were in a heated discussion with an older guy that was screaming in Jason's face.

Tall and thin, with dirty blond hair that hung around his sallow and pockmarked face in greasy strands, whoever the guy was, it was obvious, by his inability to stand without swaying and his slurred words, that he'd hit the bar early and well.

Jason took a step forward and Cole grabbed his arm, trying to get them both to calm down. Another shout with waved arms added to the mix was my cue to get involved. I blew out a breath and climbed the stairs to the stage.

Jason was one of my oldest friends, we'd met at a Savannah area music store and become friends over a love of guitars and rock music, We had truly bonded over the realization that both of us would rather have been anywhere but home.

Jason, because his mom was an addict, and me because my dad was overbearing and controlling, and my mom chose to clean out closets rather than confront him. That cleaning out closets was her way of hiding her drinking was a subject no one in our house raised.

For all of my issues with family, at least I had them. Jason's mom was never sober long enough to be a parent and Jason had never known his father; his mom wouldn't even tell Jason his name. Jason's life had been much harder than mine and it showed in a lot of ways but, his inability to control his temper had affected me most. More than once I'd entered a fight because he couldn't keep from running his mouth and, judging by what I was seeing on stage, history was about to repeat itself.

"Hey, guys, what's going on?" I smiled and patted Jason on the back as I wracked my brain for something to say that would diffuse the situation.

Jason shrugged my hand off and pulled the toothpick he was always sucking on from his mouth to use as a pointer. "Ian! This idiot busted my bass-"

"You lyin' sack of crap! Your lousy gear was already-"

A clash of symbols rang out, followed by a shout. "Break it up!"

All eyes swung towards the drum kit. A tall, red-haired lady stood with a drumstick in her hand and a scowl on her face. She raised her arm and pointed to the exit.

"Warner, you've been warned already; get out. Bad Opera, off the stage." She looked at her watch. "Meeting with Eclipse in-"

"Who are you to tell me...?" The old guy stumbled over to the drum kit; his lips set in a nasty sneer. "I ain't listen' to some groupie wh-"

"That's enough!"

My eyes widened as Chad Crawford, lead singer for Eclipse and apparently, my ex-girlfriend's father, stepped out from the wings. He nodded at the redhead.

"I got this, Nikki." He turned to the belligerent drunk. "Richard, why are you here?"

"Schad! Buddy, I'm lookin' out for-"

"You have no responsibilities on this tour. Go enjoy your vacation-"

"But Schad, you need me to-"

"Nikki is doing a great job as our tour manager." Chad grabbed Warner's arm and started walking towards the edge of the stage. Chad said something to the guy and then walked back to the lady by the drum kit. Before Warner continued down the steps, he turned and glared at Chad's back, an ugly snarl twisting his face.

I watched him stumble out the lounge doors and then turned to my bandmates. "What the heck was that all about? Jason, you have got to control your temper, dude."

Jason scowled and dug in his pocket, pulling out the little plastic bottle that housed his whisky–soaked toothpicks. "Man, I didn't do anything!" He flipped the toothpick with his tongue as he nodded at Cole. "Tell him, that dirtbag knocked over my-"

"Jase!"

Jason huffed but stopped talking.

"Look, we'll sort out your gear, just don't get into any fights, okay?" I shook my head. "Especially not with a member of Eclipse's crew!"

Jason snorted. "Rick Warner is a junky that has been riding Chad's coattails for years; he's not part of the band!"

I frowned. Jason acted as if he knew the guy. I shook my head and sighed; I didn't need the complication. "Does it matter what he does or doesn't do? He's with the band in some way, you heard Chad!" Jason started to argue, and I threw up my hand. "I don't want to hear any more, man! Just don't embarrass us."

The woman, Nikki if I'd heard correctly, caught my eye and waved us over. "Come on, looks like we're gonna meet Eclipse." We started walking towards center stage.

From the corner of my eye, I could see that Jason's face was still set in a pugnacious expression. I gritted my teeth. That temper was going to ruin him and, if I wasn't careful, he'd take the rest of us down with him.

"Jason?" I stopped and waited until he'd made eye contact before lowering my voice and whispering. "Shake it off, dude. This is our shot, don't mess it up so early in the game!"

We stared at each other for several seconds. The toothpick he was never without flipped back and forth across his lips as he chewed on the tip. I wished he'd never found the novelty item. Soaked in whisky, he sucked and chewed on one constantly, and it drove me crazy, but they seemed to help him burn off nervous energy, and if it kept him calm ... He blinked and removed the toothpick, drawing a deep breath and releasing it slowly.

Thank God, he was calming down. I smiled. “Take another, and relax.”

I waited another minute. “Good?”

Jason nodded. “Yeah man, let’s do this!”

I smiled. That was more like it! With all of us on the same page, we moved to join Chad Crawford and the rest of Eclipse for our first rehearsal meeting.

My pulse quickened and my thoughts narrowed, blocking out everything but the coming concerts. Bad Opera was getting the chance of a lifetime and I was letting nothing get in the way.

Down in the Doldrums

Tina

I SIGHED AND SANK onto the rattan bar stool, letting my gaze wander around the pool deck. The kidney-shaped pool was filled with bikini-clad women laughing and flirting with men out to impress them. Scattered amongst the potted palm trees were lounge chairs filled with couples holding hands and murmuring soft words or reading books in companionable silence.

Staccato bursts of boisterous laughter rose above the din created by the pool's waterfall as groups of friends swapped stories and sipped brightly colored drinks around umbrella-covered tables. Everywhere I looked, people were having a good time. They'd taken a rock and roll-themed cruise for a chance to party with their favorite bands and forget about the real world awaiting them back home. For them, the day held the promise of nine fun-filled days on a cruise to paradise.

I snorted. More like nine days on a floating version of Dante's inferno.

"What'll you have?"

I stared at the bartender and tried to stop the words that tumbled from my mouth.

"Whiskey Sour."

The bartender grabbed a low-ball glass, added a generous shot of whiskey and a splash of sour mix, and then slid it towards me before scurrying off to wait on the crowds clamoring for refreshment.

It'd taken less than two minutes. A few clicks on a clock and I was once again staring down my demon.

My breath left in a whoosh. What was I doing?

I pushed the drink away and stared at the tiny palm trees painted on my bright blue fingernails, mesmerized at how they appeared to dance in time with my shaking hand.

I reached across the gleaming teak wood bar. "Stupid, stupid, stupid ..." Fell from my lips in a hoarse whisper, but, as if possessed of free will, my trembling hand closed around the slick glass and brought it to my lips.

"Crap!" Cold, lemon-colored liquid slopped down the front of my dress. I was batting a thousand in ways to destroy a vintage outfit.

"Oh! Do you get a buzz quicker that way?"

I stopped daubing cocktail napkins across my chest and turned toward the unwelcome, would-be comedian.

The words to verbally flay the woman alive were on the tip of my tongue until I registered the twinkle in her green eyes.

My lips twitched. Had I not been Jonesing for a drink, the girl's comment would have cracked me up.

I smirked. "I got an email sayin' it's the latest thing."

The woman's eyes widened. "Wow! Did you check that out with Snopes?"

I snorted and shook my head. She presented the picture of innocence, except for the telltale twitch at the corner of her mouth.

"You always such a smart Alec to strangers?"

The twitch turned into a grin as the woman offered her hand. "I'm KC Anderson. Now we aren't strangers." She shrugged. "And yeah, that's me. Pretty much always a smart mouth."

I snorted and shook the proffered hand. "I'm Tina Crawford." I crumpled the soggy napkins into a wad and tossed them across the bar before turning my barstool, so I faced KC.

"Ya know, if you hadn't been so funny, I'd have ripped you a new one. Today has not been a good one."

"It's the first day of our cruise! That can never be a bad day."

I snorted. "Can if you run into an ex-boyfriend, and his sort-of fiancée."

KC's eyebrows rose. "Ooh, I take it back. That'd ruin anybody's day." She took a sip of her Margarita and then brushed salt from her shirt. "Um, what is a sort of fiancée?"

I stared at the frosty glass filled with lime green slush. Frozen margaritas were one of my favorites. My mouth puckered at just the thought of knocking back the tart drink.

Maybe I could get away with one, surely one wouldn't —-

KC cleared her throat. "You want one?"

I jerked my eyes away from the temptation and shook my head. "Nah, I uh, I kinda quit drinking."

KC cocked her head to the side and clicked her tongue. "Ya got a thing for the indecisive."

I frowned. Somewhere in this conversation, I'd lost the thread; probably while I was near to drooling over the drink. "Sorry?"

KC smirked. "Sorta fiancées and kinda on the wagon; you got a pattern going."

I laughed. "I do at that." I waived the bartender over and ordered a ginger ale. "Thanks, KC."

KC wrinkled her nose. "For what?"

"If you hadn't distracted me with your wisecracks I'd be on my way to getting wasted."

KC laughed and raised her glass. "Well, glad to see my wise tail is good for something after all!"

I grinned. "You should market yourself. Laugh your way to sobriety with KC Anderson. It'll be huge, you'll make infomercials."

KC chuckled. "Oh yeah, I can see it now." She raised her hands in an arc motion. "My life story on the Bio channel: The Rags to Riches Story of KC Anderson: From Cook to Counselor."

I laughed. "Hey, you're a chef?"

KC shook her head. "Nah, I'm just a cook in a little café in Port Wentworth, Georgia. No chef by any means."

I stared. "That is so weird! I'm a chef and assistant manager at a café in Savannah." I shook my head. "It's a small world, huh?"

KC drained her glass. "Yeah, crazy coincidence." She raised her hand to summon the bartender and a gleam of gold and fairy-like tinkling drew my attention.

"That is so pretty!" I pointed towards KC's wrist. "I used to wear a charm bracelet! What all do you have?"

KC lowered her arm so I could examine the bracelet. There were dozens of charms, among them a spatula, a sea turtle, a peach, and intertwined letters K and C.

I cocked my head. "I get the others, but what's this one for?"

K.C.'s brow furrowed. "Um, it's my name."

I frowned. "But I thought your name was Casey."

K.C. laughed. "It is." She drew the letters K and C in the condensation of her glass.

I snorted and gave herself a mock slap to the forehead. "Don't mind me, it's been a long day."

K.C. smirked. "So I've already heard." She fingered her sea turtle charm for a second, twisting the little gold creature around until its green eyes caught the light. "So you said you work in Savannah? Which restaurant?"

"The Cosmic Café. We're over by Forsyth Park."

KC frowned. "I've heard of that ... oh I know! I heard about it on the news. Wasn't that place somehow wrapped up in that mess that ended with a shooting during the Saint Patrick's Day parade?"

Tina nodded. “Well, kind of. The café wasn’t but my friend Ivy was, she owns the Cosmic, and I ...‘oh, ‘scuse me, KC.”

The sound of Lil’ Miss Can’t Be Wrong drifted from my purse. I dug around in my voluminous bag and pulled out my phone.

“Hmm, speak of the devil. Hey, Ivy! I was just talkin’ about you.” I moved the phone away from my mouth and whispered to KC. “I gotta take this. It was nice talkin’ to ya, maybe I’ll see ya around.”

KC nodded. “Yeah, nice meeting you.” She waved and then held up her hand in a stop motion. “Hey! If ya don’t have dinner plans, how about we meet up?”

“Hang on a minute, Ivy.” I lowered the phone. “Umm, I think we’re assigned seating at dinner, and I’m supposed to have dinner with my—“

“Oh, that’s ok,” KC’s smile faded. “I didn’t mean to impose or anything.”

I felt like I’d kicked a puppy. “Don’t be silly! I can’t do dinner but how about we meet after. Are you planning on going to the Eclipse meet and greet tonight?”

KC’s face fell. “Nah, those tickets are extra and way beyond my budget.”

I nodded and made a quick decision. This girl’s humor had saved me from a big mistake, thanks weren’t enough. “Well, you can be my guest if you like.” I had planned to skip the event after finding out Warner was on board but maybe with a friend around ...

KC's face lit up and I knew I'd made the right call. "Oh my God, are you serious? I mean, what do I wear, I don't know- "

I laughed and slipped off the bar stool. "The band put their pants on one leg at a time, just like us, so 'do you, Boo.' I'll meet ya outside the Alchemy Lounge around nine?"

She nodded and I headed for the relative quiet of the leeward deck. "Sorry about that, Ivy. You still there?"

I listened to her rapid string of questions as I searched for an unoccupied deck chair.

"Yeah Ivy, I'm listening or tryin' to. You're talkin' a mile a minute- "

"Well, I'm sure your cellphone, provided by the Cosmic Cafe I might add, is now roaming and that isn't cheap, and you kept me waiting for ten minutes!"

"Nah, couldn't have been more than five."

"Whatever! I'm not made of money you know. Food prices have gone through the roof, I'm worried about the supply of poultry products because Mr. Henderson lost his battle with cancer and I don't see how Mrs. Henderson will run that farm by herself, and don't even get me started about Jaime. His lawyers are hounding me to pay back the loan; I'm getting like six phone calls a day!"

I propped my feet on the deck rail and stared out at the sea. “Tell the lawyers to go play in traffic! You haven’t got a pot to piss in so what are they gonna do--”

“Must you be so blunt?”

I snorted. “Uh, Ivy? Did you forget who you called?”

A peel of laughter burst through the phone’s speaker. "Thanks, Tina, I needed the laugh."

I smirked. “That’s me, the supplier of levity and butt of all cosmic jokes. Glad I could be of service.”

I waited until the laughter died. “So, Ivy, you want me to join this conversation, or did you just call to rant?”

A loud huff came down the line. “I called to see if you were all right. Did you speak to your father yet?”

“Uh ..., kind of.”

I rolled my eyes as Ivy started ranting again. I held the phone away from my ear, but still caught words like, be responsible..., the whole point ..., grow up.

“Ivy?” I waited until she’d run out of steam. “I’m having dinner with Chad tonight and going to the meet and greet.”

Ivy huffed. “Well, why didn’t you say so?”

I snorted. “You didn’t let me get a word in edgewise.”

Ivy launched into another round of issues with the Cosmic Café and I half-listened as I debated telling her about running into Ian Buchanan.

On the one hand, Ivy knew the whole sorry tale, on the other, she knew how much Ian affected me and she'd worry about backsliding.

I bit my lip and decided my need for a sounding board outweighed Ivy's peace of mind. "So, uh, guess who else is on board?"

Ivy drew a deep breath and sighed. "Oh God, who?"

"Ian Buchanan, and his fiancée ..."

A harsh intake of breath came down the phone line. "Oh honey, are you all right?"

I snorted. "What do you think? Not only is he here but so is that S.O.B. Richard Warner!" I thumped the arm of the deck chair. "What did I do to deserve this kick in the teeth from karma?"

Ivy huffed. "Tina, it isn't karma. Tell your dad about that Richard guy, that will solve so many of your problems!"

I snorted. "Oh yeah, just drop that in over dessert, shall I?"

Ivy clicked her tongue. "Look, I know none of this is easy and I admit, right now, this is more than you need emotionally, but you can do this! You've been sober for three months and you know Dr. Marsden thinks so many of your issues can be resolved by just making up with your dad ..."

"Oh yeah, just making up with him."

"I'm sorry, I wish I was there with you ..."

I sighed. "Thanks, wish you were, too." Silence sat on the line for several seconds before I cleared my throat.

"Uh, but I did make a new friend, well she talked me away from a drink after I ran into Ian anyway."

"Oh thank God, I love her already! What's her name? Are you meeting up with her again? That's what you need, a friend to keep you on track and-"

"Ivy! Slow down, girl." I laughed. "Her name is K.C. Anderson and get this, she's a cook at a restaurant over in Port Wentworth. She's really funny, too."

"Well, there ya go! You have lots in common. So just hang out with her as much as you can when you aren't with your dad and – oh crap, Tina I gotta go, Pete burned the rolls."

"Oh man, make some more before the dinner crowd, and don't worry about me, I'll be fine-- "I trailed off as the line went dead. "I hope."

High and Dry

Tina

THE SPAGHETTI STRAP ON my dress slid towards my elbow for what must have been the twentieth time as I headed for the elevators. I mashed the button and shoved the stupid thing back into place, again.

"You'll snag the crochet if you keep that up, ask me how I know."

I turned to find KC standing behind me. I grinned and then my eyes widened. "We're wearing the same dress!"

KC laughed. "Well, almost. You got the short version, and they are different colors ..."

I shook my head and laughed. "What are the odds?" The elevator arrived and we stepped on. "I take it you love Izzi's boutique, too."

KC nodded. "Yep, bought a bunch of new clothes for my trip," She smiled at a man standing near the control panel. "Deck six, please."

"Yeah, I didn't go crazy, but a vacation requires at least one new outfit, or it isn't a vacation! I gotta tell ya, you are rockin' that red."

KC's face lit up. "Thanks!" She twirled a little and giggled. "Never had a long dress before ..., feel like a princess!"

I smiled but didn't crack a joke. Something in her face told me she wasn't used to dressing up, not that I considered the style of dress we were both wearing as formal or even semi-formal wear. "I tried on the red, but I just don't have the complexion for it," I grinned. "And too, lime green is a favorite color of mine; you should see my closet!"

KC smiled. "That dress you had on yesterday was awesome, lime looks good on you but here, hold this." She handed me her clutch bag. "Need to tighten that strap."

A few seconds and my wardrobe malfunction was a thing of the past. "Oh my gosh, thank you!" I handed her purse back. "Was driving me nuts!"

KC shrugged. "No problem, what are friends for?"

I grinned. She really was a nice person and Lord knew I would need a friend while dealing with my dad and now all of the other baggage trying to fall on me. "So, are we still on for after dinner?"

Her eyes widened. "Are you kiddin' me? I can't wait!"

"Excuse me."

A couple interrupted to exit the elevator and I realized we were on deck six. "Let's go, KC. We'll get to jabbering and ride this thing all the way to the engine room!"

She laughed and followed me out. There was a line at the hostess station, but we didn't notice. Our conversation turned to the music scene in Savannah. We had mutual friends and barely noticed the wait until we were interrupted.

"Kristina Carol honey, you don't have to wait in this line, our table is this way."

I glanced around to find Drew Alton, founding member and lead guitarist for Eclipse, standing at my elbow.

KC's eyes widened and I cringed. I had hoped to keep my connection to the band low-key. Still, nothing I could do now. "Hey, Drew. I didn't know. This is my friend, KC."

"Hey! Nice to meet ya, darlin' ..." Drew smiled at KC and then huffed at me. "Come on honey, they're all awaitin' ..."

"Oh gosh, I'm sorry!" I glanced at KC and grimaced. "I'm sorry, gotta go but ..." I dug in my bag and pulled out an engraved card with the Eclipse logo on it. "In case we miss each other after dinner, this will get you into the meet and greet, okay?"

Her eyebrows rose but she took the card. "Wow, it's a VIP pass! But what about you? How will you get in?"

Drew snorted. "You kiddin'? She's Cha-"

"I'll be fine, KC." I rushed to cut Drew off, even though KC had to have suspected I at least knew the band unless she wasn't a big enough fan to recognize Drew; it was usually my dad that got the fanfare, so it was possible.

I smiled at her. "It's fine, I have another ticket. Find me in the Alchemy Lounge after dinner then?"

KC nodded so I nudged Drew to get moving before he said anything more revealing.

"So, how have you been Uncle Drew? Still building hot rods?" We might not have been blood, but Drew Alton and his wife were like family to me.

Drew laughed. "Been great, kid, and of course I am, even bought into a shop putting out custom rides up near Charleston."

I smiled and let him weave us a path through the dining room. I'd missed him. When I'd cut my dad out of my life, it'd ended up being the whole band and the way of life. I glanced at him. "So you and Kay are still over in Summerville?"

"Uh-huh, you know Kay, spending all my money on her horses. She'd love for you to come by." He guided me around a table and then pointed towards a short set of stairs. "We're up there at the captain's table." He rolled his eyes. "In the spotlight, just to eat!"

I laughed and climbed the steps. Most of the band were already seated, along with some officers and other people I figured had been deemed worthy. I didn't see Nikki which was a bit odd if she was dating my dad and I had gotten the vibe that something was going on between them. I made a mental note to quiz Chad about it later.

I smiled and glanced around the table. "Evenin' all. Hope we haven't kept you waiting?"

My eyes widened as I looked down at the table. Ian and his band had been included; I wouldn't have thought an opening act was high enough on the totem pole to dine with the stars.

Not that Eclipse members thought themselves high and mighty, but Rob Thornton, their longtime manager, had always pushed the superstar exclusivity angle.

"Punkin, you look gorgeous, as usual!" I cringed as my dad's effusive greeting drew all eyes. The men rose from their chairs and Chad held the one intended for me.

Drew took a seat across from Ian as my table mates murmured assurances that we were still waiting on a few others. I greeted my dad and accepted an embossed card from the waiter. "Mmmm, what's on the menu for tonight?"

"It all looks good," Chad grinned. "We'll see if it's up to your standards."

I shook my head; why did everyone assume a chef couldn't eat out without critiquing the meal? I studied my choices. My dad was right, it all sounded great, but the vegetarian option looked particularly intriguing. I handed the menu back to the waiter, with a request for ginger ale.

I jumped as Chad leaned closer and murmured. "Feeling seasick?"

I blinked. "Um ..., no. Why?"

He shrugged and sat back. "Just noticed you didn't order alcohol and ginger is great for an upset stomach. It's also an antioxidant and anti-inflammatory but being we are on a ship I figured ..."

I stared at him and then laughed. He really had committed to his healthy lifestyle. "You've changed." I sipped my water and smiled, thinking of what my mother would have said about the health-conscious Chad Crawford.

Chad snorted. "Told you that."

I smiled. "Yes, you did. I'm just noticing it's true."

He grinned. "You ever do yoga?"

I gulped to keep from spraying a mouthful of soda across the table. "Uh, yeah Chad, I practice at least three times a week."

A bright smile lit up his green eyes. "Cool! Our suite has a private garden. Join me tomorrow morning and we'll welcome the sun!"

I bit my lip to keep from laughing. Could I do it? Yoga with my dad? Not even Dr. Marsden would expect that level of dedication.

"Uh, we'll see." I racked my brain for a safe and distracting change of subject. "So, I talked to Drew. He seems pretty settled back in the Low Country. How about you?"

My dad took a sip of something I suspected was an herbal and fruit shrub; I bet he gave the bartender the recipe. The mental picture occupied me until he nodded, drawing my attention. "Yeah, I thought I told you. I've got a place on Dutch Island ...," He grinned. "And I bought a boat."

A bubble of laughter burst out, drawing several pairs of eyes. I swallowed and toned it down a notch. "You so didn't!"

My dad chuckled and nodded.

"After last time?" I snorted. "Is that a good idea?"

He laughed. "You sound so much like your mother." He shook his head. "I quit drinking, remember? I also took boating lessons; no danger of running aground again."

I grinned. "I'm sure every landlubber on the Georgia coast thanks you for your consideration."

He laughed and started to reply when the captain joined the table.

"Ladies and gentlemen, I am Captain Stroud and I thank you for dining with me this evening." He raised his glass, and everyone followed suit. "May you all have a fun and memorable voyage."

The captain took his seat and tipped his head towards us. "Mr. Crawford, Ms. Crawford. I hope you're finding your suite satisfactory?"

I bit back a laugh. Since we were staying on a private floor in the owner's penthouse, complete with a private deck, hot tub, butler, and concierge there was not much chance we wouldn't be satisfied. I nodded and let my dad make small talk.

"Please captain, call me Chad, and the suite is amazing. The views are spectacular. I was just telling my daughter about my plan to do sunrise yoga on the deck and ..."

I tuned their conversation out and munched on my salad while I observed the new person my father appeared to be. The last time I'd eaten with him in public he'd been stoned out of his mind on God only knew what. Most likely bourbon and oxy. I snorted. He'd been barely coherent and what was understandable was belligerent.

His transformation was amazing; it was just sad that it'd only come at the shock of his friend's death. Thinking back on how bad my dad had been, I was grateful for Ivy's intervention before my life went as far off the rails as his had.

I sighed. Not that being grateful made my task any easier. At some point, I had to reconcile with my dad, not just be friendly. Dr. Marsden insisted I wouldn't be emotionally free until I told him the truth of why I'd broken ties with him.

The threads of bad memories started to rush at me. I brushed them away by focusing on the low hum of conversation floating around me.

My father was chatting with a couple around his age that proclaimed themselves huge fans, and Rob Thornton was regaling them with stories from Eclipse's many tours. The antics were funny, and Rob was a good storyteller, though he had to stop and sniff or wipe his nose every five minutes. I frowned, wondering if he was coming down with a cold. I made a mental note to keep my distance and hoped it was just allergies.

I let my gaze wander. The dining room was opulent but understated. Shades of white and cream with bursts of nautical navy kept the focus on the bank of windows overlooking the ocean. The room was full, but I looked for KC anyway. My gaze went around the room twice without falling on her, though I did manage to make eye contact with the woman Ian was involved with. I wondered why she wasn't with Ian but, if the cold and hate-filled look she sent me was an indication of her personality we were all better off without her.

She tipped her nose at me and looked to my left. I followed her gaze and saw Ian and Drew in an animated conversation. I smiled as I caught the gist; they were in the weeds over guitars. The discussion was way over my head, but I enjoyed watching the two men's faces as they discussed their passion. Ian, of course, kept drawing my eye. Even if I hadn't known him intimately, his shining eyes and parted lips, the way he leaned into the table to speak ... it was obvious he was in heaven, and I couldn't have been happier for him.

A twinge of guilt hit me. I pushed it aside, but really, I should have introduced Ian when we were dating; even if I hadn't been speaking to my dad, the same hadn't applied to Drew. Older, hopefully, wiser, and out of the party life, I could acknowledge that I'd been selfish.

The main course arrived, and Ian made eye contact with me as he leaned back to give the waiter room. He flashed me his megawatt, dimpled smile. I raised my glass in salute. I turned my attention back to the conversation at the head of the table as the captain's words reached my ears.

"Chad, I just finished your autobiography, and I have to tell you how ..." Captain Stroud huffed a laugh. "How impressed I am with the way you've reclaimed your life. From an all-consuming chemical addiction to an author of clean-living books," he shook his head. "It's a remarkable achievement."

My eyes widened and I stared at my dad. He'd written a book. Chad Crawford. I'd missed a lot over the last ten years.

The super fan couple across from us, Marie and Brad, if I had heard right, made a joke about getting older or something. I smiled and when the conversation paused I elbowed my father and teased. "A book?" I winked at the captain. "That's impressive. And clean-living! Be careful or all of those old groupies are gonna start calling you guru."

Everyone laughed and my father mock scowled at me. "No respect from kids these days."

I grinned. "Seriously though, I knew you'd gotten clean but ..." I shook my head. "You've started a whole new life."

My dad smiled as everyone agreed but he leaned toward me and whispered. "Not a new life, Punkin, a reclaimed on; I don't want a life that you aren't in."

I caught my breath at the sincerity in his voice and the hint of tears in his eyes. I swallowed past the lump in my throat. "I ..., I don't want that either."

"Good, that's settled. Bygones, and all that ..." He smiled and patted my arm as the captain spoke to me. My father assumed our ten years apart had been caused by his drinking and lifestyle, and I had always let him think that because it was easier than telling him the truth-

"Ms. Crawford ...,"

I jumped and shook off my guilt.

"Oh please, call me Tina!"

He smiled and nodded. "Tina, what your father has achieved is remarkable but what he is doing with the young ..."

Not wanting to show even more ignorance of my father's life, I nodded in agreement and made a mental note to find out just what Chad had been up to since he'd come out of rehab.

"I agree, captain!" Brad interjected. "Addiction is taking a toll on our schools."

The conversation turned into a discussion on morality, children, and a bunch of other things I had no interest in. I concentrated on my food until a bark of laughter at the other end of the table drew my attention.

The guys from Bad Opera, along with Benny T, were teasing Ian.

"Man, don't try to deny it, you are whipped!" Jason laughed. "She kicked you out of your own cabin!"

Ian scowled at his bass player. I knew Jason, slightly, from my time dating Ian. I'd thought they were close friends, but if looks could kill ... I snorted and thought Jason would be wise to occupy himself with the toothpick he had hanging from his mouth instead of trash-talking Ian. Jason scoffed and sat back, chuckling as Benny T took over the ribbing. I frowned and tried to piece together what had happened.

"Like Linus man, dragging your blankie as you beg the spare bed in Jason's cabin!" Benny snorted. "What were you thinkin'? Dude, everybody knows you can't hide the side piece on a cruise ship!"

"That's just it, he wasn't thinkin', not with his brain at least!"

Ian smirked and flipped Jason the bird. The guys laughed harder.

My eyes widened and I gasped as the truth dawned. "Oh my God Ian, did your fiancé break up with you because of me?" I shook my head and tried to figure out what I could have done to cause them to fight. "Whatever I've done, I'm so sorry ..."

Benny and Jason started to laugh again but a snarl from Ian made them duck their heads and resume eating.

"You've nothing to apologize for, Tina. This thing with Judith," he snorted. "You didn't cause this."

I frowned. "Well, why did your fiancé kick you out of your cabin then?"

He ignored the snicker from Jason and rolled his eyes. "It's not- she wasn't my fiancé Tina, and the cruise is booked so there weren't any other cabins-"

"Wait, I'm confused. You and your girlfriend had a fight-"

"Uh-uh, not my girlfriend, a woman I dated a few times." He huffed and shook his head. "Look, it's no big deal, the guys are just messin' with me."

I licked my lips. From what he'd said, and what he hadn't said, it sounded like they weren't a couple but the snooty woman I'd met was trying to force the issue. I ignored the flash of pleasure that idea gave me. "You, um, you didn't break up because of me then."

Ian smiled. "Nah, like I said, we just dated a few times, and she got the idea to-never mind, it's a long story, but none of this is your fault."

I bit my lip and nodded, though it all seemed a bit odd to me. Why would the woman have come on the cruise with Ian if they weren't a couple? I was missing something. I started to question him further but Drew got his attention and the men all started talking about the concert, so I let it slide, it was no business of mine, no matter how much I wished it to be.

The conversation had turned to music and Ian was laughing and trading quips with Drew and the band; professionally, it looked like his ship had come in. When he'd broken ties with me and moved to L.A., I'd been devastated but there was no denying it had been a wise move, musically. I'd followed his career and been overjoyed when he won an Indie award. His reputation was preceding him, the proof was in the invitation to open for Eclipse.

All of Ian's dreams were coming true and I was happy for him, but I couldn't lie to myself; I still loved him, probably always would, and how pathetic was that?

Tears pricked my eyes. I sniffed and shook my head. This was a road I had no business going down. I drew a deep breath and took a bite of the three-cheese polenta with wild mushroom ragu I'd ordered. The perfect blend of mozzarella, asiago, and muenster coated my tongue, and the hint of Aleppo pepper balanced the creaminess. Lost in thoughts of adding something similar to the winter menu at the Cosmic, it took a nudge from my father to draw my attention to the fact that the captain was speaking to me.

"I'm sorry," I smiled at him. "I was miles away. What did you ask me?"

Captain Stroud smiled. "It was nothing, I just said we've been neglecting you. Marie is a teacher, and Brian is a principal, I just wondered what occupies your time and energy."

An imp must have been sitting on my shoulder because I glanced at my father and then grinned. "Oh, I'm just a cook."

My dad snorted. "Sure wrote a lot of hefty checks to educate a cook!"

I laughed at him and then apologized to the captain, whose face showed his confusion. "Sorry, I'm a chef, soon to be a partner in a Savannah restaurant."

His eyebrows rose. "Oh ho!" the captain continued. "Should I worry about internet reviews of our cuisine?"

I laughed. “Not at all!” I waved my fork at my nearly empty plate. “Everything I’ve eaten so far has been divine. In fact, I was lost in thought because I’m planning to steal this dish for our winter menu.”

He smiled. “I’ll be sure to pass on your compliments to our chefs and their staff.”

“Oh yes, please do!”

The captain turned to address the other diners, leaving me to finish every last bite of my meal. If I wasn’t careful, I’d need a whole new wardrobe when I got home.

“That good, huh?”

I jumped as my dad leaned in and whispered.

I grinned. “What gave me away?”

He laughed. “Oh, I don’t know, maybe those little yum noises-what the-” He stiffened, and half rose from his chair, looking around the dining room.

“Something wrong?” Captain Stroud frowned and started to rise.

“Nah,” Chad shook his head and settled back into his seat. “Thought I saw a fan that’s been bugging me ...”

“If you are having a problem with someone on board ...”

Chad shook his head and smiled. “No, no, nothing like that.” He took a sip of water and shrugged. “Just looked like someone the band had a problem with, overzealous fan, you know?” The captain nodded. “It was a long time ago, though. Haven’t had that issue in years.”

Captain Stroud smiled. "Well good to hear, but if you should need anything, please don't hesitate to ask."

Chad said that he would, and the topic changed to the decadent dessert cart being wheeled around the table.

Dad and Drew started swapping stories of the good ol' days, enthralling the other diners as we waited for our turn to choose dessert. I'd barely taken a bite of a chocolate mousse when a commotion at the hostess station drew everyone's attention.

My stomach rolled and my father cursed.

Richard Warner, barely able to stand, was harassing the poor hostess as Nikki Hardy attempted to steer him from the dining room. They would have succeeded if Richard hadn't caught sight of my father. I shuddered as his voice rang out over the room.

"Chad, Shad!" He pulled away from the crew and, remarkably quick for someone so drunk, staggered his way through the maze of tables before stumbling up the steps to hover over the back of my father's chair. Nikki was right behind him, rambling apologies as she tried to pull Ricky away.

I flinched and leaned as far away as I could without falling out of my seat. My heart started to pound, and my mouth went dry. Ricky leaned closer and his hot, rancid breath fanned across my cheek. I bit back a gag and tried to rise but my father's hand suddenly clasped mine, holding me captive.

I swallowed and met his gaze, begging to be let go. He frowned, glancing between me and Ricky.

"Chad, Schad! D'choo know what these idiots did?"

"No, and I don't care-"

"I'm so sorry, Chad!" Nikki tugged on Ricky's arm. "Come on, you sorry son of a -"

"Get off of me, you bi-"

"That's enough!" Chad gave my hand a slight squeeze and then rose, helping Nikki guide Richard from the table. "You're making a spectacle of yourself, and we talked ..."

I took several deep breaths and tried to calm my racing heart as my dad and Nikki led Richard away. I glanced at the horrified diners and forced a shaky laugh. "And that, folks, is why I gave up drinking."

My joke defused the situation, and everyone resumed their chatting over dessert. Ian was sending me some questioning looks but I ignored him, concentrating on pushing my mousse around while I willed away a full-on panic attack; no way I could eat now.

Tip of the Iceberg

Tina

THE CAPTAIN AND OFFICERS were excusing themselves when my father returned to the table. He didn't sit, merely leaning over to ask if I was finished. I jumped at the chance to leave, feeling like everyone was staring at me after the spectacle of Warner.

We left the dining room and I started to head towards the Alchemy lounge, but Chad shook his head.

"Don't you have to get in there?"

"Doesn't start for a few minutes yet. Let's go out to the deck and talk."

The way he said talk made me a little nervous, but I wasn't feeling up to a horde of people, so I agreed. He put his hand to my back, steering me to a quiet spot at the railing.

I stared out at the water as Chad leaned his elbows against the rail and sighed. "You wanna tell me why you're afraid of Rich?"

I stiffened. Crap. I should have chosen the lounge full of fans. I was not ready for this conversation, might never be ready. I decided to brazen it out. "Uh, I don't ..." I laughed. "I don't know what you mean. I'm not-"

"Stop it, Punkin'." He rose to his full height and turned towards me, taking my hand. "I'm not the self-absorbed drunk anymore, I notice things, especially where you're concerned. That's twice now Warner's come around and you get scared and run away or try to, what gives?"

My mouth went dry, and I looked around, desperate for a distraction when Ian's snobby, 'not girlfriend' stepped out on deck. The woman stopped and glared at me before walking passed.

My father snorted. "What was her problem?" And there was my distraction!

He shook his head and met my gaze. "Back to Rich. What has he done-"

"It's not him, Chad it's uh," I bit my lip and wondered if I was opening more cans of worms, but my dad seemed determined ... with silent apologies to my ex, I plowed ahead. "It's uh—it's Ian."

My dad leaned back against the rail and frowned. "Ian. The kid fronting Bad Opera?"

I nodded, feeling lower than pond scum.

"What does our opening act have to do-"

"We used to date!" I rushed on before he could think it all through. I was glad he'd stopped drinking, but it was easier to fool a drunk Chad Crawford. "And we didn't leave things in a great place when we split and..." I was struggling, and his face was getting that suspicious look I think they teach before you take a baby home from the hospital.

"Uh... And uh, that woman that just walked by?"

Chad nodded. "Yeah, what about her? She was staring daggers at you."

I laughed. "Yeah, that's because she's Ian's fiancé, or sort of anyway..." I was rambling and I knew it. Flop sweat was starting to form. "She kicked Ian out of his cabin, and I think she blames me for their problems." Now I was in left field and stretching any semblance of the truth, but no turning back now.

"Why would she do that?"

I shrugged. "Think she sees me as a threat because this afternoon Ian was trying to get me to meet him for drinks or something after the meet and greet... just to catch up I think but..." I sighed. "It's just a mess, Chad."

I was busy digging my hole and didn't notice that my dad had switched gears until it was too late; I'd laid the story on too thick.

He cleared his throat, and I met his gaze. His expression was stern, and his shoulders were squared. He looked ready to fight. I prayed the deck would open up and swallow me.

"Huh. I've seen the way he looks at you, Kristina Carol..." He nodded, seeming to be convincing himself of my lie. "If that woman he's engaged to has noticed and it sounds like she has... Yep, he's causing you problems." He frowned. "You want me to fire him, Punkin'?"

Oh my god! "Geez Chad, no!" One little lie and now I'd made Ian's idol hate him. I was so going to hell, and definitely without the aid of a hand basket. "It's no big deal."

Chad cleared his throat. "You sure it isn't going to be a problem? Because I'm not going to have you upset..."

I sighed and ran a hand through my hair. "It's not like that, Chad. Seriously, Ian and I are fine."

My dad still wore a mulish expression. "Punkin' when guys get dumped..." He nodded his head like he'd settled something with himself. "Yeah, I'll have a word with Ian, tell him he has to let it go—"

"Chad, no!" I wanted to climb in a hole, or better yet, dive overboard. My father was in full tilt protective mode and for all the wrong reasons. "Look, I appreciate that you care, but just leave it alone."

"Can't do that, Punkin,' it just leaves tension and that will interfere with the music." He patted my hand. "Don't you worry about it, I'll be low key, but he has to understand—"

"Chad, Ian broke up with me!"

My dad frowned. "Huh? But you said—"

"No, you assumed." I smiled. "Look, I do appreciate your concern, honestly. Feels good to know you'd defend me..." Now, I silently added. Ten years too late— I was not going there.

I shook my head and focused on my father. "Ian and I do not have any problems it's all in that silly woman's head."

Chad nodded but his expression still showed disbelief. "So, uh, why did you two split?"

I sighed. A lie was ready on my tongue but the last one had gone way too far, and I was exhausted. God only knew what trouble I'd cause if I told another whopper. "Ian was tired of my drinking."

My dad's eyes about popped out of their sockets. "You have a drinking problem, Punkin'?" He slapped his forehead. "The ginger ale! That's why you were drinking it."

I nodded but really, what was there to say?

He folded his arms across his chest and gave me a hard stare. I had hoped for an end to the whole sorry conversation but no, I wasn't going to be that lucky. My dad went from concerned defender dad to stern, Father Knows Best, dad. "How long has this been going on and what are you doing about it? How long have you been on the wagon?"

Something about his tone just rubbed me wrong. I mean, where did he get off with that accusing stare? Before I could stop myself I blurted out. "Bit rich, coming from you."

He cocked his head, and a scowl darkened his face. "What's that supposed to mean young lady?"

I snorted. He was laying the Ward Cleaver on thick. "You were a raging alcoholic and drug addict for almost fifteen years, or was it twenty?"

He glared at me. "You implying it's my fault you have a problem?"

"You think it's not?"

He blew out a breath. "Always the parent's fault, eh? No personal responsibility, no owning up to your failings. Nah, just blame it all on your parents."

I rolled my eyes. "Not parents, just you."

He threw up his hands and backed away. "I don't have time for this." He stomped towards the Alchemy Lounge but turned back to meet my glare. "I thought we were getting somewhere kid, but you..." the anger left his eyes, replaced by sadness that cut me to the quick.

"You need to grow up, Punkin.' I'll see you around."

He disappeared into the crowd milling in front of the lounge, and I stomped my foot, holding in a shriek.

"You want to hit something?"

I jumped and turned around to see KC standing across the deck, half-hidden by shadows. I frowned, wondering just how long she'd been standing there but lost my train of thought as she continued.

"I can grab a pillow, or I think there's a punching bag in the gym."

I frowned, trying to grasp ..." Wha- oh!" I laughed and flopped into a deck chair. "I get it, funny."

KC sat on the end of my chair. "You don't look like you find it funny. Wanna talk about it?"

I smiled. "How much did you hear?"

KC shrugged. "Just a bit at the end about blame and growing up."

I snorted. "You heard enough, then."

KC's eyebrows rose. "So, Chad Crawford is your dad?"

I drew a deep breath and sighed. So much for anonymity. "Yeah, but I don't broadcast that."

KC grinned. "Oh, I can see why!"

I laughed. "Yeah, I guess you can." I sighed and rose, holding my hand out to KC. "Come on, let's go to the meet and greet."

Her eyes widened. “You’re still gonna go? After that fight?”

I shrugged. “For us, that was a minor skirmish and yeah, I don’t want you to miss out because of my dysfunctional family.” I frowned. “Or would you rather go by yourself now? I mean, it’s okay, you won’t hurt my feelings.”

KC snorted and took my hand, letting me pull her to her feet. “Please, what kind of friend would I be if I abandoned you to play fangirl? I mean, going in there is the last thing you want to do, right?”

I smirked. “That obvious?”

KC grinned. “I think you need a soak in the hot tub counting the stars. What do you say?”

I laughed. “That sounds perfect, I’ll grab my suit and meet you at the one outside the spa, okay?”

“Sounds like a plan.”

I hugged her. “Thanks, ...” I laughed. “Gotta warn you; I might not be the best company.”

KC smirked. “That’s okay, I know all about difficult fathers.”

The Cut of One's Jib

Ian

DINNER CONVERSATION WITH DREW Alton had me flying high but, five minutes after I left the dining room, Judith Fogarty got in my face and badgered me about Tina, playing rock music, and disappointing my dad ... she burst my bubble of happiness before I managed to shake her off.

All evening my phone had blown up with messages from my dad; it hadn't taken Judith long to carry her tales. The whole situation was a mess I didn't want to deal with, but the reckoning was coming soon, and I couldn't avoid a confrontation for much longer.

I shook off the gloomy thoughts and entered the Alchemy Lounge, heading towards a cluster of friends talking by the end of the bar. I pushed the Judith mess away, freely admitting I was being cowardly, and joined Benny T as he waited for 'show time.' We were swapping road stories with Drew Alton and bass guitarist, Cliff Harris when Chad Crawford walked into the lounge.

It was obvious, even before he spoke, that Chad was in a foul mood. His eyes were hard, like pieces of jade, and his mouth was set in a thin line. Drew cracked a joke to him, but Chad ignored him, turning his frosty gaze onto me. He never said a word, but man, it was clear I was on his crap list.

Benny T shot me a puzzled glance. I shrugged. No idea what I could have done to tick him off but, when the band's manager came to say the event was kicking off I figured it was time to cut and run; Chad stopped me with a hand to my chest as I walked by.

"Ian, have a word?"

My mouth went dry. I nodded, 'cause what else could I do? From his expression though, I figured I was about to get canned.

"Uh, sure uh Mr. Crawford ..." he stared at me, arms folded over his chest. I felt like a kid, being asked to confess before receiving punishment.

Chad glanced over at the entrance where the crowds were pushing in; they'd be forming lines at his table in seconds, yet he seemed in no hurry to speak his mind.

I fought the urge to volunteer a confession. It was like standing before the principal with your friends, waiting to see who would crack first.

Another glance in the direction of the signing table, then he sighed. "You dated my daughter."

It wasn't a question. "Uh, yes sir ..."

"You broke up with her."

My eyes widened. Was I in his black books for dating Tina or dumping her? His face offered no clues, so I went with the truth. "Um, yeah, I did."

He nodded. "You love her."

Oh geez, another statement. I rubbed the back of my neck and tried to decide if there was a right answer to a question he didn't ask.

"You're engaged to that doctor."

My eyebrows rose. Now that was a statement I could deny. "Uh, no sir, I'm not."

It was Crawford's turn to look surprised. "Tina said- "

"Yes sir, uh, Judith introduced herself as my fiancé, but we aren't, I mean..." I blew out a breath. "Thing is, we were only casually dating and then I broke it off, but she decided to invite herself-" I glanced at the lines of people waiting for autographs. "Uh, shouldn't you ..."

He followed my glance and huffed. "Yeah, I gotta-look, don't mess around with my daughter's feelings. Pick a girl, kid."

I gulped and nodded. "Yes sir."

He slapped me on the back and smiled. "Good. Women ain't nothin' but trouble; my daughter excluded of course ... he snorted. "We'll talk later."

Whew, that had been intense. I still didn't know what he'd been angry about, but he seemed to have resolved his issue without me and I wasn't gonna re-poke that bear.

I did wonder why he'd said I loved Tina. I did, but how did he know?

I shook my head; the whole day had been full of unexpected twists and turns, and I wasn't up to figuring it all out.

Benny and I were going for a drink once his gig was over, so I decided to kill time and do some promo for my band. I logged in to Bad Opera's social media account and set up my phone to live stream.

I was walking around, doing spontaneous interviews with fans when I decided to show my followers the backstage areas where our equipment and dressing rooms were located.

The back halls were mostly deserted but as I got closer to one of the equipment rooms I could hear what sounded like an argument.

I ended the live stream and was turning around when a cry rang out followed by something falling. I ran towards the sound and stumbled to a stop as Eclipse manager, Rob Thornton exited the room where our gear was stashed.

His face was red and sweaty, and his shirt tail was hanging out on one side, not usual from what I'd seen of the man. He sniffed and glanced at me and then back to the half-opened door.

"Everything all right, Mr. Thornton? Thought I heard someone yell and-"

"Yeah, yeah kid, it's all good. That drunk, Warner? He was fumbling around back here and knocked over some equipment but-"

"Anything broken? You need me to -"

"Nah, go on back to the lounge, I called security, he's dealing with Warner, and I'll tell Nikki about the equipment."

I nodded and was about to leave when the door opened, and Richard Warner, the jerk who'd knocked over Jason's, equipment, stumbled out. His lip was bleeding, and one eye was already swelling; no way were his injuries caused by falling into or having equipment fall onto him.

I frowned. Jason had ranted for almost an hour when he'd told me what happened to his bass. I didn't like the guy just by reputation. Still, I wasn't gonna see anyone get roughed up, though I found it hard to believe the manager would stoop to that kind of violence.

"Hey, man, you need a hand?"

Warner was bleary-eyed and unstable on his feet. He started to answer me when a throat clearing drew his attention to the doorway behind him. Richard's face paled and he hunched his shoulders into a protective stance.

I followed his gaze and frowned. The guy standing in the entry was big, not nightclub bouncer big but you could tell by the way his suit jacket stretched that he was muscled. His sandy-colored hair was crew cut and by the hard look in his eyes ... he had law enforcement written all over him or ex-military.

I nodded a greeting and pretended not to notice the guy's knuckles were red and looked to be flecked with blood. The tension was thick, Thornton and Warner were fidgety, and the big guy stared at me without blinking.

I forced a smile and pointed behind me. "Well, if you got it under control, Mr. Thornton, I'm gonna head back ... meeting friends for drinks soon."

A greasy kind of smile lit Rob's face; in another circumstance, I could see him trying to sell me a used car, one that had a blown engine. "Oh yeah, kid, you go on, enjoy yourself!"

He moved and put his hand on my back, guiding me down the hall away from Warner and the big guy. Whatever was going on, I wanted no part of it. Richard was on his feet and whatever he'd gotten himself into he'd have to get out of.

Thornton stopped at the end of the hall and motioned for me to continue. I looked over my shoulder and noticed Richard was following after us. His progress was slow, whether from being worked over or drunk I couldn't say.

Thornton turned around and I noticed he'd stopped to talk with Warner as I pulled my phone from my pocket and reconnected, preparing for a final live stream. I was leaning against the wall watching the circle spin as the page tried to load when Warner's voice reached my ears.

Most of what he said was slurred and I was paying little attention until his voice got louder.

"Big man ... keep messin' ... b'low dry up-you ..."

I straightened and strained to hear; it sounded like he was threatening Thornton.

Warner coughed and Thornton said something I couldn't make out. Richard laughed. "Fix ...sh'you'll be beggin'!"

Warner's voice was getting louder and a quick peek around the corner showed he was staggering his way towards me. I moved toward the lounge before I could get caught up in any more of his drama.

When I got back to the main lounge, the lines had broken up and people were milling around in small groups. I was live streaming with followers when Drew and Chad joined me. Bad Opera fans got an exclusive with the two rock gods and then I signed off.

"Thanks, dudes, might go viral with this."

Chad laughed but Drew was clueless.

"See, if enough people watch and share this video, then-"

"Excuse me, Mr. Crawford?"

A waiter interrupted my tutorial, handing Chad a white envelope with the ship's logo embossed in the corner.

Chad frowned and turned it over. "Huh, wonder who it's from?"

Drew Alton leaned over his shoulder. "Well, ya won't figure it out that way, open it!"

Chad laughed and ripped the seam with his fingernail. He pulled the contents out and the three of us stared at it. "What the hell?"

One of the many glossy publicity stills offered to meet and greet ticket holders, the one sent to Chad was marred by dozens of puncture marks and a large red X running from corner to corner.

"Crap, Hoss," Drew laughed and smacked Chad on the back. "What fresh groupie hell have you gotten into this time?"

I smiled at the joke, but it faded as I caught sight of Chad's expression. Pale under his tan, a muscle worked in his jaw and his hand trembled slightly.

"Chad? Everything all right, man?"

Chad shook himself and flashed a smile, but it looked forced. "Yeah kid, just a joke." He nodded towards Drew. "Like Alton said, probably a woman I've managed to tick off."

He tossed the photo onto a nearby table. "This thing is winding down, think I'll turn in. Tomorrow's gonna be a long day."

He nodded towards me and glanced at Drew. "No late-night carousing man, we gotta show tomorrow."

Drew smirked and waved him away. "I can hold my own, old man, worry 'bout yerself."

Chad shook his head and slipped through the thinning crowd.

His expression suggested good humor and not a care in the world, but I couldn't help but notice his eyes scanned the room and he kept away from the groups milling about.

Curious, I picked up the discarded picture. A chill ran down my spine. The holes were random and scattered, with some shallow and some so deep they ripped the paper.

Whoever had done this was in a frenzy. I folded the picture and tucked it into my back pocket though I couldn't say why; something just felt off about the whole thing and maybe someone should look into it, though I had no idea who that'd be.

Still, I'd hold onto the thing and maybe hand it to Rob Thornton the next time I saw him; for now, Chad was right. Tomorrow was a big day! My band was opening for the rock and roll legend, Eclipse.

A Shot Across the Bow

Tina

A RUSTLING NEAR THE cabin door brought me fully awake. I rolled over and frowned; a white envelope was laying halfway under the crack at the door.

I groaned and rubbed my eyes. I may not have drunk too much, but staying up late with KC left me with the same hung-over feeling, and wasn't that a crock? I mean, if I was gonna wake up feelin' lousy, I should have at least gotten to enjoy the party first.

That note was fueling my curiosity though, so I shrugged off the covers and shuffled over to the door, ripping the sucker open. I sighed; it was from my dad.

Hey Sleepyhead, you missed a beautiful sunrise.

I'll be doing a sound check in the Starlight theater.

Come down and watch and we can grab breakfast after. Love, Dad

PS: sorry I lost my temper last night.

Oh man, I blew out a breath and ran a hand through my tangled hair as guilt roared through me. He was extending the olive branch even though every bit of last night's argument was my fault.

I turned the shower on and adjusted the temperature. If I'd just had the courage to tell him what happened with Richard ... ah crap, it was too early for this. I dried off and then wiped the fog from the mirror. I wrinkled my nose at my reflection and then stuck out my tongue. Suck it up, girl, Dad's right, you do need to grow up!

Thirty minutes later I was exiting the elevator on the sixth floor just like the map on the ship brochure said, but now which way did I go? I turned the glossy paper every which way, but it didn't help; did that arrow mean the front or the back? Screw it. I looked around for one of the guys in their little white short sets; there had to be an easier way to get around this boat. I'd barely crossed the atrium when a familiar voice came from behind me.

"You look lost."

KC. I laughed and turned. "That obvious?" I shook the map. "This thing is garbage, or I just suck at directions."

KC laughed and took the paper. "It's just you. Where are you trying to go? I was hoping we could grab breakfast and then try out the spa or maybe hit the pool ..."

"Ah, that sounds like fun, but I need to go to the Starlight theater."

KC frowned. "This early? I wouldn't think they'd have any shows until later in the day."

I fidgeted with the strap of my purse. "I, uh have to meet my dad. He's doing a sound check and then we are having breakfast."

The light dimmed in KC's eyes. "Oh, right. I understand." She pointed down at the map. I followed her finger, and got distracted as I noticed KC's nails were the same shade of light blue as mine, she even had a palm tree on her ring finger. I was just about to comment when she tapped the map.

"So, we are here at the atrium, facing starboard." She glanced at me and snorted. "Come on, I'll walk you down there."

I grinned. "I really do have a terrible sense of direction."

KC laughed. "Probably that chauffeur lifestyle you grew up with."

I forced a smile, snarky comments like that were why I never told people about my dad. "Yeah, you may be right. Don't know what I'd have done without you."

KC grinned and nodded towards a sign on the wall. "You'd have found it eventually, just follow the arrows." She stopped outside a row of ornately carved doors. "Through there. According to the map, the theater takes up two deck levels at the back of the ship."

I gave her a quick hug. "Thanks so much, KC. I'd better get in there ..."

KC shrugged and scuffed the toe of her sandal in a semi-circle on the royal blue carpet. "Have fun then, guess I'll see ya around."

Guilt slammed into me. It was obvious KC didn't know anyone else on the ship ... and it wasn't like I didn't enjoy her company ...

"Hey, I can't do breakfast but what about a late lunch? Maybe around two?"

The change in KC was electric and a smidgen of unease crawled through my mind. No one's happiness should have been dependent on me!

"Super! Wanna try that little French Bistro up on deck twelve? I've heard they make a fab Croque Monsieur."

I grinned. "Oh yum, I can't wait!" I waved and headed inside. "I'll meet you there around two."

The theater was dark but there was enough light for me to realize I was on the balcony. I looked over the rail and saw my dad and the crew on the stage, so I was definitely in the right place, now I just needed the stairs.

I found my way to the orchestra seating and took a seat in the third row with Eclipse manager Rob Thornton. He smiled at me and continued yammering into his phone, so I tuned him out and studied the activity on the stage.

Dad and Drew were nowhere to be seen now, but Benny T was tightening his drum kit and chatting with a roadie and Cliff was discussing something with his tech.

"In three, two ..." A lighting tech adjusted something at the back of the stage and gave a thumbs up. Seconds later the light and slide show began running through its program.

I sat back and let the familiar scene swaddle me like a favorite blanket. I hadn't realized how much it all meant to me until I'd cut it from my life. With Dad's apology fresh in my mind, I had to admit that he'd well and truly changed, and not just in beating his addictions but in maturity overall. As a child, he had been like a big kid, the life of the party drunk or not.

Mom had been the rock, the steady guiding force that made sure I had regular meals, routine daily life, and discipline when I needed it. Dad would stroll in from a tour or whatever band activity had kept him from home and completely upset the apple cart. When Chad Crawford and, more often than not, his entourage were in the house there were no rules, it was just one big vacation.

In the end, it had driven my mother to leave, declaring she had to have stability for me. For years I had blamed myself for the divorce and the loss of my father's attention, but when I reached my teens and realized how wild his lifestyle truly was, I'd understood that his irresponsibility and his affairs were the true cause of my parents' break-up and that mom had only been trying to keep me safe.

I shuddered, remembering my sixteenth birthday party. Mom had begged me not to go, but I had been ecstatic to have Dad host a party for me.

He'd flown me to California on a private jet. A private shopper met me at the airport and soon my father's limo was filled with boxes from Rodeo Drive's most exclusive boutiques. It had been an incredible, modern fairy tale kind of day with the promise of a gala event the following night. Dad's home was palatial, and the entire backyard had been transformed for my party.

It was an all-day affair beginning with a star-studded pool party. I'd sashayed around in a bathing suit my mom would never have allowed, reveling in the attention, especially from the men.

The black-tie gala dinner blew my mind. The extravagant food displays, elaborate decorations, and famous illusionist entertainment ... I had been at the center of a whirlwind evening most only dreamed of experiencing.

As the evening wore on though, the tone changed. Gone were the designer gowns and gourmet menu; exchanged for a ribald rock-n-roll club scene. The champagne still flowed but so did the bottles of booze and drugs.

I gulped as my memories or lack thereof swamped me. What happened during the after-party was hazy at best. Lots of men, from up-and-coming stars and several, now well-known, movers and shakers in politics and business danced attendance on me.

But it was Richard Warner and his crew of roadies and techs that had made sure I never saw the bottom of a glass or the pass of a joint.

I'd been too young for the after-party, not that Dad had interfered. He'd disappeared with the lucky groupie of the night just as things ramped up, leaving me to dance and laugh into the wee hours of the morning completely unsupervised.

I squirmed in my seat, trying to push back the flood of memories and worse, the things I was only guessing had happened; I was not ready to address the emotions attached to that long-ago night.

I stopped the walk down memory lane and forced my mind back to the present, focusing on the lighting crew as they tweaked their part of the show and checked equipment.

"Hey Cliff, you and Benny got a set list preference?"

Dad stepped from the wings and hollered at his band-mates. I half stood, thinking to greet him before the checks got rolling, but jerked to a stop as Warner ambled from the opposite wing and proceeded to run into and knock over equipment as he hollered for my dad.

"Hey man, watch it!"

"Ah, for God's sake, Warner!"

Nikki Hardy rushed across the stage and halted Warner's progress as she confronted him. Her face showed anger and she was waving her hands and pointing off stage, though her voice remained level; I'd have been screaming at him.

I drew a shaky breath and sank back into my seat. Rob made a disgusted noise and muttered something before taking his phone call to the back of the theater, leaving me alone.

He was over twenty feet away, but my pulse still quickened, and I was panting like a backyard mutt on a dog day in Savannah, but I fought my usual instinct to flee from anyplace that Warner inhabited. It was past time that I dealt with my fears.

Grow up, Tina! He's across the room, he's no threat!

He's no threat ran through my mind like a mantra as I watched the scene on stage unfold.

Nikki was trying to get Warner to leave but he ignored her, batting her arm away and yelling for my dad. He started to walk around Nikki. She stepped in front of him, and Warner pushed her aside, causing her to lose her balance and fall into the drum kit.

My dad rushed over and helped Nikki to her feet. Dad said something and Nikki nodded. He then turned to his personal assistant.

Even from my seat,I could tell my dad was furious. He strode across the stage and grabbed Ricky's arm.

"Drunk again!" Dad looked Warner over and frowned. "What else are you on?" He shook his head and pointed towards the theater doors. "Doesn't matter, we talked about this. You don't show your face unless you are sober, now get out!"

Even without hot mics, my father's voice reverberated through the theater as he laid into Richard. Dad walked across the stage, forcing Richard to move with him. At the steps, he stopped and motioned for Warner to continue. Richard steadied himself with the handrail and then looked at my dad.

"sChad, I was just- "

"No! I'm done. If you can't stay sober, you stay away from me and this band, am I clear?" Chad moved closer, his chest almost touching Richard's. "And don't you ever put your hands on Nikki again!"

The mulish but good-natured drunk attitude changed like someone had flipped a light switch. Warner drew himself up to full height. His eyes were narrow slits, and an ugly sneer twisted his mouth.

"Your memory going Mr. Big Star? Forgotten how you became the big man?" He spit in Chad's direction and then turned, and stiffly walked down the steps as he yelled. "You owe me!"

Dad threw his hands up and shook his head, ignoring Richard. He checked on Nikki again and then addressed the crew. "Sorry everybody, that will not happen again."

I released a pent-up breath and willed my pulse to a normal rhythm as I processed what I'd just witnessed. My father had stood up to Warner! He'd finally addressed his behavior and set a boundary for him being in his life, I was floored.

The drama of Richard over, Nikki and her crew got back to work setting up and the four band members converged center stage, conversing for several minutes before breaking up.

Benny and Cliff moved into conversation by the drums, Drew adjusted his guitars, and Dad came down the front steps to stop in front of me.

"Hey Punkin, glad you made it."

I smiled but said nothing, just stood and put my arms around his waist, squeezing lightly.

Chad's arms enfolded me as a nervous laugh escaped him. "Not that I'm complaining, but what's this for?"

I gave him another squeeze and stepped away. The hug was for many things but shutting Warner out of his life was top of my list, though I wasn't quite ready to open that Pandora's box by saying so.

I shrugged. "I'm sorry, Dad. You were right, I do need to accept responsibility for my actions and, well, thanks for not letting the argument fester."

Chad's eyebrows rose and worry lines disappeared from his brow. "You called me Dad!"

I nodded and started to answer but he continued.

"And wow, you're reaching a level of self-awareness it took me too many wasted years and broken relationships to achieve." He smiled. "Proud of you, Kristina Carol."

I ducked my head, but couldn't deny the thrill at having his praise even if it did embarrass me. I shuffled my feet and then pointed at the stage. "Uh, don't you have a sound check?"

Dad nodded. "Uh–huh, the Warner mess derailed things," he rolled his eyes, but I just nodded in understanding; I wanted nothing to do with any conversation that involved Richard Warner.

Dad shrugged and glanced at the stage. "Looks like we're about to get started." He glanced at me. "We're gonna try and get it dialed in with three songs." He nodded towards the sound board. "We've already done the individual levels so it's just a matter of the fronts, monitors, you know how it is ..."

I nodded. "Well, I'll just hang with Rob," I grinned and waved at the older man. Rob had returned to his seat. Shoulder hiked to prop his cellphone to his ear, the older man was sniffing and blowing his nose ... I decided to move down a few seats. I did not relish getting whatever funk he had.

Dad snorted. "Cool." The house lights flashed and an announcement for the first round of checks rang out. "Gotta go Punk. Hang tight."

I took my seat and watched as the band took the stage. Minutes later, the pounding rhythm of one of their biggest hits, Firestorm, poured through the huge speakers, and I let myself get lost in the music.

Dad's estimate had been optimistic because, by the time they got everything dialed in to his and Drew's satisfaction, I was starving.

I waited until Drew walked away before mounting the stairs and joining Dad center stage.

"Hey, pretty girl, you as hungry as I am?"

I laughed and patted my stomach. "I need food!"

He laughed and set his guitar back on its stand. "I hear ya. Just let me tell my tech- "

"Hey, you guys! Look out- "

We looked around. I wondered who was yelling, and then a scraping, metallic sound rang out above me. I looked up. “Ooomph, what the ...”

Something or someone had shoved me. I stumbled backward into a stack of amps as the sound of grating metal and breaking glass filled the theater.

There was an unnatural quiet and then all hell broke loose.

“What the hell- “

“Hey lighting, you trying to- “

I rubbed my head, a nasty goose egg was already forming, and untangled myself from the pile of amps and cords.

Debris was everywhere. It was like a bomb had gone off! I was in shock, just looking around trying to get my bearings when I heard my Dad shout.

“Oh my God, Drew!”

My eyes widened. Dad was kneeling in the spot where we’d just been standing. Drew was on the ground, groaning. I rushed over and knelt on his other side.

“Don’t move, Drew!” Chad looked up. “Somebody get a doctor!” He brushed away pieces of metal and glass and urged his friend to stay down. “Can you tell me where you’re hurt?”

Drew grimaced. “My arm, man.” He reached across his body and tried to pat his left arm.

“Whoa man, stay still! We got help comin’.”

I held his right hand. “He’s right, Drew. Try not to move in case something is broken.”

Drew snorted. “Honey, my arm burns like a son of a sailor; you can bank on something being broken.”

I gulped and squeezed his hand. “Let’s pray it’s just a sprain or something, Drew.”

“You’re lips to God’s ears, honey.” He muttered a curse and closed his eyes, leaving me to focus on the mess surrounding us.

Twisted metal and shards of glass lay scattered over the stage, along with wires, cables, and colored wood that my gut said were the remains of Dad’s prized guitar, Mary Jane.

The bulk of the debris was in a radius around where Dad and I had been standing. Drew had saved our lives!

I gulped and met my father’s eyes. What happened? I mouthed my question so Drew wouldn’t hear.

He shook his head and glanced down at Drew. He started to speak when the theater doors slammed open, and a flock of ship’s crew ran towards the stage.

Dad and I stepped back as the ship’s medical staff evaluated Eclipse’s lead guitarist.

I kicked at a strip of metal. “Was that a light, dad?”

Dad glanced over and then back at Drew. “Yeah, looks like a par can.” He looked up and scratched his head. “These things don’t just fall, though. Somebody screwed up or ...”

I nodded. "Dad, if Drew hadn't pushed us out of the way ..."

He nodded. "I know, Punkin'."

I shivered and slipped my hand into his, murmuring. "Is Uncle Drew gonna be all right?"

He squeezed my hand and then put an arm around me. "I think so," He nodded towards the medical team as they moved Drew to a stretcher. "Looks like they secured his arm, so it probably is broken ..." he dragged a hand through his hair and sighed. "What the hell are we gonna do now?"

Trimming the Sails

Ian

MY BAND AND I sat on the window seat in Chad's suite and listened as he and Rob Thornton argued over solutions to Drew Alton's broken arm.

Whatever they came up with would probably impact Bad Opera's opening times but, aside from that, I hadn't figured out why we'd been told to attend.

Thornton was arguing for Full Throttle, the other headliner, to step in and Chad was not going for it.

From what he said, and what he didn't, I assumed Chad Crawford was no fan of Full Throttle and was even less impressed with their lead guitarist, Jesse Fincher.

I'd wondered at the two famous bands not socializing or holding any joint sessions, though there was an all-star jam on the final night, which was probably gonna be canceled now. With Drew Alton out of commission, it looked like all of Eclipse's gigs were off.

Since my opinion wasn't wanted or required, I tuned out and studied the room; amazing amount of space for a cruise ship cabin and complete with its own butler and some other dude whose job I couldn't figure out.

A pale and fragile-looking Tina Crawford walked into the room and drew my attention. Her honey-blond hair was a tangled mess, her dress was wrinkled and there were angry red scratches and cuts on her arms; she looked like she'd been in a war zone or at least a minor skirmish.

She curled up on the end of a couch and hugged a pillow to her chest. Her gaze traveled around the room before connecting with mine. Her smile was half-hearted, and she looked so lost and sad I had to fight my instinct to go over and hold her; Chad and I were cool now, but his warning to 'pick a girl' was fresh in my mind.

Not that there was an actual choice to be made. Tina and I were old news and there hadn't ever been news with Judith; the only thing left to do was give her that memo.

Thinking about the best way to get the snobby doctor out of my life without upsetting the uneasy truce with my dad was derailed as Chad's voice rose on a forceful no. The room got quiet as Chad and Rob Thornton squared off in the middle of the room.

"But Chad, there's no other way!"

Chad waved his hand and made a disgusted noise. "We are not canceling the concert." He stalked across the room, stopping a few feet from where I was sitting. "Hell, Rob! It's the reason all of these people took the cruise!"

Rob sighed. "I realize that Chad. But if you aren't willing to let me fly someone in or ask Fincher to play, then what else is there?"

Chad pursed his lips and shook his head.

Rob threw up his hands. "This is gonna take all day, I'm ordering lunch."

Tina gasped, drawing my attention. I tried to catch her eye, but everyone started talking and milling about, blocking my view.

I joined her on the couch. She was perched on the edge, staring at the phone.

"Something wrong?"

She looked up and offered me a small smile. "No, I'd just forgotten a lunch date and now I realize I don't have her phone or room number."

"Her?" I shouldn't have been happy to hear that, but who was I kidding? I had it bad for Tina, always had, always would.

She rolled her eyes. "Yes, her. KC. I met her the first day out and we've become friends ..." she bit her lip and glanced at the room phone. "I wonder if they can connect me to her room, or maybe leave a message?"

I was about to suggest she call the restaurant they'd been planning to meet at, but Benny T stood up and cleared his throat, drawing everyone's attention.

"Uh ..."

Chad cocked an eyebrow. "Problem, Benny?"

He shook his head. "Nah, I just, uh had a thought about a guitar player ..."

Chad nodded. "Well, out with it, no one else has suggested anything useful."

Benny shuffled his feet and glanced over at me before looking back at Chad. "Uh, not sure I should-" he shrugged. "I mean, new member and all-"

"No, you're a part of this band, Ben. You got an idea, let's hear it."

Murmurs of agreement echoed around the room. Benny nodded. "Ok, well, the band I played with a few years ago, Atmos?"

My mouth went dry as I realized where Benny T was going.

"We played Eclipse songs several times a week ..." He looked at me and I started shaking my head and mouthing the word NO.

Ben grinned and nodded. "Ian could step in."

He'd done it. I cringed as everyone turned to look at me. Several people started talking at once, but Chad's voice rose above the furor. He walked over to me and looked down.

"That true? Think you could take Drew's place?"

My eyebrows rose. "God no! There's only one Drew Alton."

Chad grinned. "Kid, not gonna argue that, but can you play Drew's parts on Eclipse songs?" He nodded towards Benny T. "He says you can."

I blew out a breath. "Man ..." I rubbed the back of my neck and wondered how to answer. I mean, of course I could play the songs, Benny was right we'd played most of Eclipse's songs at one time or another, especially the hits that would be on the set list for the upcoming concert.

"Kid? Can you do it?"

Decision time. I swallowed past the lump in my throat. "Yeah, yeah, I can play the songs ..."

Chad frowned. "Then why the hesitation?"

I shrugged and tried to put my concerns into words. "Well, people have come to see and hear Drew Alton play these songs but there gonna get me ..." I blew out a breath. "Same songs technically, but-"

"Understood." He smiled at me. "But I think the fans will understand." He snorted. 'It's that or no concert at all."

Oh, well when you put it that way. A knock at the door revealed lunch had arrived. Problem solved, everyone dived into the mini buffet as they talked and joked.

I shook my head and wondered what I'd gotten myself into and what my stepping in for Alton would mean for Bad Opera.

"You'll do great, Ian."

I jumped as Tina's hand slipped into mine and gave it a squeeze. I smiled at her. "Thanks," I snorted. "Big, big move ..."

She patted my arm. "But one you are more than ready for. Relax, it'll be fine." She walked to the buffet, leaving me to come to terms with my decision.

I filled a plate and sat near my band, bracing for their reactions; it didn't take long.

"Hey man, that's great for you and all, but what's gonna happen to us?"

I swallowed a mouthful of cheese and met Jason's glare.

"Hey man, none of this was my doing."

He rolled his eyes and I started to fire back when Thornton came back into the room.

"Chad! You can't be serious, he's the opening act, for cryin' out loud!"

Chad turned; his face marred by a thunderous frown. "What the hell does that have to do with the price of tea in China, Rob?"

To his credit, Thornton didn't back down. "We need a big name to replace Alton, can't have a nobody kid take the stage with-"

"A nobody kid?" Chad's volume dropped to just above a whisper and the room got deadly quiet.

Chad's lip curled as he stalked towards his manager. "A nobody kid." He snorted. "Gettin too big for yourself, Rob. We were all 'nobody kids' at some point!"

Thornton started to speak but Chad waved him to silence. "I called Ian a kid, but I've seen him play," he snorted. "Drew and I had to approve Bad Opera as the opening act!"

Thornton looked a bit sheepish, though he still seemed unconvinced. "I, uh, I understand Chad, and I didn't mean to be insulting ..." he turned to me and offered a smile. "No offense son, nothing against you personally."

I held up my hands and shook my head. "Hey, none takin, I'm just here to play my gig and help Eclipse if I'm needed."

Rob nodded. "Well, I appreciate that attitude." He looked at me for several seconds; I got the feeling he was sizing me up. He nodded. "You think you're up to this? Stepping into Alton's shoes, playing with Eclipse?"

I nodded. "Absolutely, I can play, I don't have any doubts about that. I know every signature lick, every one of Alton's intros. But for the rest of it, you're going to be getting me, my take ..." I shrugged. "Just wanna be sure that's understood."

Chad grinned and clapped me on the shoulder. "Point taken and approved." He glanced at Rob. "It's decided, Ian will step in for Drew."

Decision made, everyone relaxed and enjoyed their food, cracking jokes and making plans for shore excursions.

I bit into my club sandwich and watched Tina from under my lashes while I pretended to listen to Jason and Cole worry about me playing with Eclipse. She was chatting with Benny T, and they were both laughing at something.

Jason and Cole were arguing, with Jason insisting that I couldn't do both shows and I was just about to step in and settle the issue when the phone rang, drawing my attention back to Tina.

She looked around, but no one made a move to answer it. She shrugged and picked up the receiver.

Her whole body went rigid and even from across the room, I could see her face had lost color. What was going on?

I set my plate on a side table and rose from my seat. I'd only moved a few feet towards Tina when Rob stopped me. I sighed and focused on the concert details, filing her strange behavior in the back of my mind.

Chad, Cliff, and Benny T. joined us, and we hammered out the details for the remaining events.

"I'd like a day to rehearse, get in sync with the band ..."

Cliff nodded in agreement as I glanced at Chad. "Is it possible to push tonight's concert back?"

He nodded and turned to Rob. "Get with the promoters or whatever and flip the concert to tomorrow night."

"But Chad, the unplugged show is tomorrow-"

"Well, push it farther out then. Let's do the unplugged tomorrow night, I can do it by myself, and if Drew is feelin' up to it, he can join me and we'll shoot the bull," he snorted. "Fans will love it." He tipped his head towards me. "That will let Ian work with us tonight and tomorrow."

Murmurs of agreement came from Cliff and Benny T. Cliff cleared his throat. "That sounds good, Chad." He glanced at Benny and then at me. "We'll run through the set basics then tie it all together with the crew."

Chad nodded. "Yep, sounds like a plan." He looked at Rob. "Make it happen."

"Okay Chad, if you're comfortable with that." He sniffed and pulled his phone from his pocket as he headed for the door but turned back around and questioned.

"But what about Bad Opera? How are they going to open? Do I need to find a replacement?"

My eyes widened and Jason started muttering under his breath. I jumped in before he said something he, and I, would regret. "Ah ..., Chad? I can still open with my band, no reason to sideline them ..."

Rob frowned but it was clear that Chad understood what I wasn't saying. He glanced at Jason and Cole, and then met my gaze and nodded.

"Yeah, that'll work." Chad turned to Rob. "Bad Opera will play as scheduled." He paused and cocked his head, thinking. "Uh, maybe cut the set short and tone down the energy-" He snorted. "Nah, you're young, just cut the set by about 20 minutes and we'll stretch the set change time so you can have a short break."

He looked to Nikki Hardy. "Problems with that, Nik?"

She grinned. "Problems with my crew draggin' ass? Please ..."

Everyone laughed and then, having their marching orders, they filed out a few at a time until it was just me, Chad, and Tina. Chad and I discussed a few minor details about the concert and then he yawned and excused himself for a nap.

"You're lookin' tired, too, Punkin. Get some rest, or at least some sun, you look like a ghost."

Tina's lips formed a weak smile. "Gee, thanks Dad. Bet you get all the ladies with those compliments."

He smirked and left the room, hollering that he was going to visit Drew at seven if she planned to join him.

Tina moved to the window seat and patted the space beside her. I accepted her offer. She was putting on a good show, but up close the stress of the day was clear. Her face was pale and the cuts and scrapes from the lighting accident stood in stark contrast.

"I should go, you really look like you need to rest."

She snorted. "What is it with you musicians and compliments? Rumors say y'all are lady killers!"

I grinned and leaned back against the window, letting my shoulders sag. I drew a deep breath and then released it; it had been a tense morning.

"Whew, some day, huh?"

Tina smiled, though it didn't reach her eyes. "And it isn't even halfway over."

I nodded, but let silence fall between us. She wasn't acting right. The falling light and Alton's injury had shocked her, I'd seen it when everyone first came to the suite, but she'd been coming around, she'd laughed with Benny T while they had lunch ... lunch!

"Who was on the phone?"

Tina jumped and stared at me. "Um, wh ...what? I don't-"

"Don't blow me off, Tina." I shook my head. "I remember seeing your face when you answered the phone. Someone upset you. Who was it?"

Tina started to shake her head. I glared at her, and she rolled her eyes and then sighed. "That's just it, I don't know who it was." She shrugged. "Maybe it was a wrong number ..."

"I don't get it. If you don't know who it was, and think it was a wrong number, then why did it bother you?"

She smirked. "Nothing gets past you." She chewed on her bottom lip, her gaze flitting around the room, before coming back to me. "It, uh, actually may have been a wrong number, at least I'd feel better if it was, but-"

"Tina, what did they say? It's clearly bothered you."

She nodded. "Yeah, it did. They uh," She swallowed and started again. "They said, you're next."

"What?" I leaped from my seat and turned to face her. "Why didn't you say something then? We could have traced the call or-"

"Ian, stop." She huffed and looked at the carpet. "I didn't say anything because I thought ...,"

I placed a finger under her chin and nudged until she met my gaze. "You thought what?"

She huffed. "It occurred to me that it might have been your doctor."

I blinked and sat back on my heels. "Judith?"

Tina nodded.

"No, that's ..." I stood up and started to pace as I ran Tina's idea through my head. I'd seen the looks Judith gave Tina, you'd have to be blind not to see that she was jealous, but did that translate into making threatening phone calls?

I glanced at Tina. “I get where you’re coming from, but I just can’t see it.”

“Well, I don’t want it to be her,” She shrugged. “I don’t want to cause trouble between you and your fiancé-”

“She’s not ...,” I sighed. My cowardice over the Judith situation was just digging a deeper hole. Time to set the record straight.

“Tina, I have not now, nor have I ever been engaged to her or anyone else ...” came close with you once, my treacherous brain silently added.

I shook away cobwebs of what might have been and focused on the situation; someone was threatening Tina. “Look, with Alton getting hurt ...” I dragged a hand through my hair. “Everything is crazy today and probably tomorrow, too. But Tina ...,”

I sat beside her and grasped her hand. “Can we meet and talk? Maybe go ashore at St. Thomas or something?”

She bit her lip and for a moment I thought she’d refuse but she blew out a breath and nodded. “I’d like that, Ian, only ...,”

I frowned. “Only what?” Jealousy reared its ugly head. Was she involved with someone? I beat my inner monster down by reminding myself that if she was I had only myself to blame for letting her go; truth it might have been, but it was still a bitter pill.

I lost my train of thought as she started to speak. "I, uh, I've missed you." Her words came out in a rush, almost like it was against her will.

I cocked an eyebrow and fought to keep the self-satisfied smirk off of my face; I doubted she'd appreciate it. "Is that a bad thing?"

She chuckled. "No, well ... I don't know." She squeezed my hand and stood up. "We didn't leave things on the best of terms and now ..."

"Now?" What was she trying to say? My stomach knotted with nerves. Was there someone else?

"Um, it's just complicated right now."

Complicated. If that wasn't a word women used as an all-encompassing excuse, I didn't know what was. "Complicated how?"

She frowned and I guessed it was from my tone. I knew I sounded grumpy. Too bad.

Her lips pursed and irritation was clear on her face. "If you must know, I am here to resolve some issues with my dad and, as much as I'd like to renew our friendship ..." she shrugged. "I just have a lot of emotional stuff on my plate right now."

Friendship? That wasn't the word I'd have used to describe what I was thinking and what was all that about her dad? I opened my mouth to ask for clarification when Tina started talking.

"Look, can we do this later?" She shook her head and walked to the couch, perching on the edge. "My mind is just ..." she shrugged. "All over the place and right this minute all I can think about is that call, you know?"

I nodded. She was right, I'd gotten distracted by her pretty face and my desire to pick up where we'd left off, but now wasn't the time. "Yeah, I understand. We'll play it by ear and get together when you're comfortable."

She smiled and it was finally a genuine, relaxed, Tina Crawford smile; the one that lit up her face and made you feel ten feet tall when she directed it at you.

I snorted. Man, I had it just as bad as I did two years ago! I wasn't uneasy about it though, she seemed to have matured and I had, too. Maybe we would get another shot, but for now, I respected her need for space and too, I was getting a bad feeling about that phone call.

"Tina, that call. It was a woman, right? I mean, you thought it was Judith ..."

She nodded. "Well, I'm not sure if it was a male or a female to be honest. The voice was muffled and there was a lot of background noise." She grimaced. "I really don't know who called."

I frowned. Wait a minute, a few minutes ago she was claiming it was Judith. "Well then, what made you think it was her? You can't go around accusing people of stuff like that without- "

"I'm not!" Tina rose to her feet. "I wasn't going to say anything, you were the one that pushed me."

I snorted. "So, it's my fault you're making false accusations?" Crap. I regretted the words as soon as they'd left my mouth.

Twin spots of color appeared on her cheeks and her eyes sparkled. She was beautiful, I'd give her that. Wrong in this instance and always stubborn, but gorgeous while she was at it.

"For the last time, I am not accusing her or anyone else!" She ran a hand through her tangled mess of blond curls and sighed. "Look, just forget about it. It was probably a prank." She walked to the door and opened it. "You'd better go, I need to get cleaned up and nap, and you need to get set up to practice."

I shook my head. "In a minute." I ignored her glare and paced the room as something nagged at me. I didn't particularly like Judith Fogarty, wished every hour that I'd never let myself get roped into a second date with her, much less letting the woman invite herself aboard, but I knew without a doubt that she wouldn't stoop to nasty phone calls.

Still, my mind was sounding alarm bells ... I snapped my fingers as it came to me. "Ah hah!"

Tina stared. "What?"

I smiled. "I'll bet it was the angry groupie."

She closed the door and frowned. “The what? Talk sense.”

I grinned and joined her by the door. “Last night at the meet and greet a waiter delivered an envelope to your dad.”

“What was in it?”

“A publicity photo of him with tons of holes poked into it and a big red X. Looked like it was drawn in lipstick.” I snorted. “Alton teased him and said Chad had ticked off a groupie.”

I smiled. “So, there you have it. A jealous woman.” I squeezed her hand. “Tell your dad when he wakes up because I don’t think this should be ignored.”

Tina pulled her hand away and once again opened the door. “Well, what else can be done? It’s a huge ship and we have no idea- “

I raised an eyebrow. “You and I don’t, but your dad likely does.”

Tina frowned. “Why would you say that?”

“Think about it, probably someone he’s had a relationship with, and it was a bad break up.” I shrugged and ignored the anger sparking in her eyes. “I’m just saying! And if not a relationship, then a crazed fan and he probably has an idea who that is, you know?”

Tina’s eyes widened. “Last night, at dinner!”

“What about it?”

"Dad suddenly rose in his chair and was looking around the dining room." She shrugged. "He dismissed my questions, said he thought he'd seen a troublesome fan ... maybe he did see this person."

I nodded. "With everything that's happened, that makes the most sense." I walked through the door and then turned. "Tina, just in case, don't leave this floor alone, okay? Wait and go with your dad ..."

Tina's lips pursed. "What? I'm not going to be a prisoner in here! Why should I? If your theory is correct, this nut is mad at dad- oh my God."

"What?"

Tina raised a shaky hand to her face. "What if, oh God ..."

Her face had once again gone deathly white. "Tina! What are you- "

"The light, Ian, the light! What if it wasn't an accident?"

Bottoms Up

Tina

THE OUTER DOOR CLOSING brought me to a semblance of consciousness. I moaned and rolled over to squint at my phone; eight o'clock.

My eyes were gritty, and my mouth felt like it was stuffed with cotton. The slightest lifting of my head sent it spinning and my stomach churned an accompaniment in four/four time.

I wanted nothing more than to roll over and bury my head in the pillow at least until noon but with consciousness came memories of last night; I had to get up if only to distract myself from the disaster that had been the previous evening.

I struggled into my robe and ambled into the lounge, my only goal a giant bottle of cold water and a Goody powder. I felt a momentary thrill at having achieved my objective until my gaze landed on a half-empty bottle of bourbon laying on the carpet beside the coffee table.

"Ah hell ...," I gulped back another wave of nausea and averted my eyes to the endless expanse of ocean pictured through the double windows framing the bench seat.

I chugged water like it was nectar of the gods and tried to keep my mind from wandering back to the series of poor decisions I'd made last night. Unfortunately, the universe and karma had teamed up to prevent any evasion.

It had all seemed mundane after waking from my nap. Dad and I had decided to give tea and sympathy to Drew. We'd spent a few hours with him, chatting over a room service meal but, the day had been too much for him and we'd left Drew to slumber in the arms of painkillers.

It was barely ten o'clock and, after an afternoon nap, neither of us had been ready for bed. Nikki had called as we were making our way back to the suite and Dad had decided to join her in the movie theater.

He'd invited me, but I'd had no desire to be a third wheel, no matter how much I was coming to like Nikki Hardy. Dad had shrugged and told me to stay out of trouble.

I'd had every intention of a long soak in the hot tub and then curling up with a new thriller I'd downloaded to my e-reader. But what was that saying about the best-laid plans?

The hot water and gentle bubbles had relaxed my muscles, but my mind refused to settle. Every time I closed my eyes I saw the shattered remains of the Par can and Drew's arm in a sling. Then there was the whole creepy phone call to consider.

Who could have delivered that menacing message, and why? Had it been meant for me or was I just the unlucky one that answered the call?

I sighed and pushed my questions to the back of my mind. I had no answers, no idea how to get any, and I still hadn't mentioned any of it to Dad.

Trying not to dwell on the accident had the unfortunate consequence of letting my mind focus on the kiss Ian had planted on me before slipping away.

Taken by surprise, I'd been unable to react until he was halfway down the hall. I'd yelled his name, but he'd just looked back, flashed me a wicked grin, and hollered that he'd see me later.

So many emotions swirling around me, it was no wonder I couldn't relax. What had Ian meant? Was he looking to get back together or was this just a little vacation hook-up? And what about the snooty doctor? Where did she fit into the puzzle?

Ian hadn't really explained their relationship beyond saying they were not nor ever had been engaged and that told me precious little! I sighed and let my head fall back against the padded rail.

The sky was an inky black canvas dotted with zillions of shiny white dots. I was a bit surprised the light pollution of the ship allowed such clear star viewing but the sky was so bright, almost cluttered with stars, that it made me slightly dizzy.

I averted my eyes, focusing on the darker expanse of water directly in front of me as I tried to quiet my mind, but questions just kept circling and the more I fought thinking about them, the faster they seemed to spin.

What had that kiss meant? Why had he done it? Beyond what Ian might or might not want, where did I stand? Just thinking about my feelings for Ian set my pulse racing.

Could I enter into another relationship with him? My mouth went dry, and I swallowed past the lump in my throat. Ian's rejection two years ago had sent me into a tailspin that, without Ivy's intervention may well have killed me.

I loved him, I had never stopped, but I wasn't sure that was enough now; I feared giving him my heart and getting it trampled again. My pulse raced, keeping pace with my whirling thoughts.

An attempt to stop my rising anxiety only made it worse. My chest was tight, and I couldn't get a full breath into my lungs. I closed my eyes and tried to use the meditative breathing the therapist had taught me, but it was no use; I couldn't shut off my thoughts.

I'd always used a couple of drinks to sort out my nerves but, thanks to Ivy's ultimatum that was off-limits. Experience from the past few months said that the longer I sat alone and quiet with my thoughts, the worse the desire to drink would be.

Back home, I would have left my loft and walked along River Street or visited with friends when the company of my own thoughts threatened to swamp me.

I pushed myself out of the hot tub and toweled off. A walk around the ship would stand in for the sites of Savannah. I peeled off my wet bathing suit and slipped into a sun dress. With the cabin key card tucked into my pocket, I set off to explore and hopefully chase my demons away.

With no destination in mind, I had decided to start at the main public deck and work my way back to my floor at the top of the ship.

Stepping from the elevator onto deck six, I ambled around the multi-storied atrium wondering which direction to take, before I remembered that the Starlight Theater occupied the entire back end of the ship on decks six and seven.

Since I didn't know what lay at the front of the ship, I set out to my right and soon found myself in a carpeted hallway gazing at a gallery wall of paintings for sale.

The muted ringing of bells and laughter bounced off of the ivory-colored walls, drawing me further down the hall. I turned a corner to find myself standing outside of the Galaxy Casino.

I'd never gambled before, but a quick walk around told me standing at a whirling and ringing machine pushing a glowing red button wasn't going to distract me from my tumultuous thoughts.

Putting a trip to the casino off until I could go with a group, or at least until my mind wasn't troubled, I exited by a side door and found myself staring at a stairwell.

A few minutes later, my wandering had landed me on the promenade of deck seven. The thumping base of subwoofers announced the location of the Nebulous Night Club better than any sign. I turned away and headed towards a row of duty-free shops and another display of art.

The late hour meant the coffee shop, and boutiques were closed so I did a bit of window shopping, made a mental note to return for a better look at a rack of dresses I'd spied, and then called for the elevator.

According to the little map posted next to the buttons, decks eight through eleven were just cabins. The bands were staying on decks fourteen and fifteen, leaving me with just two more opportunities for distraction.

I shrugged and pressed twelve, praying I'd find something interesting to occupy me until I got drowsy. A quick glance at the directional signs outside of the elevator said I'd find nothing to suit my current needs but, before I headed to the final public deck, I took a quick look around.

Behind floor-to-ceiling glass walls, the spa lay in darkness. I moved to my right, following the corridor past the hair salon, library, and fitness center before finding myself outside on the pool deck.

Open to the sky and deck above, the pool deck was fairly crowded for the late hour and, judging by the music blaring from above, I guessed they were the overflow from the concert taking place on deck thirteen.

Uninterested in striking up a conversation or sitting alone watching happy couples flirt, I located the stairs and made my way topside.

Here, at last, was the distraction I'd craved. The deck teemed with people and, judging by the level of dancing and general carousing, the booze had been flowing for quite a while.

I pushed through the crowds of happy people and found a spot by the forward rail. I had a good view of the band on stage, yet I was far from the temptation of the bar.

The music was loud and the lyrics crude; a hallmark of Iron Heart, the band opening for Full Throttle. I listened for a while, but the band wasn't holding my attention and the crowd was getting rowdier.

Back in my partying days, I'd have been right in the middle of the wet t-shirt and chugging contests springing up in tandem with the raucous music, but now ... returning to those days held no allure.

I wound my way through the throng, smiling and saying excuse me more times than I could count, and avoiding more than one set of wayward hands.

It was all in good fun, it was just no longer my scene. Despite the boisterous crowd, I had felt safe until an arm snaked around my waist from behind and hot, rancid breath wafted across my cheek.

"Weeelll, lookee here what I caught."

I didn't need to turn my head to know who held me captive. Even if his slurred drawl and weasely tone hadn't been etched into my memory, the skull tattoo and the missing tip of the ring finger on his left hand would always announce Richard Warner to me.

I swallowed through a wave of nausea and tried to step out of his grip, but his arm tightened and he jerked me back against him. My heart started racing and my breaths came in short, shallow bursts as I felt his body press intimately against my back.

The thin material of my dress did nothing to disguise Warner's interest in me and my anxiety amped up. I thought my heart might explode from my chest and tunnel vision was starting to form. Knowing I had mere seconds until I passed out, I fought against my panic, drew a deep breath, and dug my nails into the forearm wrapped around my waist.

Warner yelled and his grip loosened enough for me to twist around, though he still maintained a hold on me.

"Get off of me!" I screamed as I placed both hands against his chest and shoved. People started reacting to my shout, with several men and a few women coming to my assistance and demanding Warner leave me alone but my attention was solely on Warner.

His mouth went slack, and his eyes were wide as he flailed and tried to regain his balance to no avail; he fell backwards into the crowd, which parted enough to allow him an unimpeded journey to the deck.

I backed away, shoving people aside in my desire to distance myself from Warner and the invectives he was hurling at me. Once I was clear of the mob, I ran to the elevator as fast as my shaking legs could carry me and didn't begin to relax until I was safely behind the locked door of our suite.

"Oh my God ..." I swallowed past the lump rising in my throat and rose from the window seat as my memories of last night continued to filter back to me. The headlong flight back to the room was clear but after that, everything was a bit hazy.

The last thing I remembered with any clarity was pacing the living room of the suite, being unable to stop shaking, and wishing I had someone to talk me down.

I had started to call Ivy, but it was so late, and I wasn't sure about connections and charges so I gave up. It crossed my mind to call Ian or even my dad but, in the end I picked up a bottle of bourbon.

"Oh God ...," I swallowed hard and shuffled back to my room to dress. My memories after picking up the bottle were vague, but one thing was pretty clear; at some point my dad had returned to our suite and found me more than comfortably numb.

An image of me laying on a deck chair, singing along to my playlist of sappy love songs rose in my mind, followed by Dad replacing the bottle in my hand for a glass of water and then suggesting I sleep it off.

I dreaded seeing him and the recriminations I was sure to see in his eyes, but I also knew it couldn't be avoided. I checked my phone, but found no message from Dad.

Figuring it was better to get the scolding over with, I fired off a request to meet in an hour and jumped into the shower.

The notification ping sounded as I was drying off. I winced as I read his text. The final sentence told me everything I needed to know about how my dad felt about what he'd seen last night.

Breakfast with the band now setting up for tonight's gig.

Meet for late lunch ... if you can stand the sight of food.

Whether or not I could choke down any food was debatable, but avoiding Dad was not. I dug through the dresser and pulled out a pair of red shorts and a red and white polka dotted t-shirt. I'd bought the outfit because it was cheerful and today, my mood needed all the help it could get.

Through Thick and Thin

Tina

LUNCH WITH DAD ENDED up being postponed when they ran into technical difficulties with the sound equipment. Grateful that the reckoning had been delayed, I spent the afternoon dozing on our private deck.

More sleep, combined with a light lunch of fresh fruit, had left me feeling closer to normal. However, now that I was within minutes of joining my father, my anxiety was climbing.

I entered the dining room and breathed a sigh of relief. Dad was seated with Rob Thornton, Cliff, Benny T, and the guys from Bad Opera, though Ian was conspicuous in his absence as was Nikki Hardy.

Either way, Dad and I weren't dining alone, which meant I had an eleventh-hour reprieve: I was pretty sure he wouldn't broach the subject of my fall off of the wagon until we were alone.

"Good evening everyone ..." I took the empty seat next to my dad. Jason Young was seated to my left. I smiled at him. "Have you ordered yet?"

Jason shook his head and removed his toothpick to answer. "Nah, we just sat down." He handed me the drinks menu. "Here, the waiter will be around for our drinks order so, pick your poison."

I reached out to accept the laminated card and jumped when Dad plucked it from my hand and murmured. "Oh, after last night, I'm thinking a little detox is in order, don't you?"

I stiffened and met his gaze. I'd expected to see mockery in his green eyes but all I found was worry, tinged with sadness.

Great, I'd disappointed him. A ton more guilt was added to the self-inflicted load I was already laboring under. I licked my lips and lowered my voice. "Sorry, Dad. What, uh ... I don't remember-"

"We'll talk about it later. "A gentle smile curved his lips, and he patted my hand.

With that, he turned and started talking to Rob Thornton about some recording studio, leaving me in the last place I needed to be; alone with my thoughts.

Nikki arrived as the waiter was taking our orders. She smiled at me and then nodded to Jason. "It's all set.

Jason gave her a thumbs up. "Man, that's a relief. Thanks, Nikki!"

"It's all good, just sorry it happened ..." Nikki glanced at her menu, missing my Dad's frown.

He cleared his throat. "Ah, Nik? What's going on?"

Nikki placed her order and then met my dad's gaze. "Oh, it's ... taken care of, Jason's bass was broken, and I got him a loaner from Cliff."

Dad's eyebrows rose. "How did that happen?" He smacked the table with his palm. "Who was it? We can't have careless crew-"

"It wasn't my crew ..."

Dad frowned. "Who then?"

Nikki sighed. "Warner."

Dad's lips tightened. "Drunk again?"

Nikki pursed her lips and nodded.

Dad gritted his teeth and then looked at Jason. "I apologize. Send Rob the repair bill or the cost of a new one if you prefer."

Jason's mouth dropped open. "Wow, uh thank you Sir, but you don't have to-"

"Yes, I do." He glanced at Rob. "We gotta do something about Warner, he's out of control."

Rob snorted. "Been saying that for years, Chad."

"Well, now I'm saying it!" Dad scowled. "I'm not the one that insisted he come along ..."

Rob held up his hand. "Alright, alright, no need to get excited. Can't do anything until we dock ..." Rob dug into his dish of pasta. After several forkfuls, he looked up and chuckled.

"Heard Warner got knocked on his ass last night after he got too friendly with a girl at the Iron Heart gig."

Dad snorted. "Good, maybe it knocked some sense into him."

Talk of Warner had driven my appetite away, especially after Rob mentioned last night. I pushed my food around and kept my head lowered, hoping no one noticed my discomfort.

Conversations swirled around me for several minutes, and it lulled me into complacency. I jumped when my dad leaned over and murmured in my ear.

"Still feeling sick?"

My gaze shot to his. "Uh, still?"

He cocked an eyebrow. "You really don't remember last night."

I closed my eyes and winced, shaking my head. "Nope and something tells me I really don't want to."

My eyes popped open as he laughed quietly. "Dad! It's not funny!"

He nodded in agreement. "Since you have supposedly stopped drinking, you're right, it isn't funny."

"I did-" Nikki glanced over and frowned, prompting me to lower my voice back to a whisper. "I did quit drinking!"

Dad's eyebrows arched. "Then what was last night all about?"

I gulped and looked back down at my plate. What could I say? Hey Dad, you know that friend that y'all were just talking about being knocked to the ground by an irate girl? Eh, that was me ... oh yeah, that'd go over really well with dessert.

"Come on, let's get out of here."

My head snapped up and I met his gaze. He was already rising from his chair and making excuses to the others, leaving me no choice but to follow.

I let him lead me from the dining room and up the stairs to the deck above. Dad had said we'd 'talk about it later and, since I didn't want within twenty feet of the worms in that can, I avoided eye contact and remained silent.

My dad, however, pulled out the proverbial can opener.

"So, last night when I got back from the movies ..."

I tipped my head back and blew out a breath, bracing for the lecture I was positive he was about to deliver.

He surprised me by grabbing my hand, swinging my arms like we'd done when I was a child. "It's okay you know."

I cocked my head and met his gaze. "How so? I'm supposed to be on the wagon, Ivy will be-"

"Your friend that owns the restaurant?"

I nodded.

"What's she got to do with your sobriety?"

Reluctantly, I told him all about the little incident at Christmas and why Ivy had made me promise to quit drinking.

He chuckled. "As stupid drunken decisions go, I have you beat by a mile, Kiddo!"

I laughed. "Not helping, Dad."

He grinned. "I know." He sighed and steered me toward an empty spot near the railing. "Seriously though, no one can make someone else get clean. It has to be your choice ..."

"It is my choice, well mostly, I mean I still don't think I have a full-blown drinking problem, but I do use drinking to unwind, and when I'm stressed-"

"And that's what leads to substance abuse! You have to learn better coping skills-what drove you to drink last night? When I left, you were planning to soak in the hot tub and then order dessert from room service."

I bit my lip and looked at the deck beneath my feet in an attempt to stall. What could I say that wouldn't lead to more questions I didn't want to answer?

I searched for an innocuous response and congratulated myself when one of the conversations with Ian popped into my head.

"I was relaxing in the hot tub when I got to thinking about some things Ian said." Remembering how my little white lie concerning Ian had spiraled out of control, I hurried to clarify before Dad could jump to conclusions. "It was after you left to take a nap."

Dad frowned. "What did he say that upset you?" He shook his head. "I'm tellin' ya Punkin, if he is causing you to drink, he'll have to go-"

"No!" I shook my head. "It's nothing like that." He looked skeptical. "Honestly! Nothing to do with personal things, Dad. Ian and I were talking about the light falling-"

His brow furrowed. "What about it? It was an accident-"

"That's just it, Dad. Ian and I are wondering if it was an accident ..."

"What? Why would you think-"

"Ian told me about that picture with the holes in it."

His mouth snapped shut on whatever he was going to say. "Y'all think the two incidents are related? Why? Totally different things ..."

I shook my head. “Not when you add in the phone call.”

“Phone call?”

I sighed and told him about the creepy call during lunch. As expected, he got irritated.

“Why didn’t you tell me?” He dragged a hand through his hair? “I can’t help you if you don’t-“

“I didn’t want to worry you before a gig!”

His mouth dropped open, and his eyes showed shock. “What? Why- Tina, I have been performing for over thirty years. I’m not sure there is anything that can put me off of my game.”

I shrugged. “Maybe, but it’s just speculation. I was gonna tell Rob to check into it.”

That mollified him and he let the matter drop, or so I thought. We were both staring out to sea when he came back to my drinking.

“So, how did you thinking about a series of questionable incidents lead to downing almost a fifth of Jack?”

I winced. There was no easy answer to that question, if I were truthful we'd go down the road that ended with Warner.

“Uh, ...” No ideas presented themselves, so I did what I did best; avoid and obfuscate.

“Let’s walk, okay?”

We strolled along, chatting about an excursion on Saint Thomas and the gala dinner dance being held later in the week. To my surprise and relief, Dad didn't press me for more discussion about the previous night.

Our meandering led to the pool area. I stiffened and slowed my pace as we drew closer to the outdoor stage. The crowds were getting heavier. Alcohol was flowing freely, and general rowdiness was becoming the norm; just like last night.

Since being on board, I'd noticed several times that the main pool area, with its numerous bars, was always crowded and more often than not had a bunch of wild party people creating a ruckus; the main reason I had avoided swimming.

Since my dad's band had been around for decades and most of the fans I'd seen sporting Eclipse gear were in the over forty age bracket, I had to assume the wilder bunch were on the cruise to support the other headliner, Full Throttle.

Without thinking, I mentioned my observation to Dad.

"Pretty much accurate." He waved a hand towards a spontaneous wet t-shirt contest. "Not gonna say we weren't wild like this once, but as Eclipse mellowed so did our fans." He laughed. "Still can't figure out why the management teams thought a combo tour with Full Throttle was a good idea."

He laughed. "That band hasn't calmed at all. Nikki was complain' yesterday about how hard it was to manage our bunch once they started mixing with the other-ah, for cryin' out loud..."

I looked where Dad was staring and shuddered. No surprise, Richard Warner was smack dab in the middle of the wildest group of yahoos, and from the looks of it, he was the ring leader.

Dad snorted. "Guess I owe the Full Throttle guys an apology. Pretty clear who's encouraging all this mess ..." he sighed and started towards the group.

My mouth went dry and all I wanted to do was run or maybe warn all of those girls partying with him. My fear won out.

I put a shaky hand on Dad's arm. "Dad, can't you just leave it? You-" I gulped and forced words past the lump in my throat. "You told him to stay away when he's drunk so ..."

Dad frowned and his eyes narrowed as he looked at me. I tried to hide my trembling, but the scene around the pool was triggering things I'd prayed to forget and my body was reacting against my will; it was clear my Dad had noticed.

"It *is* Rich, isn't it." He nodded in answer to his own question. "You said it was Ian and I-" he glanced at the wild crowd and then back at me. "What is it with you and Warner, Kristina?"

I bit my lip and shook my head. The look on his face said I wasn't going to fob him off this time but I tried anyway. "I don't know what- Dad!"

He ignored my sputtering, taking my arm and steering me away from the raucous crowds. Once we were settled against the ship's railing overlooking the bow he turned to me.

"Can we just stop the pretense?" He crossed his arms over his chest and looked down his nose at me. "I noticed it several times; you try and run away, heck you did run the first time! So what is it, what's he done to you?"

I don't know! I silently cried. Tears started to spill from my eyes. I blinked them away and turned to look out over the ocean.

We were miles from land. I was used to being close to shore and seeing pelicans, dolphins, other birds but this far out, there was nothing but the gentle swell of waves against an endless blue sky.

"Kristina, what is it?"

I jumped as Dad's hand fell on my shoulder. It wasn't so much that I didn't want to tell him as I didn't know how to tell the sordid tale, but Ivy and the shrink were right, it was time to get it out and let the chips fall where they would.

I turned and forced a smile for my dad. "Could we uh ...," I motioned in front of me. "Could we walk and talk?"

His lips pursed and his gaze searched my face for several seconds before he agreed and gestured for me to lead the way. I started walking, staring out at the ocean as I collected my thoughts.

I swallowed my fears and settled on a place to start. "What do you remember about my sixteenth birthday party?"

Dad huffed. "That it was a big 'to do' lots of industry people, whomever Thornton thought should be invited really, and it cost a fortune. Why? What's this got to do with your issues with Richard Warner?"

I licked my lips. "Uh, you don't remember the after party-" I shook my head. "Nah, of course you don't, never mind, it's not-"

"What after-party? Where was I?"

I glanced at him and then down at the wooden deck . "Uh, you left with some woman ..." I shrugged. "I don't really know where you went or-"

His hand went out in a stopping motion. "Hold on, just stop running and tell me what is going on."

I sighed and came to a stop, though I avoided his gaze, choosing to pick at the polish on my nails.

My tactic lasted all of two seconds. My dad nudged my arm. "Look at me."

It took willpower but I complied, then wished I hadn't. His forehead was creased as he frowned. I could see his confusion but also his concern; it was the latter than made my stomach roll.

This was too much. Too *emotion'y'*. I huffed and looked out to sea. Why did I have to do this? My life had been great; one breezy day after another.

Until your drinking threatened the Cosmic Cafe and Ivy, the best friend you've ever had, reached the limit of what she'd tolerate.

I really wanted to punch my inner voice; she wasn't helping a darn thing! I wanted light and fluffy in my relationships, I needed it. With Ian. Most of the time with Ivy, and especially with my dad.

The last thing I wanted was a deep, dark delving into my psyche and traumas; it was easier to blow them into corners and wall them off than to put them under a microscope, and easy was my middle name-

"What happened at this after-party, Kristina?"

His question jarred me from my inner pity party and my gaze rose to meet his. The emotion I saw there sent it flitting away, landing across the deck, where Warner and a girl were in close, intimate contact.

She was lying on a deck chair, and he was leaning in as he said something that made her laugh ... a case of the stares set in, and unable to move, my mind drifted to memories from that long-ago birthday...

The music has been changed from club techno to slow jazz, I wonder who is in charge of the radio? My mind doesn't stay on that track long, I'm stumbling around the pool deck, steering clear of the hot tub where two couples are doing things that make me never want to enter that water again.

I move on, then stop because I've forgotten where I am heading. A swig from the bottle in my hand. A voice calls my name and I peer into the shadows, cocking my head because I can't quite make out who is motioning me forward.

I shrug, and I am once more shuffling across the concrete, though this time I have a destination. I glance around, most of the crowd is gone or scattered to more private and darkened corners of the yard, like the one I am headed for.

I am so sleepy. My eyes are closed to slits that I use to find my way, but my energy is fading fast; I need to sit down before I fall down.

Ah, an empty lounge chair in a nice, quiet spot. I flop down and carefully place my almost empty bottle on the table beside me, before lying back staring at the stars, though it is really dark now, almost pitch black.

Someone has turned out most of the lights, either that, or I am so wasted I don't know my eyes are closed.

I grin at my own joke and then flinch as a calloused hand runs up my leg and disappears under the hem of my very short dress.

"Hey, baby girl ..., you feelin' no pain?"

Hot breath on my face, the rank smell makes me gag and I turn away. I want to get up, to leave, but my body doesn't want to listen to my brain.

The last thing I remember seeing is the grin on Richard Warner's face as he shoves me over and joins me on the lounge chair ...

I swiped at my eyes and stared at the deck, absently noting I needed a pedicure. My dad's breaths were coming in staccato bursts and anger was radiating from him in waves.

From the corner of my eye, I can see his hands are clenching and unclenching ... I didn't know what to say, my ready quips to lighten a moment had fled and all that remained was a God awful tension that had my brain begging me to flee.

Dad cleared his throat and I made the mistake of meeting his eyes. Oh God, tears were trickling down his face but his jaw was clenched and a nerve jumped in his cheek.

I closed my eyes and gulped. What had I done? How was this a solution? Ivy and that stupid therapist ...

"Kristina," his voice broke, and I just wanted a hole to open up and swallow me.

He cleared his throat and slid his hand into mine, I wasn't sure which of us was shaking, but I squeezed and the movement slowed.

He returned my squeeze. "Are you-" He drew a deep breath. "Are you telling me that Warner ra-"

"Don't say it!" I pulled my hand away and wrapped my arms around myself. "Please, it's over and done-"

"He needs to be in jail, he needs to pay for what happened-"

"That's just it, Dad, I don't know what happened." I met his gaze. "Can we just let it go? I'll just keep avoiding him and we'll call it a day ..."

He shook his head. "I can't-wait." He stared at me, his mouth dropping open. "Is this why you stopped talking to me? Stopped taking my calls?" He ran a hand through his hair. "Just dropped out of my life?"

I shrugged and nodded. "Pretty much."

His eyes welled with tears. "You blamed me ..." He looked out at the sea, muttering. "I should have been there ... always drunk ..."

The wind carried his words away but I heard enough. I hugged him from behind, laying my cheek on his back. "Please don't, it wasn't your fault."

He stiffened and then turned, hugging me before pulling back to look at me. "Not my fault? How can you say that? If I hadn't been a selfish drunk -" He shook his head. "I'm just grateful you're giving me a second chance ..."

I bit my lip and thought about what he'd said. Had I blamed him? Not consciously. I'd never thought about it. My decision to cut ties with him had been because he was friends with Warner but maybe …

"Dad …," I sighed. "Please don't blame yourself-"

"How can I not?" He threw his hands up and started pacing. "If I had been more responsible-"

"Yeah, see that's not …" I gritted my teeth. This was why I hadn't wanted to bring it all up; now what was I to say to my dad? I'd never intended-

"Dad, I never blamed you, okay?"

He snorted and his face showed disbelief.

"All right, maybe a little, subconsciously?" I shook my head. "But that wasn't why I stopped talking to you and stuff." I shrugged. "I was just immature and didn't know how to tell you that your friend creeped me out and so I just …"

"You blame yourself!" His tone was incredulous.

I met his gaze and nodded. "Well yeah, I mean, no one made me drink and smoke their crap, probably popped pills, too." I shook my head. "No tellin' what all I took that night but no one forced me. Ultimately," I shrugged. "It's my fault …"

His jaw set and his eyes blazed with anger as he turned to look at Warner, still partying by the pool. "Not force maybe, but he knew what he was doing and knew you were too young to know better …"

Before I could blink, Dad was striding across the deck, fists clenched and murder in his eye.

Oh God, what had I done?

I ran after him, trying to pull him to a stop. “Dad, wait, what are you-”

“Go back to the cabin, Kristina.” He shook off my hold and increased his stride.

“What? No way!” I stepped around a bunch of drunk girls flirting with some of the ship’s crew and wove my way through the dancing, laughing crowd.

“Warner!”

Oh no. I hopped up and down, trying to see over the crowd. My heartbeat stuttered; Dad had reached his friend.

“Please! Let me through!” I shoved at a guy trying to make a pass and rushed over but I was too late, Richard Warner was on his butt. He glared at my dad as he swiped at the blood flowing from his nose.

“What the hell, Chad?”

Warner tried to get to his feet, but Dad leaned over him, one hand gripping a fistful of his t-shirt. "Tomorrow. You leave tomorrow and I don't ever want to see or hear from you again!"

Dad shoved him back to the deck, grabbed my hand, and pulled me towards the door that led to the Alchemy Lounge.

“Dad.”

He ignored me, pulling me a little when I slowed.

I dug in my heels, and he stopped.

Finally! "Dad, was that wise? I mean, it's probably all over the Internet now!"

He scowled. "Punkin' do you think I care? Now come on, I gotta get set up ..."

I rolled my eyes but followed him into the lounge. I was about to start in on him again, but Drew was waiting by the stage and, while I figured he'd hear about Dad's fight at some point, I wasn't in the mood to go over it all again.

"Hey, Uncle Drew." I hugged him, avoiding his arm. "Should you be up and around?"

He grinned. "Eh, pain killers are keepin' it to a dull throb."

Dad frowned. "Man, you don't have to do this, go on back to your room and rest."

Drew waved his hand. "And leave you to tell the truth? Get out of here!"

We all laughed, though Dad's seemed a bit forced to me. I didn't regret telling him what had happened, but I wished the timing had been better.

I hoped he could push my sordid tale from his mind enough to get the job done ...He still looked angry to me, though Drew didn't seem to notice.

Dad motioned for Drew to follow him down to the stage. "Well come on then, hard head, let's figure out what I'll play, and you can jabber about."

I started back up the aisle, intending to find a seat in the back, but Dad turned and grabbed my arm. "Huh-uh, Punkin' you're gonna sit where I can see you."

I frowned, was overprotective Dad what I now had to look forward to? I wanted to protest but, after what I'd thrown at him ... I allowed him to lead me to a seat in the front row. "You know, with the lights, you won't be able to see me anyway."

He scowled. "I can see enough to know you're safe."

I sighed. "Dad, you just knocked him on his rear, and I did it to him last night." I snorted. "Warner isn't likely to mess with either of us again."

His eyes widened. "That was you?"

I nodded, wishing I'd kept that little fact to myself.

He crossed his arms over his chest and glared at me. "So that's what caused you to drink last night."

It wasn't a question, but I nodded anyway.

His eyes were flat and hard as he held my gaze. "How did he get near you? He can't access our deck ..."

I glanced at the stage where Drew was trying to get the stool and microphones situated with one hand. "Uh, Dad?" I tipped my head towards the stage.

He followed my gaze and sighed. "I gotta get up there ..." He turned and pointed at me. "You, just park it in that seat and don't-" He pursed his lips and studied my face before continuing.

"Look, don't go off by yourself right now, okay? Between the crazy crap with the light and stuff and now Warner-" He dragged a hand through his hair. "I don't think he'll try anything but just ..."

Worry was etched on his face, making him look his age and that bothered me enough to not protest the coddling. I nodded and gave him a quick hug. "I'll be right here."

He exhaled and I could see most of the tension ease from his shoulders and neck. He mounted the stage, calling for Drew to stop before he injured himself again.

I tuned the men out and looked at my emails. Almost two hours before showtime, then another two for the actual performance. It was gonna be a long night.

Calm Before the Storm

Tina

JUDGING BY THE LAUGHS and smiles from the audience, the Unplugged show was a hit. My dad and Drew were a great team, always had been. The founding members of Eclipse were so attuned they often finished each other's sentences.

I laughed and snapped pictures along with the audience over the many stories made more special for me as I'd lived through several of them.

I shifted in my seat and glanced around, once again looking for any sign of KC. I'd managed to convince Dad it was safe to use the restroom and taken advantage by searching the crowd for my friend. I sighed and settled back in my seat. The evening was wrapping up. I was putting away my phone when Dad started to tell one last story.

"This cruise is special to me. All of these events are really, but this one is personally special because my daughter has joined me and," he shrugged. "Well ..., we haven't seen each other in a while."

My head snapped up as my mouth dropped open. Surely, he wasn't going to tell all of these strangers –

"When you get as old as dirt, like me," Dad paused as the audience laughed. "True story. When your bones start to creak and your hands have to work just a little harder to reach those chords, you find yourself getting sentimental, nostalgic." He strummed the guitar lightly, picking out a fairy light melody that made me swallow past a lump forming in my throat.

"Sometimes you yearn to be young again, want a chance to make better choices." He shrugged and continued to play. "Other times, you want one last day with loved ones long since passed."

The melody deepened as chords were added. "And sometimes ...," He looked up and nodded towards the back of the lounge. The lights dimmed to one spotlight and Drew left the stage.

"And sometimes, that nostalgia is more like a bone-deep ache to mend the chords of broken relationships you damaged in the selfishness of youth."

"This little song takes me back," he smiled and there was a wistful sadness to it that brought tears to my eyes. "So long ago now, she was just a tiny thing, maybe four? Five?"

My eyes widened as a spotlight fell on me. I met Dad's eyes and frantically shook my head in little, hopefully unnoticeable, movements, as I silently urged him to regain his senses and not do what I was so very sure he was going to do.

An ear-splitting grin lit his face. "Come on, Punkin' if I play it, you gotta sing it; them's the rules."

The audience erupted in applause and Drew was suddenly beside me, taking my hand and nudging me to take the stool he'd just vacated.

"Oh my God," I whispered as I dragged my feet. "Uncle Drew, he's lost his- "

"Get up there, Lil' Bit. You'll break his heart if you don't."

I gulped. Drew was right, I couldn't do that to him, especially after the crap I'd laid on him recently. I sucked in a breath, cleared my throat, and took the stage.

The audience applause surrounded us in a cocoon of white noise as my father leaned over, kissed my cheek, and whispered, "Still know the words?"

My mouth was dry, but I swallowed a few times and nodded.

"Good. I'll play the intro twice then you come in- "

I shook my head and he laughed. "All right, I'll just nod for you to start."

I flashed a nervous smile and settled on the stool as a tech adjusted my microphone stand. The applause died back as Dad started playing.

I drew several deep breaths and watched for Dad's cue.

"*Little sea turtle crawling across the sand, you're going the wrong way, ...*"

The tune had become a bedtime song, sung by us whenever his schedule allowed him to be home.

"Use the light of the big bright moon to find your way back ..."

We'd been walking on the beach one morning, the sun had barely broken the horizon. We'd come across a nest of sea turtles. Tiny footprints indicated the hatched eggs had made their trek back to the ocean. We'd followed the tracks down to the shoreline and stumbled upon one little turtle going the wrong way.

Five-year-old me had asked why the baby turtle was alone and my father had said that mama sea turtle's laid their eggs in nests and then returned to the sea, leaving their babies to hatch and find their way back to the ocean alone.

I cocked my head and smiled as a break in the verse showcased the sweet, lilting notes of the melody.

"Turtles leave their babies, but humans never do ..."

Younger me had been wide-eyed at the idea that a mama would leave her young. I'd fearfully asked if that would happen to me and Dad had smiled and taken my hand, continuing our beach stroll.

Dad's deep voice fell in to harmonize with mine. *"Never, no matter how far you go, no matter how high you fly ..."*

My throat tightened and I had to break off. Dad finished the song.

"Even when you leave the nest, you'll never walk alone ..."

The audience erupted in applause, but I only saw my father. He set the guitar back on its stand and picked up a small box from the table beside his stool.

He stepped back to the microphone and the applause faded.

"Thank you." He turned to me and held out his hand, nodding to the bright blue box sitting in his palm.

"My baby turtle is all grown up and flying solo most of the time,"

I opened the box and gasped. Nestled on the black velvet was a platinum sea turtle pendant.

"Look on the back."

I glanced at Dad and then followed his instructions.

You'll never walk alone, love Dad

I choked back a sob and managed a watery smile. "I ..., it's beautiful," I whispered.

His smile could have lit the ship. "Here, let's put it on."

I nodded and presented my back, lifting my hair as he slid the fine platinum chain around my neck.

With a shaky hand, I traced the delicate shell, inlaid with emeralds and diamonds, and wondered what I could say. The song, the audience's presence, the inscription ... I was overwhelmed.

I turned and met his gaze. He didn't bother to hide his love and guilt slammed into me. I had held a grudge for ten years, ignoring him for the most part and, when I couldn't I'd been cutting and cruel.

Yes, he'd been selfish. Yes, he'd been an addict. Yes, he'd been irresponsible and, when I'd needed him most, he had been remote and unavailable emotionally.

I realized now that his lack of interest when I'd come to him about Ricky, was due in large part to him starting the road to recovery from his addictions. Even though my problem had never gotten to the level of my father's, I could be honest enough to admit that fighting an addiction took every bit of mental and physical strength a person had, and it hadn't been fair to just walk away from him.

I stood on tiptoe and whispered, "I'm sorry, Daddy."

He froze for a second and then engulfed me in a hug. "S'okay, Punkin' I'm more sorry than I can ever be."

I shook my head and returned the hug. The audience was applauding furiously, the sound penetrating my bubble of emotion and making me aware our private moment was becoming a spectacle.

"Don't be, Dad. I ... we need to talk," I looked around. "But not now, okay?"

My dad wiped at his eyes and laughed. "Yeah, later." He turned to the microphone and thanked the audience for indulging him in his old age.

The last thing I wanted to do was take my seat and have hundreds of eyes staring at my back. Decision made, I asked the tech to let my father know I'd be waiting in a chair on the deck outside the lounge and slipped through a side door.

I followed the short corridor and turned, exiting onto the deck. A few couples stood by the rails or sat huddled in chairs, but I was able to find a quiet spot a distance from them. I stood at the rail, staring out at the water and watching the moonlight bounce on the waves as I tried to regain control of my emotions. Sounds of happy concert-goers reached my secluded spot and I realized the show had ended. My cozy nook was quickly surrounded, and several people were giving me smiles and nods of recognition. I had no desire to make chit-chat with fans, so I sidled into a darker corner.

I was texting my whereabouts to Dad when something rammed into my back, pitching me forward. My stomach hit the railing, knocking the wind out of me.

"Hey! What the- "

My words were cut off as someone tugged on the chain of my new necklace. My neck burned as the metal cut into the skin. I clawed at the chain as I struggled to draw in air. My hand closed around the little sea turtle pendant. I jerked forward and the chain snapped.

My attacker leaned over, their hair brushing against my cheek as they whispered something that sounded like *time* before they shoved me once more and ran off.

Screams filled the air as people noticed what had happened, but all I could focus on was my need for air and my raw and burning throat. I stumbled back from the rail and into a growing crowd of onlookers whispering and holding up their phones.

My legs were shaking, my vision was beginning to turn black, and all I could focus on was finding my dad. I fought to remain on my feet and made it to the archway that led to the ship's interior.

A cry of relief escaped me as Dad came rushing down the hallway, a uniformed crew member right behind him. His arms went around me just as the deck rose to greet me and everything went dark.

Loud voices and fast, jerky movements brought me awake. I swallowed and then moaned as my bruised throat protested.

"Lay still."

I opened my eyes and realized I hadn't been unconscious for very long because I was laying on the deck, with my dad kneeling beside me. I met his gaze and started to speak.

He shook his head. "Don't try and talk." He raised his head and shouted. "Someone get the doctor!"

Dad on his knees by an injured person, yelling for medical help was a déjà vu moment I could do without. Crowds were pressing closer; the camera flashes were creating eerie shadows across their faces ... Oh God!

I grabbed my father's arm and pulled myself up. I leaned in and whispered. "Viral video straight ahead, exit stage left!"

Around the Bend

Ian

I HELD TINA'S HAND and tried to keep a lid on my rage. Not that she'd of noticed. Whatever the doctor had given her, Tina was feeling no pain. She was also barely coherent. I'd stopped responding to her drug-induced observations and she'd dropped off into a restless sleep, leaving me time to absorb everything.

In one hour I'd gone from no more care in the world than filling my stomach with pizza, to the realization that I could have lost the love of my life.

I'd been in rehearsals with Cliff Harris and Benny T for most of the day and hadn't seen Tina. I'd texted her around lunch, the last time I took a break, and she'd replied that her day was being spent lounging in the sun, and then she would be attending the Unplugged Show with her dad.

My gaze drifted over her sleeping form. She had scratches on her face. They were fading, which told me they were probably from the incident with the light, but the ring around her neck was not. Her creamy skin was marred by an ugly red rash, and there were claw marks on the sides of her jaw and cheek.

My grip on her hand tightened; she should have been safe! What kind of lunatic was running around on this ship? For that matter, why had Chad allowed her to be alone?

The door opened, drawing my gaze. I glared as Chad stuck his head around the frame. "Who did this? Why was she by herself? What is being-"

"Not here, kid." Chad jerked his head, indicating I should follow him into the lounge.

When I'd arrived, the spacious living area had been packed wall to wall with people, from the ship's medical crew and security people to Eclipse management personnel. The crowd had thinned out while I sat with Tina, leaving just Rob Thornton, the chief of security, and a woman in scrubs that I assumed was a nurse.

I followed Chad farther into the room and perched on the edge of the window seat. My leg bounced as I tried to expel the nervous energy running through my body. I jumped as Rob Thornton stuck a glass in my face.

“Here son, you’re white as a sheet.”

I sniffed the glass and shook my head. “No thanks, I don’t drink.”

His eyebrows rose. “For medicinal purposes, ”

I shook my head again and he shrugged, knocking the shot back himself.

“No?" He swiped at his nose with a tissue. "Well, suit yourself.”

Chad waved Rob away and pulled a chair closer to my seat. “Doctor says she’ll be fine-“

“Fine? This should never have happened!” I jumped from my seat and started pacing. “Why was she alone? Why is this ship allowing someone to run around causing-“

“Whoa now, this was an isolated incident and we are -“

“Bull crap!” I rounded on the security chief. “Don’t even try that! How much has to happen before you guys start looking for the nut that’s doing this?”

Penshaw shot a quick glance at Rob. I frowned as the band manager gave a very slight shake of his head. It reminded me of the night I'd stumbled upon the two of them with Warner during the meet and greet. I was pondering the reason for the security chief and Eclipse's manager to be so tight when Penshaw launched into his damage control spiel and distracted me.

"I can assure you," he met my gaze and then looked at Chad. "The cruise line takes any incident of violence seriously! We are actively looking at surveillance footage and will certainly keep you informed-"

"What about the light? Y'all figured out who did that?"

Penshaw frowned and turned back to me. "Sir, I was given to understand the mishap with the stage light was a case of laxness on the part of a crew member. Are you suggesting it wasn't an accident?"

I rolled my eyes. "Uh yeah." I turned to Chad. "Didn't Tina talk to you?"

Chad nodded and started to reply when Rob Thornton interrupted.

"What's this all about, son? That par can falling was someone not doing their job, and-"

"No, well maybe but ..." I blew out a breath and tamped down on my anger. When I felt capable of being civil I told them about my suspicions.

"So, you're saying someone is targeting members of the band?"

I met Rob's incredulous gaze. "Maybe?" I shook my head. "I don't really know. Before this, I'd have said Chad was the only target."

Rob scoffed. "I think you're reaching, son." He looked over at Chad. "You really think someone's got it in for you?"

Chad sighed. "Man, I don't know. Until now, I'd assumed it was all random but ..." he shrugged. "That publicity still of me with the holes in it?" Chad snorted. "Not ashamed to say that sent chills down my spine. I didn't think any more about it though and certainly didn't connect it until the kid laid it all out. Now? I gotta admit, he has a point."

Rob's eyebrows shot upwards. He held Chad's gaze a few seconds and then nodded. "Okay. If you think so ..., let's say the theory has merit." He glanced over at Penshaw. "What can be done?"

The security chief cleared his throat. "We take safety concerns seriously-"

"Yeah man, we've heard it already. Just tell us our options."

I stifled a laugh as Chad's interruption caused the big man to sputter and stammer.

Penshaw straightened his shoulders and puffed out his chest. "Yes, well ... being on the locked floors is a measure of safety already provided but, we can add to this by providing a security detail for all band members when they are in unrestricted areas of the ship." He met Chad's gaze. "Of course, to ensure the highest levels of safety, we'd ask that all of you remain on these floors when not engaged in activities related to your performances-"

"Now hold on a second!" Chad jumped to his feet. "We can't hide out up here, people took this cruise to mingle with the band and we can't just-"

"I understand, Mr. Crawford, but we can't assure your safety in open environments that allow unrestricted-"

"Okay then, scrap the security idea, for me at least. If the others want it they can get with you."

"Chad, what about Tina?"

He looked at me and nodded. "I'm on it, kid. She's gonna stay on this floor if she isn't with me or you, you good with that?"

I nodded. "Sounds good."

Chad hammered out a few more details with Rob and the security chief but Tina had been my only concern so I tuned them out. I stuck my head around her door to find Tina still out for the count. Having her remain on the locked deck let me breathe easier but a frisson of unease hit me as I watched her sleep.

Tina looked like a butter wouldn't melt in her mouth angel while sleeping but I had to wonder how loud the fireworks would be when she woke up and learned of our plans for her safety.

Smooth Sailing

Tina

I GROANED AND forced myself from bed. The pain meds from the doctor had worked their magic to a degree; my throat was raw, but I could now speak above a whisper. I rubbed my neck and winced; that had hurt.

I stretched and walked to the bathroom to look in the mirror. I leaned in and examined the angry red skin of my neck. The chain had left a rope burn but there were also bruises forming. I sighed. No way could I go out in public looking like that.

After twenty minutes of make-up application and then removal, I gave up and went searching through my clothes for a way to hide the damage. There were no turtle necks in my warm-weather clothes, but I did find a blue silk scarf that had been brought to tie around a sun hat. I tied it several different ways before settling on a simple knot with the ends hanging free.

I felt silly until I'd paired it with a gauzy sun dress and a pair of espadrilles. Satisfied with my outfit, I plopped the straw hat onto my head and headed out the door.

"Ms. Crawford?"

I turned as the floor's concierge rushed towards me as I waited at the elevator.

"Yes?"

"Ma'am, I was instructed to serve you breakfast in the private garden."

I frowned. "Who told you to do that?"

"Mr. Crawford, ma'am." He motioned towards the suite. "If you'd like to return to the suite, I'll place your order and prepare your tea."

My father. I snorted and shook my head. He was going into overprotective dad mode, about ten years too late. "Uh, thanks, but I'll grab something later." I pressed the call button. "You, uh, don't happen to know where my father went?"

The young man hesitated. I smiled. "It's all right, you aren't going to keep me here and my father shouldn't have asked you to try."

He sighed. "Ma'am ...,"

I gave the guy credit for reading the situation accurately because he didn't argue. The elevator dinged and I stepped in as I pulled out my phone.

Dad replied as I'd expected. I fired off a reply that I hadn't come on the cruise to sit in a cabin, no matter how luxurious.

My phone pinged as I exited the elevator. Hmmm, he and the band were running through the setlist in the Mojo Lounge. I bit my lip and looked at the big 'you are here' board.

"I always seem to find you needing directions."

I jumped and spun around to find KC at my elbow. "KC! Just in time to rescue me again."

KC didn't laugh at my joke. In fact, she wasn't smiling at all. Her mouth was set in a hard line and I fidgeted under her stare, wondering what was wrong.

"Um, enjoying the cruise? I looked-"

"You mean when I'm not being stood up?"

My eyes widened as I realized what she was mad about. "Oh my gosh! You didn't get my message?"

KC frowned. "What message?"

"After the lighting accident I tried to contact you but we never exchanged-"

"What accident?"

My mouth dropped open. "You haven't heard?"

KC shook her head.

"Wow, I just figured ..." I told her about the light falling and then the nutjob attacking me. "So you see, we never exchanged phone numbers and I didn't know how- I left a message with reception. I thought they'd-"

KC shrugged. "Yeah, sure. I mean, you don't really owe me an explanation-"

"Don't be silly! It was terrible of me." I laughed. "I'd of been cussing a blue streak if someone had left me sitting in that restaurant."

KC's lips twitched and then spread into a grin. "Well, I never said that didn't happen ..."

I chuckled. "Good, I deserved it!" My phone chimed, reminding me that Dad was waiting. I glanced at the text and then smiled at KC.

"Hey, I'm meeting my dad for breakfast and then I'm gonna try and convince him to explore St. Thomas, you wanna tag along?"

Her eyes widened and she looked everywhere but at me. I frowned. What was wrong-

"Uh, thanks, that's really, um but I can't."

I glanced at her but all signs of nervousness were gone. Huh, I must have imagined it. I shrugged.

"Oh, bummer. Are you sure?"

KC nodded. “Yeah, feel like a headache is coming on, probably should stay out of the sun.”

“Oh, that’s too bad! Maybe we could meet later? Join us for dinner.”

KC shuffled her feet and looked down at the floor. “Uh, maybe. I’ll let you know how I feel.”

She looked uneasy or maybe it was self-conscious. I tried to figure out what was wrong but KC pulled out her phone, drawing my attention.

“Um, you could give me your number, you know, so we don’t miss each other again.” She shrugged and fidgeted with her bag. “I mean if you want …”

“Oh! Yes, good thinking.” I pulled up my contacts screen. “Give me your number and I’ll message you.”

I smiled as her reply appeared on my phone. I saved her number to contacts and then met her gaze.

“There, now we won’t have to look for each other-oh, speaking of which … I looked for you at the Unplugged concert last night, I saved you a seat.”

KC shrugged. “Thanks, but I decided not to go.”

“Ah, sorry you missed it! Dad and Drew told a bunch of stories … man those two were trouble with a capital T in their youth! Oh, and Dad played several songs he hasn’t done in years-It was lots of fun.” I fingered my scarf and laughed. “Well, at least until some deranged fan decided to try and strangle me!”

KC snorted. "Yeah, sounds like I missed an awesome time, and getting choked was the cherry on top!"

I grinned. "Oh, you totally did! I mean, who doesn't want to get strangled by their own necklace?"

KC smiled. "You do know how to party!" She shrugged. "But, just as well I didn't go, I don't like being in the spotlight."

I frowned. What did she mean? Had I told her about Dad bringing me up on stage? I replayed our conversation, pretty sure that I hadn't mentioned the whole song and necklace-an alert sounded from my phone, making me jump.

I glanced at the message and rolled my eyes. "I better go, KC. Dad is fretting and if I don't get to the restaurant quickly, he'll probably send out a search party."

KC's smile dimmed as she gave me a half-hearted wave and turned to leave. Her shoulders were drooping and everything about her body language suggested she was unhappy.

Guilt slammed into me. What kind of friend had I been? I mean, granted, canceling plans hadn't been my fault but I still felt responsible, and it was clear she was on her own ...

"Hey, KC?"

She turned and raised a brow.

"You sure you can't join us?"

"Nah, I'm just gonna find a shady spot and read."

"Well, if you're sure ..." Her jaw was tight, and something just felt off about my friend's mood. She'd been frosty when we bumped into each other, then when I'd explained, she'd seemed to thaw but I still got the feeling she was ... resentful? I couldn't put my finger on it, but she was definitely down in the dumps.

I suspected she really needed a day of fun and laughter but if she refused to come ashore-I bit my lip and then made my decision. "If I can't convince you to come into St. Thomas, how about we plan a beach day tomorrow in St. Maarten?"

Her eyes lit up at my suggestion and a genuine smile lifted her mouth. "That sounds great!" A frown drifted across her face. "Only, are you sure? I mean, every time we make plans-"

"Girl, of course, I'm sure. Nothing else could possibly go wrong."

She snorted. "Oooh, never say never!"

I laughed and shook my head. "Nah, it'll be fine. We can make a day of it. Look around the island, grab lunch, then soak up some rays."

KC grinned. "Okay then, I can't wait!"

I waved and headed toward the restaurant. A tiny voice in the back of my mind pointed out that nothing on the cruise had gone as expected and perhaps KC was right to suggest I not tempt fate but I shoved the gloomy Gus voice into a closet of my mind and locked the door; from here on out, it'd be smooth sailing.

Set a Course

Tina

THE SUN WAS HIGH overhead by the time Dad and I got ourselves together and made our way off of the ship. We'd docked at the Havensight Pier and were assured the walk into downtown Charlotte Amalie was quick and easy, but Dad had insisted on taking a taxi.

The wind was whipping, which made the heat bearable but the wearing of a hat and scarf a nuisance. I gave up on the hat after Dad and I chased it across the pavement at the taxi stand for the third time, but the scarf was hiding my bruised neck and I didn't relish comments or stares.

Dad batted the material away from his face and rolled his eyes. "That thing is a menace!"

I laughed and pulled the tails free from the door of the cab. "Sorry, it has a mind of its own in this wind."

"Do you want to look around the mall or- Dad?"

He was staring back at the ship, his brow was furrowed and he looked confused.

"Dad?" I laid my hand on his arm. "Did you forget something?"

He jumped and then glanced down at me. He shook his head and smiled, though I thought it looked a bit forced. "What were you saying?"

My eyes narrowed. I glanced in the direction he'd been looking but couldn't see any reason for his distraction. I shrugged. "I just wondered if you wanted to go into that mall over there or ..."

"Nah, let's go into town."

I flipped through a tour guide pamphlet during the short ride and noted a few things we could do, but nothing jumped out at me as a don't miss kind of adventure, so I closed the book and decided to go with the flow.

We had the driver drop us off on Main street and started strolling, window shopping, and admiring the architecture. The Dutch ancestry was apparent in the arched doors and balconies, but the pastel colors were pure tropics. The tightly packed buildings in luscious shades of sky blue, mint green, and cotton candy pink made me think of sherbet.

"You're right, and with this heat ice cream sounds great." Dad pointed to a sign above a butter yellow storefront. "Gelato and an ocean view okay with you?"

"Oh yeah," I winked at him and pulled the glass door open. "But you're buyin'!"

Minutes later, cups in hand, we scoped out a shady courtyard and an empty bench. I hadn't taken more than a bite when a rustling in a nearby flower bed led me to investigate.

"Ah!" I screamed and jumped back as the largest iguana I'd ever seen skittered across the gravel mulch and climbed up onto a boulder to bask in the sun, totally unconcerned with my presence.

"What is it? You okay?"

I laughed and waved away Dad's concern as I pulled out my phone and snapped a couple of pictures.

"Look at this thing!" I shook my head and returned to the bench, handing him my phone as I finished off my pistachio Gelato.

"Wow, they're all-over South Florida, but I've never seen them quite that big!"

I grinned. "The tourist trade must keep them well fed."

A bubbling fountain drowned out the street noises and potted palms filtered the harsh sun to create a peaceful oasis in an otherwise bustling town. I slouched on the bench, ready for a mini siesta. The buildings surrounding us were different than those on the main street. Gone were the pastel shades of stucco, replaced with exposed brick and walls that looked like they were made with small pieces of gravel. Intrigued, I sat up and picked up my phone.

"Huh. Says here, one of the best materials for withstanding hurricanes is this mixture of crushed shells, coral, and bricks." I turned my phone screen for Dad to see. "Guess that's why they build with the tabby and coquina in our area, too."

Dad nodded. "Yep, thinking about using it for the retreat."

I frowned. "Um, what retreat?"

He blinked. "I didn't tell you?"

"Nope"

"Thought I did. You finished?"

I nodded and he rose, tossing our empty bowls into the trash.

"Ready?"

"Yeah, so what's this about a retreat?"

He started walking towards the end of the alley that emptied onto the main street. "Hmm? Oh, I'm gonna build a wellness and addiction recovery facility on the island."

I frowned and tried to process what he was saying but it was hopeless, I felt like I'd been dropped into the middle of a play during the third act.

"Uh, Dad? What island?"

He grinned. "The one I own!"

Now I knew he was messing with me. I nudged him with my elbow. "Dad ...,"

"No, honestly," He laughed. "I own Half Moon Hammock off the coast near Tybee." He shrugged. "Bought it over twenty years ago."

My eyes widened. "You're serious. Why did I not know this?"

His lips turned down at the corners and his eyes lost a bit of their sparkle. "Haven't talked much lately." He shrugged. "But I bought it for your mom." He glanced at me and then back to the road in front of us. "Thought maybe we'd get back together, and I'd build her a house-you know how much she loved the islands ..."

My mother had been a marine biologist, specializing in the sea turtles that made our barrier islands a nesting ground. Like my dad, she'd grown up in the Savannah area, but, while Dad had been busy forming garage bands, my mom had spent her childhood and teenage years exploring the marshes, rivers, and maritime forests of the coast; she'd gone to work for the University and been a tireless advocate for preserving our coastline until a car accident claimed her life twelve years ago.

I swallowed past a lump in my throat and grabbed his hand, giving it a slight squeeze. "She'd have loved it."

"Yeah," He returned my squeeze and cleared his throat. "I got about two hundred and fifty acres on Half Moon that are linked to the mainland by a causeway, and then another thirty on this little island you need a boat to reach ..., I named it Eclipse-"

"That is so cheesy!"

He grinned and waggled his eyebrows. "It's a prerogative of Dads to be cheesy!"

I laughed and slapped him on the arm. He smiled and grabbed my hand, swinging like we used to do when I was little.

There were a lot of jewelry shops, as well as stores hawking designer bags, shoes, and clothes ... my love for haute couture was begging me to dive in and shop until I dropped. I was about to suggest a quick peek in a shoe store when Dad cleared his throat.

"The opening of New Horizons won't be for a few years yet, but in the meantime, maybe you should look into a rehab-"

"What?" I dropped his hand and came to a stop in the middle of the sidewalk. I frowned, trying to make sense of what he was suggesting. "Um, why would I do that?"

He spread his hands and gave me a gentle smile. "Just a thought, no need to get upset ..."

I frowned. "I'm not upset, just ... I mean you hit me with that out of left field, and ... where is this coming from?"

His brow furrowed and worry etched lines around his green eyes. "You asking me that after the other night?"

I gasped. So, we were going there, again.

I bit my lip and decided to act like the adult Ivy was requiring me to be. "That bad?"

He snorted. "I've seen worse, but let me tell you, alcohol poisoning is a thing, and you had me pretty worried."

I winced. "Sorry, Dad."

He took my hand and started walking. "Not me you should be saying that too."

I wrinkled my nose. "Uh, did I puke on anyone else?"

He chuckled. "Not that I'm aware of!" He was quiet for a few seconds. "In the end, we attain sobriety when we are doing it for ourselves. Nothing anyone else says matters if you aren't committed to the journey for the sake of your own life and health."

When I didn't respond, he sighed and gave my hand a little shake. "Do you want to stop drinking for the right reasons, Punkin'?"

Did I? Easy answer was of course! But ... I blew out a breath. "Ivy won't let me buy into the Cosmic Cafe unless I stop drinking and act like I have some sense."

"That sounds like a direct quote."

I laughed. “Yeah, Ivy reached her last straw after I dragged her into that mess last Christmas.”

"I told you before, in the 'hold my beer' awards you'd only earn an honorable mention." He was grinning, which lulled me into a false sense of security.

I laughed. “Yeah, so you see, Ivy is just overreacting and I don’t really have a problem-“

“Kristina Carol Crawford ...”

I sighed. It was never good when a parent pulled out the full name card. “What? It could have happened to anyone, nothing to do with drinking-“

“Right, you’re trying to tell me you would have written that blackmail note sober?”

I pursed my lips and avoided his all-too-knowing stare. Would I have written that letter if I hadn’t been drinking spiked eggnog? If I were honest, no-well, I would definitely have been thinking it and would have had no problem saying it, but putting it into writing?

I cleared my throat and met Dad’s gaze. “What do you want me to say?”

His eyebrows rose. “Nothing.” He shrugged and started walking, motioning for me to follow. “If you do some soul searching I’m sure the answers will come to you.”

Soul searching. Great. Lots of introspection and contemplation. I was more of a jump–in and get my feet wet kind of a gal. Or course, acting before I’d thought about it was how I’d ended up in my predicament.

The day was too nice to go down the dull road of self-actualization. A shop window caught my eye. Talk of Ivy reminded me that I needed to get some souvenirs and gifts. I dropped Dad's hand and pointed at the store before walking into a little boutique. The clothes displayed in the window were a colorful bohemian style I knew would be perfect for Ivy.

I flipped through a rack of tie-dyed cotton skirts and sun dresses while Dad stood by the door, shaking his head.

"Like you don't have enough clothes ... "

I smirked. "Never! But this isn't for me. I'll just be a minute, Dad."

My gaze fell on a lavender, pink, and green swirled sun dress that would be perfect for my friend. I paid and turned towards the door.

"All set ..." I frowned. Hands on his hips, Dad was staring intently at something outside and it had put a scowl on his face.

I nudged him with my hip as I tucked the dress into my tote bag. "You keep on and your face will freeze that way."

He glanced down at me. "Wha- oh!" He snorted and pulled the door open. "Find what you were looking for?"

I nodded. "Got a dress for my friend. Still need a few more gifts but there are two more islands to visit- what were you looking at?"

"Hmm?" He glanced over his shoulder and then back at me. "Nothing important." He placed his hand on the small of my back and guided me across the street. "Let's go in there." He pointed at a sign above the door of a bright blue shop.

There, turned out to be a jewelry store where he insisted upon buying me another chain. I wasn't picky so choosing a replacement took little time. I had left the turtle pendant in my room but opted to wear the chain as I didn't want it getting lost or falling out of the tote bag I'd brought with me.

"Here, can you?" I removed the scarf and presented my back, holding up my hair so Dad could fasten the platinum clasp.

"There. Fit okay?"

I fingered the delicate chain and nodded. "Yep, perfect." I was about to put the scarf back on when Dad stopped me.

"You can leave that off you know, the marks are barely visible ..."

I wrinkled my nose. "You sure? Feel like it's a flashing neon sign-"

"Nah, it's just you, but ..." A muscle worked in his jaw and I wished I'd never brought the subject up.

"Let's go and see Blackbeard's castle or maybe Fort Christian? The book says the fort is really old and-"

"Tina."

I quirked an eyebrow and decided to pretend I didn't know what he was thinking.

"How are you feeling? Does it still hurt? Do you need-"

"Dad," I sighed. "It's fine, looks worse than it is. Let's just enjoy-"

"You could have been killed."

I rolled my eyes. "Don't be so dramatic." I shoved the scarf into my bag. "It hurt, and was definitely scary at the time but it was just some-"

"Dramatic? Kristina Carol, you were attacked!" He must have seen me roll my eyes again because he huffed and threw up his hands.

"You're downplaying this whole thing and there is a nut on that ship! I want you safe and you're ignoring the danger ..."

I blew out a breath and pursed my lips. He was right, at least about the nutjob on board the ship, but I wasn't being reckless. "Dad, I told you, I'm not gonna be a prisoner in that room!"

He started to speak so I rushed on. "However, that doesn't mean I'm not being cautious. I'm gonna pay attention to who is around and try not to be alone-though it's kinda hard to actually be by yourself on the ship!"

"I don't want you to go anywhere alone."

I huffed. The idea that I needed babysitting didn't sit well and a dozen sarcastic replies popped into my head but, we were supposed to be enjoying a day on a tropical island so I swallowed all of the snarkiness and planted a smile on my face.

"I'll try." Judging by the look on his face, arguing was clearly his intention so I opted for changing the subject.

"Smell that?" I glanced at him and grinned. "Let's get a snack." Before he could reply, I headed for a street vendor cart parked across from Fort Christian.

"Come on, Dad. Let's try pate!"

He caught up with me as I approached the order window. "What did I say about going off alone-"

"Oh come on! You were right behind me!" I pointed at a brightly colored sign. "What kind do you want- or, I know, let's sample them all!"

"Let me guess, I'm the bank again?"

I snorted. "Uh, yeah!"

Dad chuckled and pulled out his wallet as I ordered one of each variety. A few minutes later, we were carrying our street food feast over to the umbrella-covered tables situated in a little park.

I unwrapped each version of pate and broke them into two pieces. "Here ya go, dig in!"

Dad laughed and looked down at the improvised paper plate of waxed paper. "Okay, but what exactly am I digging into?"

I took a bite of flaky pastry and nearly swooned. After swallowing I grinned at him and pointed to his meal.

“Pate are like empanadas. That one on the left is a beef filling, those two are chicken and vegetable. Try them!”

He dug in and polished off a couple before picking at the last one. “What's in these two?”

I smiled. “Mmmm, that one is a conch filling and the other is saltfish. Just a warning, they’re liberal with the scotch bonnet peppers, the saltfish is spicy!”

He bit into the conch and sighed. “That is delicious. I had conch fritters in the Keys but it’s even better wrapped in this fried pie!”

I nodded. The saltfish, or salted cod really, was excellent, but a little too hot for me. I left the rest of the pate and emptied my water bottle.

“When you’re done, we could explore the fort.”

I pointed at the bright red building across the street. “Fort Christian was built in the mid sixteen hundreds and, according to the guide book, has great views ...”

Dad cleared our lunch away and nodded. “Okay, let’s play tourist!”

Fort Christian stood on a bit of a hill and the views of the harbor were incredible. You could also see an island that my book said was called Hassel. Since you had to make reservations three days in advance to tour it, the island was aptly named. Still, standing in Fort Christian with Hassel Island in the background would be a great picture.

Dad and I took a few selfies but then he decided we needed a more formal shot and asked an older couple to do the honors.

"Okay, here's the phone, you know how to work it?"

The man nodded and motioned for us to pose. I set my bag down on a display of old rum casks and walked over to the low wall to wait for Dad. He winked at our impromptu photographer's wife and then sauntered over to me.

We took a few pictures, and I went to retrieve my bag as Dad thanked the couple. I half-listened as I reached for my bag and found it lying on its side and gaping open.

"Hey, ready to move on? The Garrets said we should be sure and see something called the-something wrong?"

I shook my head and gave my bag one more search. My wallet and phone were right where I'd left them, so I shrugged and hiked the strap over my shoulder.

"Nope, my bag was open, but everything seems to be there, now what was this place?"

"Ninety-nine steps?" He placed his hand against the small of my back and guided me towards the Fort's exit. "Something about them being built out of the old bricks the European ships used as ballast."

I nodded. "Oh yeah, I read about that! Though, there are actually over a hundred steps." I pulled out my guidebook and flipped to the map. "It's a couple of blocks that way."

I pointed in the right direction, and we started walking. The smell of fried goodness reached my nose and made my mouth water.

"After this, I'm getting a snack!"

Dad snorted. "Again? You're like a bottomless pit today ..."

I laughed. "Gonna eat my way across the Caribbean!"

"Then we'd better do some walking or you'll need a post-vacation wardrobe."

"Oh, very funny-" I took off at a brisk trot. "Come on, old man, try and keep up!"

Red Skies in the Morning

Tina

WE WALKED TO THE steps made from ballast bricks but chose not to see what was at the top; the climb was steep and the weather was looking questionable.

"Tina, do you want to check out Blackbeard's Castle or –"

A drop of rain hit my nose, cutting off my reply. A glance at the sky suggested we'd be getting wet very soon. I pointed towards a covered taxi stand. "Race you!"

We laughed and sprinted across the cobblestones as the heavens unloaded. The rain beat down on the metal roof, making conversation impossible. The cloudburst was mercifully brief but after the sky cleared I noticed that the sun was sitting lower.

I checked my phone. "No more snacks and it looks like seeing the castle is out ..." I started texting Ian. "It's about time to head for the restaurant."

"Okay, I'll get us a cab."

I nodded and completed my message. After running into KC that morning, I'd found my way to the lounge where Dad and the rest of the band were putting the finishing touches on the songs they were going to do at the concert.

I'd extended the shore excursion to everyone but various excuses left us with a plan to meet for dinner at a mountain top restaurant I was dying to try.

"Ian, Jason, and Benny are on their way." I looked at Dad. "Not sure where Nikki is, have you heard from her?"

Dad nodded and held the car door for me. "Nik just left the ship. I sent her the address."

"Okay, it looks like a twenty-minute drive. Are Cliff and Drew coming?"

Dad shook his head. "Huh-uh, Cliff scheduled a massage and Drew's arm is hurting. The ship's doctor suggests a specialist, it's a bad break, so he's gonna fly home from San Juan."

"Oh my, poor Drew. I hope it's nothing permanent." I slid across the seat. "Good for Cliff, though. He was looking a bit stressed this morning."

Dad snorted and gave the driver the address. "He worries too much."

I frowned. "About Ian?"

Dad nodded. "Yeah, but you know Cliff, he's not happy unless he's over-thinking and fussing ..." His voice trailed off as he jerked around and looked out the back window.

I turned my head but there was nothing out of the ordinary that I could see. "What are you looking for?

A few seconds passed before he turned around. He ducked his head, but I saw the concern on his face.

"Dad? Is something wrong?"

He shook his head and started pointing out interesting sites along the road. I thought about pushing him for an answer but in the end, I let him change the subject.

Charlotte Amalie was a beautiful, but crowded city. Once out of that hub, the island was serene; my idea of a tropical paradise.

The restaurant I'd chosen sat at one of the highest points on the island and the road reflected that; winding through maritime forests with open patches revealing views of the bay far below. The crunch of crushed shells announced we'd arrived. The car slowed as it traversed the narrow road that led to the Old Stone House restaurant.

Evidence that we were on a former sugar cane plantation was everywhere. I peered through the window, catching glimpses of terraced fields, outlined with stacked stone walls and even the ruins of a tall, circular building I thought might have been a sugar mill. From the drive, acres of landscaped gardens were also visible.

I glanced at Dad. "This place is amazing! I hope we can wander through the gardens and I can't wait to see what the old house looks like inside!"

He smiled and nodded his head towards the front window as we pulled up to the house. "You're about to get your chance and, judging by the crowd, I'd say the food lives up to the hype."

Wide, stone stairs led to a veranda with multiple arches made of the curious mixture of shell and stone I'd seen earlier. As we approached the huge mahogany and glass double doors, I saw that the porch was outfitted as a cozy spot to while away the time before being seated. Since we'd made reservations, we didn't have to join the people seated outside on the wicker furniture. In minutes, we were escorted to our table.

Despite its name, the restaurant was housed in the plantation's former stable and the interior walls were covered in the same brick and crushed shell mortar. Arched windows and cathedral ceilings were framed in some roughly hewn wood in a warm honey color.

Dimly lit and sparsely decorated with not much more than potted palms, the atmosphere was peaceful and romantic. I could have happily dined in any of the rooms we were led through, but when we stepped out onto the back terrace I caught my breath and pulled out my phone. The flagstone ran the length of the building but was set up to host large parties, so there were only a handful of tables spaced to give each party a modicum of privacy.

Ian, Benny, and Jason were already seated at a long, farmhouse-style table, in chairs upholstered in a white fabric dotted with vivid yellow lemons. Edison bulbed market lighting was strung from one end of the patio to the other with small, square oil lantern centerpieces illuminating each dining area.

"Good evening, y'all!" Ian stood and pulled out the chair next to his so I smiled and slid onto the plush seat.

Dad sat across from me, and an empty chair to his left stood waiting for Nikki. I gave the server my drinks order and then glanced down the table, making eye contact with Jason.

"What do you think of St. Thomas, Jason?"

He chuckled and shook his head. "If the beach is anything to go by, the place is paradise."

Benny, seated on Ian's left, leaned forward and looked at me. "What he means is, it's a paradise of mighty fine women! Cuz all he did today was stare at the bathing beauties."

We all laughed until Jason accidentally sucked his ever-present toothpick down his throat. He waved away offers of the Heimlich and coughed it up, but it lowered the mood of the table.

Ian shook his head. "Jase, those things are gonna be the death of you." He snorted. "Gonna need to kick the habit man!"

Jason waved away Ian's comments and the conversation turned to the upcoming concert. I held my tongue, but Ian was right about Jason and his whisky-soaked toothpick habit.

Over the entire cruise, I couldn't recall seeing him without one of the things in his mouth. As off-putting as it was to see him flipping the sliver of wood around with his tongue, the slurping sounds he made when sucking on them turned my stomach; it was a nasty habit.

We decided not to order until Nikki arrived, so I ordered a ginger ale and then indulged in a favorite pastime; analyzing menus.

I'd chosen the restaurant because the chef prided himself on creating dishes based on traditional foods of the area. As such, the offerings were mostly seafood-based, though there were a couple of lamb dishes and one beef option.

My research had led us to delicious pate earlier, and now I wanted to try Kallaloo, a local soup made with leafy greens and okra and said to be similar to gumbo.

"Hey all, sorry to keep you waiting!"

I looked up to see Nikki slipping into the seat next to Dad. She was smiling, but there was tension around her eyes.

"Hey Nikki, glad you could come!" I sipped my ginger ale. "Did you have a hard day?"

She ordered a virgin banana daiquiri and then looked at Dad as she answered my question. "Not really, once the pest control was finished it went smoothly."

I frowned. "Pest control?"

Again, Nikki glanced at Dad. He gave a slight nod of his head and she continued. "Uh, yeah. Made arrangements for someone to leave the cruise early. Had to make flight arrangements ..." She snorted. "And convince them they wanted to go!"

Dad broke in, asking Nikki for details on the flight and I realized they were talking about Richard Warner; seemed like Dad had forced him off of the cruise!

Talking about the creep was not on my agenda so I tuned them out and, since Ian and the guys were talking guitars and music, I watched the people strolling through the gardens just off of the terrace.

The sun was setting over the harbor and the glow on the water was calling me to take pictures. I turned to Ian and waited for a break in his conversation.

"When he comes to take our orders will you get me a bowl of Kallaloo to start and the grilled lobster with a side of fungi for my main course?"

Ian nodded. "Sure, but where are you going?"

I pointed towards the steps. "I want to explore the gardens before it gets any dark-"

"Huh-uh, you're not going out there alone!"

I huffed. "What? Don't be silly-"

"He's right, Punkin' wait until we've ordered and I'll go-"

Ian rose from his seat. "I'll go with her, Chad." He motioned for me to head out and then leaned forward and told Nikki what both of us wanted to order.

I held my tongue until we came to a bubbling fountain. There were four paths leading like spokes on a wheel. Two of the options were already deeply shadowed due to the abundance of tropical foliage so I discounted them, choosing to take the path that promised good views of the distant harbor.

"You know, I'm not a child."

Ian snorted. "Oh, believe me, I am very aware of that fact!"

I rolled my eyes. “Be serious. You and Dad need to get over this paranoia because I’m not spending the rest of this trip-“

“Tina, someone tried to kill you!”

“Oh, don’t be so dramatic!” I held up my hand as he started to interrupt. “No, listen. A fan or maybe just someone out to make a buck saw an opportunity, and ...” I shrugged. “They just wanted the necklace, there is no reason to think they meant to hurt me.”

“No reason to- look at you!”

My hand rose to my neck. I’d forgotten about the mark left from having the chain tugged. I reached into my bag, determined to put the scarf back on. “Thanks for making me self-conscious-where is that thing?” I dug to the bottom of the tote but my blue silk scarf was absent without leave.

“What are you looking for?”

I looked up and scowled at him. “My scarf, since you want to point out the flaws in my appearance-“

“Oh stop it, you look as beautiful as always.” He grabbed my hand and gave a gentle tug to get me walking again.

I huffed but followed him. “Flattery will get you everywhere.”

Ian smirked. “Promises, promises.”

I shook my head at his nonsense and then dropped his hand to get out my phone. “This view is amazing!”

Ian grunted something that was probably agreement. I was too enraptured by the sight in front of me to continue the conversation.

The restaurant was perched on the mountain top. From my vantage point I could see the terraces that had once been fields of sugar cane and, farther off was the bay. I could just catch a glimpse of the sugar-white sand of a beach.

I took several photos before the sun set and then turned back to find Ian watching me. A soft smile curved his lips and the gleam in his eye was familiar and, while not unwelcome, I would have been happier about it, had he not had a sort of fiancée back on the ship.

"Ready to head back?"

I nodded but ignored the hand he extended toward me. "Yep, I'm betting our food will be waiting and I am starving."

Ian frowned but fell into step beside me. The path was uneven and, with the dim light and my wedged heels, it wasn't long before I stumbled.

Ian's hands were around me in an instant, saving me from a face plant by the simple expedient of hauling me in to rest against his chest.

My stomach fluttered and I caught my breath. Regardless of my brain's apprehensions, my body was under no such restraints.

"Um ...," I looked up and met his gaze. "Thanks for the rescue. You can let me go now ..."

His dimple flashed as a lazy grin spread across his face. "Now, why would I want to do that?"

The gleam in his eye made me catch my breath. My eyes fluttered shut as Ian dipped his head. His lips were within inches of mine when my dad's voice rang out.

"Tina? Ian? Food's here ...,"

We jerked apart as the crunch of gravel announced Dad was coming around the corner. My gaze met Ian's and I grinned.

"Feelin' a bit like a teenager right now ..."

Ian chuckled and grabbed my hand. "Come on, before your dad asks me if my intentions are honorable."

I cocked an eyebrow. "Well, are they?"

Ian smirked. "Do you want them to be?"

And wasn't that just the dollar ninety-eight question of the hour! Dad's arrival and subsequent chatter on the way back to the table saved me from having to answer, though my mind whirled with the possible implications and intentions of Ian's *almost* kiss.

We'd just passed the fountain when Dad came to an abrupt stop and swung around causing me to bump into his chest.

"Dad! What the ..., Dad? What is it?" I stepped back and studied his face. The lighting was dim, but even so, I could see his eyes were narrowed and his jaw was set.

I started to question him again but he shook his head and motioned for me to walk in front of him. I pursed my lips but continued down the path, with Ian just behind me and Dad bringing up the rear.

We were about twenty feet from the steps of the terrace when I glanced back to see Dad lagging behind. Every couple of paces he'd turn his head and look off into the darkened garden.

Something was up and I'd had enough of him brushing my questions off. Once we were seated, I caught his gaze.

"Okay, that is like the fifth time today I've caught you looking over your shoulder and acting like the hounds of hell are nipping at your heels." I scowled and crossed my arms over my chest. "What is going on?"

Dad rolled his eyes and shook his head and then took a bite of his grilled mahi-mahi. I did some eye-rolling of my own. "Dad? What's bothering you?"

Nikki frowned and glanced between the two of us. "Something wrong?"

I looked at Dad but he didn't even lift his eyes from his plate. I huffed and answered Nikki. "Several times today I've caught him looking around and looking nervous but he won't say why ..."

Nikki's eyes widened. She placed her hand on my dad's arm. "Chad? What's bothering you?"

He looked up at Nikki. His lips tightened into a flat line and he turned to stare out at the garden. For a minute, I thought he'd ignore us but, just as I was about to repeat my question, Dad sighed and turned his gaze back to the table.

"I thought I saw someone."

I frowned. "And? There are lots of someones's in the world-"

"Funny." He shook his head. "She looks like a woman that used to harass us ..."

I blinked. That was nothing like what I thought he'd say. "By us, do you mean you, our family, or the band?"

Dad sighed. "Me, you, all of the above?"

Nikki frowned. "Harassing you? In what way?"

He shrugged. "Just, creeping around ..."

Ian sat forward, looking at me as he asked. "Man, are you talking about the groupie you ticked off?"

Dad shook his head. "Nah ..., well maybe?" He scowled. "I really don't know what I mean, just ... just forget it."

I studied his expression. Dad was trying to downplay the whole thing but a nerve ticked in his cheek and tension was radiating off of him.

"No, with everything that's happened the last few days?" From the corner of my eye, I could see Nikki and Ian nodding and Jason and Benny wore similar looks of concern. "Dad, come on, we need to know."

He met my eyes and then rubbed the back of his neck and sighed. "Okay, this might sound crazy but the other night, at dinner? I could have sworn I saw-"

"Oh! I remember!" My eyes widened and I glanced at Ian. "Remember? I told you about it."

Ian nodded and then looked at Dad. "So, who did you think it was in the dining room?"

"Eh, she looked like this girl that hung around the band ... ten years ago?" He shook his head. "No fifteen, at least when it started. Rob could give the specifics, I was ..." he shrugged.

"You were perpetually drunk."

He snorted. "Don't spare my feelings, say what you really think!"

I grinned and shrugged. "I am not known for tact."

He smirked. "I know. Anyway, you were just a little kid when it started, but this chick, God! I never knew who she was, but she started showing up everywhere the band played."

"A groupie."

Dad glanced at Ian and snorted. "Nah, this gal went way, way beyond looking for a star hook-up, er ...," he glanced at me, and I could have sworn he blushed!

My lips twitched but I fought off the laugh begging to come out.

Dad rolled his eyes and continued. "Her behavior was not just a girl looking to spend time with a star."

Nikki nodded. "How so?"

Dad shrugged. "Well, you have to remember that this started before Eclipse took off. I mean, we didn't have any real security," he laughed. "Heck, most of the time we were more than willing to, uh party with fans."

I ignored the chuckles and smirks from Jason and Benny, motioning for Dad to continue.

"So this girl starts with getting backstage, but instead of just hanging out or, whatever, she kept trying to hook up with me, but I was married."

I scoffed. "Uh, Dad ..."

He thumped the table, jostling his water glass. "Don't Dad me! Despite what your mother may have said, once you were born, I tried. I tried to make our marriage work and that meant orders to the roadies and crew to not let women into my dressing room and shi, er stuff."

The tone of his voice and the look on his face told me he meant every word. Too bad my mother was no longer alive to see and hear the sober and honest Chad Crawford. I shook off a wave of sadness for what might have been and tuned in to what my father was saying.

"When she couldn't get to me, she started, well I should say these things happened and we blamed them on her because witnesses would report seeing someone that looked like her."

I blinked. I'd missed something. "What happened?"

Dad frowned. "Huh? Oh, well we'd be out on tour, hell the three of us were on vacation once, and the hotel room would get trashed, or things would be stolen."

My eyes widened. "Wow, she was stalking you."

He nodded. “Yeah, that’s what it felt like, got to the point I was always looking over my shoulder.”

“Like today.”

Dad nodded. “Yeah, I could have sworn someone was following us ... blond-haired woman ... but, it’s a small island, probably my imagination.”

Nikki’s brow furrowed. “This girl you saw today, she looked familiar?”

His brows drew together. “Eh, yes and no. It was more of an impression?” He blew out a breath. “I can’t explain ... it’s just a feeling.”

“So Dad, what happened to that stalker woman?”

He cocked his head. “Well, we’d just moved into the house on Tybee, and I had gates installed. Couldn’t see the road from the house but I got a call from neighbors complaining a woman was standing outside those gates yelling her head off.”

“Oh wow, where was I?”

He snorted. “You and your mom were visiting Grandma Sue, thank God.” He rolled his eyes. “I had to call the cops, they came and said she wasn’t mentally sound, then an ambulance came ... it was a holy mess!”

My eyes widened. “Good grief! Did you press charges? What made her stop?”

Dad shrugged. “Nah, didn’t press charges. Felt sorry for her, obviously wasn’t all there. I assume they put her away somewhere because everything stopped for several years."

He paused as the server started clearing the table.

"Then what happened?"

"Well, life went on, we were getting higher up the ladder so, if she tried to pull her stunts, I wasn't aware of it." He scratched his head and frowned. "Although, every now and then I'd think I saw her, like today. It'd be some random place, like a store or something, almost always when I was in town, never at gigs."

"So Dad, you think you've seen this woman now?"

"Uh-huh, it was just an impression. Out of the corner of my eye, you know?"

"Yes. What does or did she look like? I can keep an eye out- "

Dad shook his head. "Punkin' ..., I don't want you ..." He sighed. "I want you to enjoy yourself."

I rolled my eyes. "I am. Watching out for this woman doesn't prevent me from having a good time-"

"I think this is more of a reason you shouldn't go anywhere alone."

Dad tipped his head in agreement as I scowled at Ian.

"Oh, don't you start!"

"What?" Ian huffed. "You were attacked! That's enough to say you should have some type of security-"

"I don't need to do anything." I looked at Ian and then at Dad. "I am a perfectly capable adult and as for security

... someone looking for a souvenir to sell on the Internet is hardly a reason to call out the bodyguards."

Ian pursed his lips and looked like he wanted to argue but Nikki changed the subject by informing us that we'd be stranded on St. Thomas if we didn't get a move on. We had to pair off for the taxi ride back to the port and Ian managed to guide me into his car. We hadn't been moving more than a few minutes when he brought the subject of security back up.

I listened as he presented his case, but nothing he said swayed my opinion. I sighed. "Ian, I'm going to tell you what I told Dad. I didn't take a cruise to be a prisoner in a cabin and having someone shadowing me all over the ship would do the opposite of what you intend."

He frowned. "How do you figure that?"

I huffed. "Because that will just draw more attention to me! Look," I took his hand. "I appreciate that you care, but-"

"Care?" Ian snorted. "Tina, seeing you all banged up and lying in that bed yesterday-" He gulped and put his arm around me, pulling me closer. "You could have died."

I closed my eyes and rested my head on his chest, praying he wouldn't say any more. His actions and words made it clear he wanted to resume our relationship but did I want that?

I loved him, had never stopped really, but that didn't mean I was interested in picking up where we'd left off two years ago, in fact, that was the last thing I wanted to do. I had changed, just as I was sure Ian had. We needed to get to know the new people that we'd become and before we could begin to do that, Ian had loose ends to tie up with Doctor Fogarty.

I scooted out of his arms and he frowned.

"Do I smell?"

I laughed and rolled my eyes.

We sat in silence for a few minutes before Ian cleared his throat.

"Um, it's still early and we've already eaten ..." He shrugged. "You want to get together later?"

I bit my lip and considered his invitation. The answer to his question was a resounding yes, from my heart and body anyway, but my brain was throwing up giant red stop signs and flashing images of the snooty Doctor Fogarty.

Before I could think, I blurted out, "What about your doctor?"

Ian huffed. "Judith isn't my doctor ..., and what about her?"

Now it was my turn to huff. "Don't be obtuse, you know what I mean."

We arrived at the port and the next few minutes were spent paying cab drivers and then boarding the ship. All of us were standing in the atrium waiting on the elevator when Ian sidled up beside me and slid his arm around my waist.

"So, about getting together later ..."

I bit back a laugh as Benny T jumped in and suggested we all go to the casino. Ian rolled his eyes but was powerless to stop the momentum as Dad, Jason, and Nikki chimed in and plans were made to meet outside of the casino around eight.

Ian pulled me closer and ducked his head to whisper in my ear. "My intention was for a party of two. How about some star gazing tonight?"

I caught my breath. His words and tone promised things part of me dearly wanted but I had to know where I, and Judith Fogarty, stood.

I shook my head and started to enter the elevator but Ian's arm tightened, halting my progress. "Why not?"

Everyone was waiting on us and Ian showed no signs of releasing me unless I answered, not that I needed much pressure to agree. "All right, we can meet-"

"No, I'll come by your suite." He nudged me to board the elevator. "Remember what I said about going out alone ..."

"You promised not to walk around this ship-"

"Dad!" I rolled my eyes at Ian and my dad but refrained from giving them a piece of my mind in such a public place.

Ian and the rest of the band were on the deck just below ours. They all got off and Dad and I rode up to the top tier in silence, though there were words sitting on the tip of my tongue.

The doors opened and so did my mouth. "Dad, y'all are gonna drive me nuts with this tag-teaming over protective nonsense."

"Nonsense! Tina, this is not a joke and, at least Ian is showing some sense!"

Dad and I continued to go back and forth over his security concerns as we exited and started down the hallway. There were two suites on the top deck. The lead singer of Full Throttle occupied the suite on the starboard side; ours was around the corner.

"For the last time. If you don't agree to make sure you are not alone when not on this floor I am going to request a guard."

"Dad, that's just a bit extreme for an overzealous or greedy fan and some odd incidents."

His lips were pressed into a hard line and his eyes were glinting a bright jade. He cocked an eyebrow. "Option 1 or 2? Your choice ..."

I gritted my teeth. Men! They were blowing everything out of proportion ...

We'd turned the corner when my eye caught a flit of something blue at the end of the hall, near the door to our suite. I frowned. The color was familiar-

"What the-"

"Oh my God!" My knees started to wobble. I placed a trembling hand on Dad's arm and took back every nasty thought I'd had about overprotective fathers.

My blue silk scarf wasn't lost after all. Someone had fashioned it into a hangman's noose and draped it around the door handle to our suite.

Caught in the Undertow

Tina

ONE LEMON, TWO LEMONS... "Whoop! I won, I won!" I turned to Ian. "What did I win?"

He laughed and shook his head. "You chose the double your money option, so you've won fifty dollars. " He reached over my shoulder and started to press a button. "Hit it again-"

"No!" I grabbed his hand. "I might lose it all!" He rolled his eyes but I pressed the cash out button before he could stop me.

I took my ticket and rose from the chair. "So, how do I get my money?"

Ian chuckled and grabbed my hand. "Come on, last of the high rollers."

A few minutes later I grinned and waved my fifty-dollar bill at Ian. "Look what I won!"

"A whole fifty dollars! Don't spend it all in one place!"

I stuck my tongue out at him. "Go ahead, poke fun, but I'm up fifty ... you can't say the same!"

"True, but I only played once. Hard to keep my eye on you if I'm watching the flashing lights and spinning tiles."

He had a point, not that I'd tell him so. I also held my tongue on the obvious retort that I hadn't asked him to keep an eye on me; no way did I want that conversation to come back up.

Seconds after we'd found my scarf turned into a hangman's noose I knew the rest of my cruise was gonna be a nightmare. Dad had hustled me back to the elevator and down to Ian's room before I could blink and then he'd called the captain who came running with his calvary of security guards.

Much to dad and Ian's displeasure, I'd insisted upon returning to the cabin when they all set out to investigate, not that anyone did much that I could see. Our cabin was thoroughly searched, as was the other cabin on our deck, but whoever had left the present hadn't stuck around to admire their handiwork.

Search complete, the men had huddled in the living area of our suite and tossed around ideas for handling the situation. No one seemed to be asking the questions I thought imperative, such as how had the culprit gained access to our deck and were they caught on security cameras because they were too focused on making my life miserable. Chief Penshaw's offer of around-the-clock security was my cue to exit.

I had some definite opinions about their last suggestion but the men were in full-blown crisis mode and seemed to consider me only in the light of the victim. Several of the unsettling incidents had centered around me, but not all of them; had the testosterone not been so thick in the air, I might have pointed that out. Having been a murder suspect recently, criminal investigation procedures were not foreign to me, and, since Ivy and I had stepped up and actually found the real killer of our neighbor last Christmas, I also considered myself no slouch in the detective department.

An interesting fact about cruising that I'd not known was that there was no recognizable law enforcement; the ship's security staff were aware of the incidents but all they could really do was offer to check surveillance videos, post guards, and place the culprit into a holding cell until we reached a port, if we managed to find them.

Since there were no real cops on board, there also was no real investigation; the security team of Chief Penshaw didn't take fingerprints or even any photos! I had managed to snap a few from all angles before they'd removed my scarf. To kill time, I flipped through them while waiting for Ian and my Dad to recover enough to continue with our plans for the evening.

I enlarged my phone screen and studied the images. Whoever had tied my scarf was talented; I would have had no idea how to construct such a thing. I sighed. Aside from the noose shape, there was nothing unusual or interesting to note about a scarf hanging from a door knob.

Raised voices from inside the cabin gave me no desire to enter. I leaned against the wall opposite our cabin door to wait on Dad and Ian and started scrolling through social media. It didn't hold my attention for more than a few minutes but I'd reached the end of my patience anyway. It was nearing the time we'd agreed to meet at the casino.

I shoved away from the wall and was turning the doorknob when the phone slipped from my hand. I bent over and a flash of red by the baseboard caught my eye. I dropped to my knees and realized it was the tip of a fake, stiletto-shaped fingernail.

My brow furrowed as I considered how someone could have lost a nail. Had it caught on the door jam? Maybe they'd been startled by someone arriving and moving too fast?

How the nail tip had come off was of less interest to me than who it had belonged to. If I discounted someone stealing a key card, the obvious answer was housekeeping or someone staying in the other cabin. Only, why would any of them wish to scare or harm me?

I bit my lip and strolled down the aisle lined with slot machines as I considered the problem. I hated to admit it, but the incidents seemed personal and that meant I had an enemy on board; that admission sent a shiver up my spine. Lost in thought and not watching where I was going, I almost caused a server to drop their tray full of drinks.

"Whoa, you awake?"

Ian tugged me back against his chest and the waitress scooted past. I called out an apology and then looked around for my dad and the rest of our party. I didn't see Benny T or Jason, but Dad was playing blackjack and Nikki was standing behind him. I started walking only to be drawn up short as Ian's hand dropped onto my shoulder.

"Going somewhere?"

I sighed and looked behind me. "Not unless you are."

Ian grinned. "You're learning." He took my hand. "Lead the way ..."

I rolled my eyes. "You're enjoying this far too much."

Ian chuckled. "Having you pretty much chained to my side? Darn right, I am!"

"Whatever. Let's go see how Dad's doing. Don't want him to lose his fortune and have to move in with me!"

As we drew nearer the table, I saw that my fears were unfounded. Dad was winning so big he'd drawn a crowd. Ian and I pushed our way through to stand beside Nikki and watched as Dad won another huge stack of chips.

Everyone cheered and then groaned as Dad rose from his chair, signaling he'd finished playing. He grinned, shoved a three-inch-high stack of chips to the dealer and then motioned for the attendant to cash him in.

We were standing by the cashier's cage, tossing around the possibility of getting dessert when Warner showed up. Fearing he was there to start crap with me over our little tussle by the pool, I stiffened and started to back away, but Richard went straight for Dad.

"Think you're such a big shot!" Warner poked my dad's chest to punctuate his words. "Coward, sendin' that bitch to do your dirty work." Without taking a breath, Warner turned and looked at me. "That tramp daughter of yours been lying about-"

His words were cut off as Dad's hands wrapped around his throat. A vein bulged in Warner's forehead and his face was an alarming shade of red.

Screams from me, Nikki, and several other people standing nearby did nothing to stop my Dad. Warner started to gasp for breath.

"Dad! Let him go-"

"Chad, oh my God, you're killing him!"

Warner clawed at Dad's hands as Nikki and I shouted but Dad didn't stop until Ian stepped in.

"Chad, man, let go!"

Dad finally loosened his grip and stepped back. He threw his hands up and shook off Ian's hold. "I'm done, it's fine, just ..." Dad drew several deep breaths as he looked at Warner who was doubled over, sputtering and coughing. "Get out, get him out of here before I kill him!"

Someone must have called security because two crew members cautioned them both before walking Warner out of the casino.

Dad was pacing in a tight circle. His shoulders were stiff and a scowl marred his features. He was still blazingly angry. I was at a loss on how to help and could only watch.

Nikki put her hand out as Dad passed her but he avoided her touch. He huffed and his gaze skimmed the crowd that had formed. He rolled his eyes and then stalked towards the exit.

We all trailed after him and caught up outside the main doors just as Nikki tried again to soothe him. He shook her off, met my eyes, and then looked back at Nikki. "I'm fine, Nik I just ... let's call it a night."

Nikki started to walk with him but Dad shook his head. "I'm gonna walk it off, clear my head before I go to bed." Dad looked at Ian. "You keep an eye on Tina."

"Yes sir,"

Dad nodded and then stalked off towards the elevators.

Nikki met my gaze and raised her eyebrows. "Well, guess that's enough excitement for me!" She gave us a little wave. "See you guys tomorrow. Final rehearsals in the theater at seven, Ian."

"Will do, have a good night, Nikki."

A snort was all the reply Ian got.

"Whew, think Nikki's got the right idea ..." I shivered and leaned back against Ian, grateful for his warmth and support.

Ian placed his hands on my shoulders and leaned close to whisper in my ear. "Night's just getting started. How about that stargazing I promised?"

An entirely different sort of shiver raced through me. I turned my head and looked into his brilliant blue eyes. Those eyes held promises and intents that I wasn't sure I was ready for but my body overrode my brain and nodded before I could speak.

His lips curled into a smile that caused his dimple to flash. "Great."

We had to go up two floors to reach the Promenade deck and, once there, we discovered lots of other passengers had similar plans.

"Let's go up one more floor."

We climbed a set of outside stairs and were quickly on the pool deck. There were concerts in both the Alchemy lounge and the Stargazer theater so finding a quiet corner was easier than I'd expected.

We strolled along the deck, hand in hand. I nodded and made noncommittal sounds as Ian talked about the beauty of the night sky but, to be honest, I was only half listening.

"Penny for your thoughts?"

I jumped and glanced at him. "Oh, uh, ... nothing really to buy ..."

Ian snorted. "You're a million miles away. What's up?"

I sighed. "Really want to know?"

"I wouldn't have asked ..."

I shrugged. "Okay. Well, first, I'm worried about my dad. Think we should go find him and-"

"Nah, let him cool off." Ian swung our hands as we walked. "I would like to know what that fight was all about, though. I thought they were old friends, but Jason told me Chad and Warner got into it the day before yesterday, too." He looked down at me. "Any idea what's going on?"

I bit my lip and nodded. "Yeah ..., it's uh, something happened a long time ago and-" I swallowed past a lump in my throat and tried to force the words out but my mind rebelled at telling Ian what had happened that night.

"Hey ...,"

I met his gaze.

"You look- tell me to mind my own business if you need to. I won't be offended."

His dimple flashed as he winked at me.

I smiled. "Thanks. It's um, can I tell you later? It's kind of upsetting and it's such a nice night ...,"

His grin turned wolfish, and his arms slid around my waist, pulling me closer. "Oh, I agree. I can think of a much better use of this romantic backdrop ..."

I caught my breath as Ian's hands went wandering and his lips met mine. I wound my arms around his neck and let him deepen the kiss. The tension melted away and my body came alive as it recognized its mate.

"So long as this ends here and now, we can leave your father out of it. "

Ian stiffened and I jerked away as the snide voice of Judith Fogarty burst through my bubble of contentment.

Ian's expression was livid as he shielded me from the harpy's view.

"Wow, how is it someone that seems to know everything doesn't know when to shut up?"

Ian's voice was low and controlled, but his breaths were coming faster, and his shoulders were rigid. The good doctor wasn't particularly observant, or she'd have seen how close he was to exploding.

Ignoring Ian's question, Judith pursed her lips and continued. "I'm not going to let you continue this shipboard romance with this ..." Her gaze darted to me and then back to Ian. " This tramp, Ian. We need to resume our plans for your future. Your father and I have secured you an interview with the Dean of Music."

Ian was grinding his teeth and the tension radiated off of him in waves. One altercation in a night was more than enough; I needed to diffuse the situation.

I laid a hand on Ian's arm as I stepped around him and faced the doctor. "Um, Judith ..., I think you should-"

"I don't believe the opinion of a trollop is necessary or required."

Wow, she tossed out insults like Mardi Gras beads. The voice of my conscious said, be the better woman, ignore her, and walk away. I almost did, but then she opened her mouth.

Judith's lip curled as she sniffed and looked me up and down. "Don't you have a street corner to occupy?"

I cocked an eyebrow and snorted. "I've been called worse, by much better people."

Judith glared at me. Her lips opened and closed but no sound came out. I should have left well enough alone, but restraint had never been my middle name.

"Hmm, since you've already lost your muzzle, want me to throw a stick? You can fetch it."

Judith gasped. She raised a trembling hand towards my face, but Ian's fingers locked around her wrist before she could make contact.

My mouth dropped open in amazement at the stuck-up woman's courage. I took a step forward, intending to help her start an up close and personal relationship with the ship's deck, but Ian spoiled my fun.

"That's enough." He frowned at me until I backed up to the railing and then addressed Judith. Whatever he said made her blanch and scurry off to lick her wounds but not before shooting me a look that could kill.

I stared at the spot she'd recently vacated as something niggled at me. I was replaying the scene with her starting to slap me when Ian nudged me with his hip.

"What's wrong?"

I shook my head. "Nothing ..."

"You're frowning. Doesn't look like nothing to me."

I rolled my eyes. "I can't-ow!" I started to wrap my hand around his arm and managed to bend my fingernail backward.

I sucked on my finger, not that it did any good.

"What'd you do?" Ian tugged on my hand until I showed him my finger. "Oooh, that broke below the cuticle." He dropped a kiss on my fingertip. "Make it better?"

I wasn't sure better was the word, but his warm kiss certainly distracted me from the throb of a broken-

"Oh!" My eyes widened as what had been bothering me about Judith finally came to me.

"What?" Ian's eyes got big and he started looking around. "Something wrong?"

I laughed and shook my head. "Huh-uh, I just realized ... eh, never mind."

Ian huffed. "Tell me."

I scrunched up my nose and cocked an eyebrow. "Pretty sure you aren't gonna like it ..."

He snorted. "That's more reason to just spit it out!"

I tossed my hands up. "Okay then, on your own head ..."

He huffed and turned his hand in a 'get on with it' motion.

I shrugged. "I'd been wondering who had taken my scarf and tied it in that noose ..."

Ian frowned. "Tina, you don't need to worry, that security chief is looking at the cameras and-"

"Oh yes, I have great confidence in Mr. Penshaw." I rolled my eyes. "He brushed me off when I showed him that fingernail tip-"

"You heard him, that could have been there for days, hell, he didn't want to admit it, but it was up near the baseboard and the cleaners could have missed it ... that thing could have come from someone on the last cruise!"

I shook my head. I'd heard it all earlier, and it was as much nonsense coming from Ian as it had been from the security guy. "See how I just caught my nail on your sleeve?" He nodded, though it was clear from his frown that he had no idea what I was going on about.

"Well, my nails aren't acrylics so, under pressure, it broke buuut, hold on!" Ian started to interrupt. I shushed him and hurried on with my theory. "A fake nail would pop off under enough force!"

He sighed. "Again, it could have been there-"

"Okay, I'll give you that. It could have been there long before but, the fact that it is a red stiletto nail tip and she had that manicure the day we left port and now her nails are bare ..." I shrugged. "Just sayin' ..."

Ian shook his head. "You're just saying what, you've lost me, babe."

I bit my lip. I was ninety-nine percent certain I knew who'd left that scarf-well, I knew who the fingernail belonged to anyway, I had no proof she was also the one that had tied my scarf and hung it on the doorknob, in fact, I wasn't sure how she could have gotten onto our floor-

"Tina!"

I glanced up and met Ian's eyes. "Yeah?"

"Who do you think the nail belongs to?"

I sighed. "Well, just hear me out. I noticed her manicure the first time I met her and just now, well her nails are short and have no polish on them so she had the acrylics removed ..."

His brow furrowed. As I watched, his expression changed from puzzlement to realization, to irritation.

"Oh come on, not this again!"

I rolled my eyes. "Who else but your doctor?"

"For the last time, Judith is not my doctor!"

I cocked an eyebrow. "Ian, she introduced herself as your fiancée ..." I held up my hand as he started to interject. "I know what you said. Look at what she just did!" I snorted. "It doesn't appear that she's accepted whatever you had is over."

Ian wanted to renew our relationship in some fashion, he'd made that very clear. I felt excited, both mentally and physically, but every time I let myself think about us getting back together I'd see Judith Fogarty's face.

Not only did she act like Ian was hers but she was openly hostile towards me and I had reasonable suspicions that she was behind at least some of the things that had happened.

Ian huffed, drawing my attention.

"Tina, I told you, she's not...," He sighed and dragged a hand through his hair. "I'm not with her and I haven't been for-"

"But Ian, how ..." I winced and tried to explain my confusion. I bit my lip and decided to just say it, damn the consequences.

"Look, I believe you when you say that whatever you two had is over-" He started to speak and I held up my hand. "Hold on, let me finish. The thing is Ian, I can't ... I mean ..., what the heck happened to you?"

Everything I'd kept bottled up inside of me since running into him and meeting the boa constrictor came rushing out like a river overflowing its banks.

I rolled my eyes and frowned at him. "How could you have *ever* been with her?" I snorted. "I can't figure it out! She's not, I mean she's a nice- no I am not gonna say she's a nice person because, bless her heart, she isn't! And that is what I can't figure out ..."

Ian threw up his hands and paced in a little circle. "What do you mean, what's to figure out? She is a dried-up bitter woman who thinks way too highly of herself."

I nodded, and took a step closer to him, laying my hand on his chest as my eyes started to well up. "That's just it! The Ian I knew would have never been in the same room as a woman like her, much less have been in a relationship!"

I shrugged and stepped back, staring down at the wooden deck as I muttered. "I guess I just wonder how much you've changed and how we could ever start a relationship if that is the type of woman-"

"Hey! Hey, slow down, that's crazy talk ..." Ian placed his finger under my chin and nudged me until I met his gaze. "I am not in a relationship with Judith Fogarty and she is not the kind of woman I am attracted to, you are the woman I'm attracted to!"

My heart skipped a beat at his words but he was glossing over pertinent facts and I needed answers. "Ian, she introduced herself as your fiancé." I shook my head. "Why would she do that if she didn't think she had a claim on you?"

Ian frowned and caught his upper lip between his teeth. He started to pace again and, just as I thought he'd ignore my question he heaved a sigh and turned back towards me.

A three-quarter moon illuminated his face and I could clearly read the expression in his eyes; he looked hunted? Wounded?

I grabbed his hands. "Ian, what is it? Why were you ever with her?"

He gulped and squeezed my hand. "My dad."

I wrinkled my nose, "What about him?"

Ian sighed. "You don't know him, I never ..." he laughed and shook his head. "Hah, I just realized how alike we are. I never introduced you to my parents either!"

Oh, I really didn't want to go there! "Yea, about that. I'm sorry. It was selfish of me and, well it's a long story but ... later, later I'll tell you. Right now, tell me about your dad."

Ian tossed his head. "Eh, where to start?" He sighed. "Okay, I guess the short answer about Judith is my dad fixed us up and I didn't have the guts to tell him ..."

I frowned. "But, Ian why would your dad ever think a woman like that would be the perfect date for you?"

A laugh burst from him, though it held no humor. "Because my dad doesn't really know me; only what he wants me to be." He looked at me and snorted. "He was hoping I'd get together with Judith and she'd convince me to give up rock and roll and go back to the life he had planned for me."

My eyes widened. Give up rock and roll? The life that was planned for– "Ian, you're an incredibly talented musician."

I frowned because it wasn't making sense. I'd been around world-class musicians all of my life and Ian Buchanan could hold his own with any of them and I couldn't believe his father wouldn't have recognized that. "What life did your father have planned for you?"

He gave another derisive laugh. “From the age of five, my father has expected me to take the stage as a concert pianist.”

My eyes widened. Five? Who planned out a child’s life that young? “I ... I don’t understand. That’s too young, why would he-”

“Because I was ...” Ian huffed. “I guess you could say I was a prodigy.”

I blinked. Another thing I hadn’t known about my boyfriend. “Wow, uh ... that’s, I mean, you’re a great player but-what makes you a prodigy?”

Ian shook his head. “Nothing, in my mind, but Dad.” He blew out a breath. “My dad is also a pianist, he never made it to the concert stage, he teaches music theory and composition, well he did-”

“Ah, so he wanted you to fulfill his dreams?”

“Yes and no. I don’t think-well, maybe he was trying to live through me?” He shrugged. “I never thought about it that deeply but it’s possible.”

“So he taught you to play.”

He grimaced and dragged a hand through his hair. “Eh ..., he taught me to read music and compose but I taught myself to play ...”

He ducked his head as his words trailed off and I realized Ian was embarrassed. I laid a hand on his arm and bent my head, so our gazes met. “That’s why you were a prodigy? Because you were self-taught?”

His head bob was barely noticeable.

"Wow Ian, that's incredible! So you just sat down at the piano one day and started playing?"

"Pretty much. I played along with a recording of Satie's Gnossienne No. 1 ... it's no big deal."

No big deal? I wanted to argue that it was a very big deal to have played like that without any instruction and at that age, but Ian was clearly uncomfortable talking about his talent, so I let it go and decided to return to the discussion of his dad.

"Well, I'm sure it felt like no big deal to you, but others were probably amazed. How did your father react?"

Ian snorted and took my hand. "Let's walk. He found me playing the Satie and from there it was constant playing, instruction on reading and writing music, hours and hours of playing ... he pulled me from school so he could customize my education-"

"Oh my gosh, that doesn't sound fun!"

Ian laughed. "Uh no, it wasn't. I was nine when he got me into playing with the local symphony and then it was recording in the studio. That led to appearances around the state ... by the time I was a teen I'd had enough and insisted on going to school."

"Ooh, guessing he wasn't happy about that, huh?"

He snorted. "You would guess right. I got my mom involved though, and he had no choice but to let me ..." he squeezed my hand. "That's how I discovered rock music and electric guitar and, when I taught myself guitar and refused to play the piano again well, it all went to hell."

His voice was so soft I almost didn't catch what he'd said. I pulled to a stop and met his eyes. "What went to hell, Ian?"

He blew out a breath and rolled his eyes. "Oh man, what didn't? Dad stopped speaking to me then he and Mom started fighting over me .. They separated and Mom and I went to live with her parents."

He looked out to sea. "I broke up my parents' marriage, caused my dad to hate me-"

"Ian!" He refused to look at me so I touched his cheek and gently guided his head around until he met my gaze. "You didn't cause their marriage to fail and I'm sure your father doesn't hate you."

"Oh, trust me. After I graduated, he and mom did get back together, but when I visit he barely looks at me and, if Mom asks about my career he'll leave the house."

My heart broke for him. "Ian, that's ... I'm so sorry, but you're speaking now, right? So he's finally accepted-"

A burst of harsh laughter cut me off.

"Accepted! No baby, he hasn't done anything of the sort, remember Judith?" Ian slung his arm across my shoulders and nudged me back into our walk.

I frowned. "If your dad doesn't really talk to you, how did Judith enter the picture?"

Ian sighed. “He had a heart attack back in January. I was still living in California but, when I realized-“ He shrugged. “Mom needs me. She runs a specialty nursery and-“

“Wait, what does she do?”

Ian looked down at me and frowned. “Huh? What does who-oh, Mom? She grows herbs and stuff and sells them, which is why I came back to Savannah-she can’t run her business and also take care of Dad ...”

I’ll admit, part of me really wanted to know more about Ian’s mom and the herb growing business but I filed it away for later and stayed focused on the situation with his father.

“Ian, is he bedridden or something? Why does she need -”

“He was for a month or so. He’s been doing rehab and stuff so he’s up and around but he had to retire, and-“

“He’s driving your mom crazy.”

Ian looked down at me and laughed. “How did you know?”

I shrugged. From what Ian had described, his father sounded like a handful at any time, so I could only imagine how much worse a controlling type of personality would be if confined.

“Lucky guess?” I smiled, to take the sting out of my words. “A person that likes to have things his own way ...

he sounds like a difficult man to live with at the best of times."

Ian cocked an eyebrow and tilted his head. "Yeah ..., he's just always been Dad so I never gave it much thought ... but, regardless, now I'm back and it's taking a load off of mom."

"But at your expense!" He shook his head so I rushed on. "No, if I'm understanding this correctly, your dad has been trying to push you back to the life he wants you to live and he's using his illness to get his way."

Ian's expression turned stormy. His jaw got stiff and a nerve ticked in his cheek. I was about to apologize when he drew a deep breath and forcefully exhaled.

"I'd forgotten that about you."

My brow wrinkled as I mulled over his comment. "What about me?"

He grinned. "Your lack of a filter. No, ..." he shook his head as I started to speak. "Don't apologize, you're absolutely right! He's been manipulating me for months and sending Judith on this cruise was my wake–up call and last straw. I'm done with him-"

"Oh Ian, don't say that!" I could understand his anger and frustration but, having just ended a decade of not speaking to my father ... I didn't want him to continue down that road. "You need to tell him how you feel ... surely he'll understand that you're an adult and-"

"I've been trying, Tina." He sighed. "He's been texting me since just after we left port! Insisting that Judith is perfect for me and even worse, he's got a job lined up at the college!"

My eyes widened and I bit my lip. His father was no lightweight in the domineering department. "A job! Doing what? And he must not know you very well if he thinks that woman is a good fit-"

"He doesn't care!" Ian snorted. "Dad and Judith are allies. His hope was that I'd be attracted to her enough to be guided into going back to my classical training and he wants me to teach ..."

Since I was honest enough to admit I'd never be happy seeing Ian with another woman, I wasn't touching the Doctor Fogarty issue with a ten-foot pole. But, as far as his music career went ...

Ian had won several Indie music awards and was making a name for himself ... guys like my dad and Drew recognized and respected his talent ... it would be foolish to leave all of that behind and I told him so.

He dropped a light kiss on my forehead. "Thanks for that." His lips spread into a self-deprecating smile that pulled at my heart. He was too good of a musician, hell, Ian was too good of a person to be doubting himself and I ached to help him or at least ease his burden.

I didn't know what I could do as far as the situation with his dad went but I was there for him, regardless. I stopped and slid my arms around his waist, pulling him in for a hug.

He was quick to reciprocate and deepen the embrace. I sighed and snuggled against his chest as I considered the relationship we'd had.

I'd been devastated when he rejected my offer to accompany him to California. At the time, I'd been running from the dark things in my past with alcohol and constant partying. I realized now that Ian's seriousness and dedication to his career had been his way of running.

Older and wiser, I could look back and see that neither of us had been ready for a serious relationship. Now we were both addressing our problems and working towards solutions. I leaned back and grinned before pressing a light kiss on his mouth.

His arms tightened around my back and his lips spread into a lazy grin. "Not that I'm complaining but, what was that for?"

I shrugged and told him what I'd been thinking. "So, I guess I'm saying, welcome to adulthood."

He chuckled but his eyes reflected heat and hunger than was anything but humorous. It had been a while since that look had been directed at me and it made my stomach flutter and my knees a bit wobbly.

He pressed a series of kisses against my neck and up to my ear as he murmured. "Thinking we should mark this momentous occasion, back in your cabin, hmmm?"

I swallowed hard and fought to stay focused, but it was a losing battle. The alarm bells belonging to my logical side must have had their clappers removed because I could barely hear them. My body was responding full steam ahead.

I cocked my head to give Ian better access to my neck as I surrendered and let the current carry me away.

Dead in the Water

Tina

THE CLICK OF THE cabin door roused me from a deep and satisfying sleep. I stretched and opened my eyes and my stomach rolled as I remembered with whom I'd spent the night.

Thanking the universe for the small favor of Ian having an early rehearsal, I sprang from the bed and found my robe as my logical side launched into a lengthy lecture on the rest of my body's lack of critical thinking skills.

According to the nagging voice bleating in my skull, I lacked both judgment and self-preservation instincts and I deserved whatever might be coming by way of heartaches. Since it was my conscious ranting, I could hardly argue, though I did counter with the excuse that Ian and I were talking about the things that derailed our relationship two years ago and that, all things considered, I was hopeful we were both more mature and could sustain a healthy and balanced relationship this time around.

I shuffled into the living room and made myself a cup of tea without encountering my father, a small gift for which I was deeply grateful. Regardless of my gratitude, I'd expected to see Dad. I texted him and then headed for the shower.

Dressed and ready for the day, I'd still had no word from Dad. It'd been early when Ian left, not even seven o'clock, and I doubted that my dad would have done the same. However, a quick look around the suite and the sun deck left me puzzled.

I tracked down the floor's butler, but he'd not seen any sign of my father either. Since my dad had been in the habit of doing sunrise yoga on the private deck and then relaxing with his coffee every morning, I got a little worried and checked his room. His bed showed no signs of having been used. That amped up my concern, though I told myself he'd just stayed the night with Nikki.

I fired off another text, plus one to Ian as I walked to the elevator but then I remembered that we'd be docking in St. Maarten in a few hours, and I had made plans to spend the day on the beach with KC. A quick debate with myself ended with me deciding to just come back to the room to change and gather my beach gear. I did shoot off another text though; I was kind of surprised KC hadn't confirmed our plans.

I was standing in line at the coffee shop when my phone blew up with messages. Ian confirmed he was going to be tied up getting ready for the evening's concert and KC said she'd meet me at the gate at ten o'clock. Still no word from Dad.

Tea and Danish in hand, I decided to eat in the theater. I was concerned about having no word from Dad and I also had neglected to tell either him or Ian my plans for the day. I held my chocolate croissant in my mouth and pulled the door to the Starlight theater open. I had expected to walk into controlled chaos as the crew set up for the show but not a thing was stirring, not even the proverbial mouse.

I frowned and walked down the center aisle. The house lights were off, but the stage was lit so someone must be working. My tea was getting cold, and the flaky goodness was calling my name, so I took a seat in the front row and devoured my breakfast as I waited for everyone to filter in.

Twenty minutes later my tea and pastry were long gone, and I'd checked all of my messages, social media, and email but no one had appeared in the theater. I texted Ian, thinking maybe I'd misunderstood, and they weren't playing in the main theater, but he didn't reply, and I grew impatient.

Maybe they were backstage? I huffed and walked up onto the stage and headed to the back. Not a soul was encountered behind the curtains, and everything was quiet. I'd just decided to leave when a crash shattered the stillness and made me jump.

"Hello? Anyone there?" My heart was racing. When no one replied I walked towards the area I thought the sound had come from. Down a short flight of steps, I was standing in a dimly lit and narrow hallway that had several doors leading off of it. I walked slowly, calling out twice more and getting no answer.

The first doors I came to were restrooms. The doors were closed and a quick peek inside showed the lights were off. I kept walking. Dressing rooms were next. All but two had their doors firmly closed and locked. The others were ajar, but the lights were off and a glance inside showed nothing amiss.

I stopped and peered ahead. One more closed-door marked Mechanical, and then the last door on the left. That one was open, and light spilled onto the carpet.

The sound had been really loud and not finding anyone around was creeping me out.

"Hello? I heard something fall, is everyone all right?" I'd barely gotten the last word out when I heard rustling noises, followed by the pounding of feet. I rushed down to the open door and arrived in time to see a metal door on the other side of the room swinging shut.

I huffed, fed up with the whole situation. A glance around didn't show anything out of the ordinary. The room was being used for equipment storage for the bands. Most of the music cases and amps were marked Eclipse, though a few belonged to Full Throttle and the far corner held Bad Opera's things. I walked over to the other door. It had been closing when I walked in which meant someone had been in here the whole time.

Why they hadn't acknowledged me calling was beyond me, but a sneaky suspicion they'd been in an area they weren't supposed to be made me fire off a text to Dad and Ian. I decided to poke around while I waited for one of them to finally reply; they might not put answering me as a priority when the message was about nothing more than eating breakfast but surely they'd be alarmed that someone had been in the room with their gear.

A few of the cases were open, guitars rested on stands, and it looked like someone had begun to unpack Benny's drum kit. A series of rows had been created by the stacked cases and amps and I was scooting around a stack of front monitors when I heard someone cry out.

“Who’s there? I’m getting tired of this-“

“Tina?”

“Dad?” He didn’t reply so I scooted around a stack of cases and saw an archway that led to another room full of equipment.

Something crunched beneath my feet as I stepped through the doorway. I looked down and frowned. The white tile was littered with colorful shards of something. I picked a piece up. It was wood, reddish colored wood, and a bit of peg and wire was still attached to one end.

My eyes widened. I was holding a piece of a guitar! My dad’s voice rang out again and I yelled back as I followed the trail of bits that led me around a pile of instrument cases.

“Oh, my God ...” I gasped and backed up as my gaze stayed glued to the scene in front of me.

I screamed as a hand fell upon my shoulder.

“Tina? What in the world is going on?" I got your message-

Dad! My shoulders sagged in relief.

"I got your message, oh my God -"

With a shaky finger, I pointed in front of me. Richard Warner was lying in a pool of blood surrounded by pieces of an electric guitar.

Sailing Close to the Wind

Ian

I STARED AT THE love of my life and wondered if I could pinpoint the exact moment that she'd lost her mind. Was it when she'd texted me that she'd found, well she and Chad had found Warner lying in a pool of blood?

It might have been a few minutes later than that when I rushed down to the theater in time to find Tina standing toe to toe with the hulking Security Chief Penshaw. I'd pulled her away and tried to find out what was happening but it was chaos; Tina was yelling, Rob Thornton was arguing with the captain, and Chad was pacing like a caged lion while Nikki tried to calm him down ... I couldn't get anyone's attention.

Horrified silence descended when Penshaw's tolerance for screaming females topped out and he started to frog march Chad out of the theater. I was busy restraining Tina, but Rob stepped in and convinced the captain and security chief that the publicity would be phenomenally bad for business if they turned world–famous Chad Crawford over to the St. Maarten police.

They reached an agreement; Chad would be confined to quarters until we docked in San Juan and the FBI could conduct an investigation. All of which led to my sitting in a bistro watching Tina demonstrate her lack of mental stability.

"What are you doing?"

Tina didn't bother to look up from her scribbling. Minutes after they'd escorted Chad from the theater, she'd dragged me to the gift shop for a notebook and pen. She had then planned to return to the suite but I'd claimed hunger and diverted her to a restaurant.

"I'm making a list."

I munched on a French fry as I tried to read upside down. S E V I T ... I huffed and nudged her hand away so I could turn the page around. "Motives, Suspects, Alib- Tina, what is all of this?"

She scowled at me and snatched the paper back. She used the side of a menu to draw straight lines, forming columns the length of the paper, and then glanced at me. "I'm making a list so we can figure out who killed Warner and get my dad off of the hook."

I blinked at her and ran the explanation back through my beleaguered brain. "Hold on, who is we?" I shook my head. "Better question, why are you playing Sherlock Holmes?"

"Well Watson ..." She grinned and my alarm bells started ringing; there was a glint in her eye that made me very nervous. Not to mention I was being cast as assistant to her madness.

I held up my hand. "Stop right there. I am not your sidekick and-" Her lower lip jutted out and I'm not gonna lie, that little pout almost derailed my traitorous brain from its logical arguments. Almost.

I leaned over and dropped a quick kiss on said pouty lips and then shook my head. "This," I tapped her notebook. "This isn't any of our business and you need to keep your pretty nose out of it. The proper authorities will soon find the killer."

My love scowled at me but it didn't change my mind.

"But Ian, they don't even have the equipment to take fingerprints! They didn't block off the crime scene and not a single picture was taken as far as I could see," She fished her phone from her bag and started scrolling. "I managed to snap a few before they dragged us all out to the main theater. Nothing jumps out at me, except for this." She pointed at Warner's lifeless hand.

"See that? A yellow piece of paper. I wonder where the rest-"

"Are you serious?" I snatched the phone from her and my eyes just about bulged out of my head at the images on her screen. "Tina Crawford! What kind of- have you lost your ever–lovin' mind? You have pictures of a dead guy!"

Her mouth dropped open and then she snorted. "For a minute, you sounded just like my friend Ivy. She didn't want to investigate last time ..." She took the phone back and stared at her screen as she muttered.

"Last time? Tina ...," I sighed. "Explain yourself, please."

She tipped her head to the side and looked at me in confusion. "What's to explain?" She shook her head. "Look, we're wasting time." She waved the notebook at me. "Let's figure out who had the motive, then we'll have a list of suspects. That's what Ivy and I did last time ..."

"What last time? Girl, are you telling me you've played detective before?"

She wrinkled her nose at me. "Played?" She snorted. "Hardly! Ivy and I solved the murder of our neighbor, and this is how we did it." She sighed. "I wish Ivy was here ... she's the list maker and planner ..."

I rolled my eyes. The more Tina explained, the more confused I got. I put a hand over the paper, forcing her to stop writing and pay attention to me. "Good, now in as few words as possible, tell me about this last time."

Tina huffed. "Our neighbor, a nasty woman named Harriet, was murdered right before Christmas, and Ivy and I were the prime suspects. So, you see, I'm the perfect one to find the killer now!"

She returned to her paper as if everything made perfect sense. "Sweetie ...," I chose my words carefully because the last thing I wanted to do was fight so soon after getting back together. If we actually were together. Nothing had been discussed and I was just assuming-I shook my head and filed my insecurities away for later.

Right now, there were more pressing issues; namely, keeping Tina from being committed or, maybe it was me in danger of vacationing at the loony bin, Lord knew I was feeling a bit like Alice down the rabbit hole.

"Tina, are you saying that you and your friend were suspects in a murder case?"

"Yep, I told you that."

I drew a deep breath, mainly to keep from screaming, and proceeded to make sense of the insensible. "Ah, yes, you did ... in a roundabout fashion. How did that happen-You know what? I don't think I wanna know. Let's move on for a second." I tapped my fingers on the tabletop. "How does you being a murder suspect last

Christmas, and we will be talking about that later make no mistake, but for now, how does that translate into you finding the killer of Richard Warner?"

She shook her head at me and the expression on her face suggested I was just a bit simple-minded. I confess I was feeling that way.

"With Harriet's case, the police were convinced Ivy and I had done it and they weren't even looking for anyone else!" She shrugged. "Just like now, see?"

I started to say that no, I didn't see at all but, once I replayed the pertinent parts of the conversation I had to admit that she was making a bit of sense, or else Tina was contagious and I was just as certifiable.

I mulled everything over and then nodded. "Right then, you intend to do what?" I nodded at her list. "How does that translate into finding the killer?"

She wrinkled her nose. "I'm not sure. See, Ivy did this part ..." she waved her hand. "Once she decided where we should start, I took over and went about asking questions and stuff and then we discussed our findings, and ...I kinda thought you could help me?"

I cocked an eyebrow. "I see ...,"

There were so many things I could have, and would have liked to say but none were conducive to a continued relationship with the woman of my dreams so I bit them all back and decided to just humor my lovely girlfriend and pray she gave up her harebrained notion sooner, rather than later. I also had an inkling her father would have something to say on the subject, and I intended to inform him of his daughter's plans at the first opportunity. In the meantime ...

"Sweetie, how do you propose I help you solve this murder?"

She frowned at me and I wondered if my tone had been too patronizing because she started to reply, stopped and huffed, and then continued. "Okay, I ..., this is what I've come up with so far, take a look."

I turned the notebook around. In the suspect column were two names: Nikki Hardy and Jason Young. The column to the right listed their probable motives for killing Warner. Nikki had been knocked down by a drunk Warner and she'd had issues with him undermining her authority with the band's crew.

"You really think Nikki killed him?" I frowned. "I mean, he was hit over the head with a guitar, that took some strength and Jason? Tina, he was angry about his bass but not enough to kill the guy ..."

Tina shrugged. "Well, who else could have done it?"

I sighed and pinched the bridge of my nose as I thought about the handful of times I'd been in contact with Warner. He had been an unpleasant guy, anyone could have- "Oh! I wonder ... Nah, that's ridiculous."

Tina grabbed my arm. "What? What's ridiculous? Is it a clue? Even little things can be import-"

"Tina, baby, slow down!" I chuckled. Her eyes were glowing with excitement and she was talking so fast that her words ran together. "I was just thinking ... the night of the meet and greet ..."

I told her about seeing Warner, Thornton, and Penshaw in the equipment room and my impression that Warner had been roughed up by Penshaw. Of course, Tina ran with it.

"Wow, so Penshaw and Rob are suspects, too!" She scribbled the names down. "See, we're a great team!"

I snorted but didn't correct her. I didn't think any of the people on her list had killed Warner, although I also didn't agree with Penshaw that Chad had done it. My only real interest in finding Warner's killer was so that Chad would be released and the concert could continue.

The bonus for me was that if Tina was occupied chasing shadows it might keep her out of the authorities' way, so I wasn't going to dissuade her. I was just about to ask her how she intended to spend the rest of the day when a girl stalked up to our table and glared at Tina.

"There you are! I waited for you at the gate!"

I blinked. With her long blond hair and high cheekbones, the woman would have been stunning, if not for the death glare coming from her jade green eyes.

"KC! Oh my gosh, I'm so sorry, I totally forgot after finding-"

The woman's hands were clenched and her long red nails reminded me of claws. I braced to intercept as she raised one shaking hand and pointed towards Tina's chest but, at the last minute, she tapped her fingernails on the table instead.

"Let me guess, something more important come up? Again?"

Tina's eyes widened. "Yes! Haven't you heard? My dad has -"

"Of course, always about your dad!" She snarled and rolled her eyes. "Never mind, it's obvious where I rank in your priorities. I don't know why I bother-I'm going ashore. See you never!"

The woman turned on her heel and stomped out of the restaurant. I raised my brows and looked at Tina but she'd returned to her notebook as if nothing had happened.

"Tina? Babe, who was that?"

She lifted her head and blinked. "Huh? Oh, that was my friend, KC."

"Your friend seems pretty angry, don't you think you should go after her?"

Tina frowned. "What? No." She waved her hand in dismissal and started writing again. "She's not really a *friend*, friend." She shrugged. "I mean, I met her the first day of the cruise. I like her an all, but she's a bit clingy, and this is important!"

I blew out a breath. The woman was really angry and something about her made me a little uneasy but before I could think any more about it, Tina tapped her finger on the notebook page.

“Okay, I think we need to find out where everyone on this list was this morning, you know, alibis and stuff- ooh, I wonder if Penshaw has searched Warner’s cabin yet ... think I’ll go their first and-“

“Tina! You can’t-“

“While I’m doing that, can you find out where Jason was?” She shoved her things into her bag and rose from her chair, not letting me get a word in. “Then we can meet back at ... hmm, your cabin or mine? Let’s do yours, then we can compare what we’ve found and then go see what Dad says, okay?”

She dropped a quick kiss on my cheek and scampered out of the restaurant before my head had stopped spinning. I heaved a sigh and wondered just what I’d gotten myself into.

Getting Underway

Tina

I RUSHED FROM THE restaurant eager to start my investigation, only to find myself standing at the elevator not knowing the location of Warner's cabin. A quick text to Dad got me the cabin number, and loads of questions I ignored, but now I had a new issue; how to get into the room.

I proceeded to deck ten hoping for inspiration and, the stars were aligning in my favor because, as I rounded the corner leading to Warner's cabin, I just about tripped over the housekeeping cart.

"Miss, are you all right?"

I smiled at the young girl with an Eastern European accent. She fell all over herself apologizing and checking to make sure I wasn't hurt and I assured her everything was fine but something stopped me from asking her to open Warner's door. I continued down the hall, wracking my brain for a reason she should let me in when an obviously drunk couple staggered out of the elevator and bounced off of the hallway walls until they came to their cabin. Eureka!

I knocked on Warner's door and then started shouting for him to let me in. A glance over my shoulder revealed my plan was working, the little housekeeper was watching me, concern written on her face.

I poured it on thick. "Ricky! Pleeeease, I just need my phone ..." I faked a sob and kicked the door for good measure. I slid down the wall, burying my head in my hands, and pretended to be upset. A few seconds passed and, sure enough, I felt a gentle tap on my shoulder.

"Miss? Miss are you okay? Can I help?"

I hesitated and then sniffed a few times before raising my head and meeting her gaze. "Oh, uh ..." I managed another dramatic sob. "I ... this is so embarrassing!"

I looked at Warner's door and bit my lip. "See, I hooked up with this guy last night, and ...," I shrugged and pulled a sad face. "I left my phone in his cabin and now he is avoiding me or something and I don't know what I'm gonna do and-"

"Here, you come ...,"

She motioned for me to rise and walked over to the door. After knocking a few times with the standard 'housekeeping' announcement, my helpful friend pulled a keycard from her pocket. The click of the lock was music to my ears. I kept my sad face on until the door closed behind me and then did a little happy dance. My pirouette revealed Warner was either a slob or someone had already searched his room.

The cabin was fairly large for an inside room. A full bathroom on my left, a coffee bar, and a mini-fridge just outside the bathroom door, along with a closet. The main living area held a king–sized bed, a built-in dresser, and a desk area, followed by a loveseat and a floor lamp on the far wall.

I gazed around the room and wondered where to start. The ladder-backed chair was overturned and the desk drawers were pulled open, as were most of the bureau drawers. Cushions were half off of the loveseat and the bed linens were in a twisted mess at the foot of the bed.

I blew out a breath, wished for a pair of surgical gloves, and then started pawing through the dresser drawers. Underwear, socks, t-shirts ... I found nothing but clothes in the first three drawers.

I opened another drawer to find a pile of wadded-up jeans. I pushed the wrinkled denim around but saw nothing interesting.

I was just about to move on when a rustling noise stopped me. I frowned and nudged at the bottom pair of jeans. The noise sounded like paper. I pulled the pants from the drawer and shook them out; my reward was a crinkled piece of yellow paper half balled up and, proving my instincts were golden, the paper was missing a corner.

I smoothed it out and frowned.

KaliSeb San Juan 3:30 23b

I bit my lip and tried to decipher the chicken scratched words and what they might mean. The housekeeper's voice rang out as she announced her presence to the cabin across the hall, telling me my time was almost up.

I shoved the note into my pocket and continued to poke around. The desk revealed nothing interesting so I moved on to the sofa. I didn't see anything worth my time but my OCD tendencies kicked in and I just had to return the cushions to their proper place.

As I lifted the back cushion to tuck the seat cushion under it something blue caught my eye. I was reluctant to stick my hands too far down the back of a cruise ship couch, but my curiosity overrode my squeamishness. I removed the cushions and bent down. In the crease of the cotton fabric that lined the couch frame, there were four capsules, two blue and two yellow.

I retrieved them and then plopped down on the other sofa cushion to examine my find. The capsules were standard pharmacy issue except there were no markings of any kind denoting content or dosage. They felt light in my hand and, on a hunch, I flipped on the floor lamp and held one up for closer inspection.

Empty. I twisted one capsule just to be sure, but I was correct, there was nothing in the capsules. I scratched my head. Now, why would Warner have empty drug capsules? If they actually belonged to him at all ... Time was running out so I added the capsules to my pocket and turned to the rumpled bed.

Oh man, I totally did not want to touch those linens! Being in Warner's room at all creeped me out but for my skin to come into contact with ... gross, just gross!

I stared at the bed for a couple of minutes before I got up the nerve to move closer and nudge the sheets around.

Aside from some stains that I had no intention of examining, the bed held no secrets. A quick look at the bedside table came up empty, too. I checked the coffee bar and fridge. The closet held shoes, a few shirts, and a jacket. On to the bathroom.

If the bed had grossed me out, the bathroom made me want to vomit. It wasn't so much the mess as the smell;

the stench of Warner's cologne filled the small room and brought back a rush of bad memories. I swallowed past the lump in my throat and forced myself to look around.

Bathing products in the shower, toothbrush, and razor on the counter ... I didn't see anything worth me remaining- my gaze fell on a leather shaving kit tucked beside a stack of folded towels on the shelf beneath the vanity top.

I unzipped it and gasped. My hands trembled as I pulled a roll of hundred-dollar bills from the bag. A myriad of reasons for why Warner might have had that much cash on him danced through my mind, but my wild hunches became fact when I dug deeper into the bag and produced a plastic bag full of white powder.

I was staring at the bag that I was assuming contained drugs, trying to decide what action I should take when a knock at the door brought me to my senses. I pulled out my phone, snapped pictures of the money, drugs, and capsules, and then put it all back into the bag, zipped it closed and pushed it back onto the shelf.

The door swung open just as I reached for the handle. I smiled at the timid housekeeper, waved my phone as I shouted my thanks, and skipped back to the elevator. I couldn't wait to share my discoveries; Ian and Dad would be so surprised!

Learning the Ropes

Ian

After Tina left, I sat at the restaurant for another ten minutes contemplating the whole sorry mess the cruise had turned out to be. Falling lights, threatening phone calls, attempted stranglings, and now a flippin murder; if it weren't for bad luck, none of us would have had any luck at all!

A notification chimed from my phone. A quick look showed my father wanted to pummel me with questions about Judith. I was not in the right frame of mind to deal with him and, since he wanted to talk about the good doctor ... hell, I was never in the mood to do that.

I sighed and rose from my chair; now was as good a time as any to appease my girlfriend and her crazy ideas but, if I were gonna play private eye, I'd do it by the pool. I shoved the phone into my pocket and headed back to my cabin for a pair of swim trunks.

I'd just come out of the bathroom when Jason returned. He grunted a reply to my greeting, and I caught a glimpse of white on his temple.

"Hey man, what happened to you?"

Jason sniffed and shook his head. "Cut myself."

My eyebrows rose. The location of the bandage ... it was a difficult place to accidentally cut yourself. "How did you manage that?"

He shook his head and flopped onto his bed, crossing his arms beneath his head. "Accident."

I rolled my eyes. Getting answers from my friend was like pulling blood from a stone.

"I assumed that what happened?"

Jason snorted. "Careless while changing a string on the bass Cliff loaned me."

I nodded. "Lucky. That's pretty close to your eye."

"Yep." He grunted and sat up, swinging his legs over the side of the bed and resting his arms on his knees. "Man, what's going on with the concert? I got back to the theater, and nobody was there, well, none of the band. That security guy and his crew were messing around on the stage and in the back rooms."

"Concert is postponed until our last night at sea. We'll work out another rehearsal time as soon as they give us the all-clear for using the theat-"

"Dude! That blows." He jumped up and started prowling around the room. "This whole damned cruise has been a shit show!" He snorted. "So much for furthering our careers ..."

"Jase-" What to say? I agreed with him, but stoking his smoldering temper into life was never a good idea. "We'll still get to open for Eclipse, it's just gonna be a few more days, and ..." I shrugged. "Not like there's anything we can do about it. I mean, we have to respect that a guy was killed today-"

"Respect! Guy should have been done in a long time ago!" He threw up his hands and started rummaging in a dresser drawer. "You gonna swim? I'll get changed ..."

I nodded and he went into the bathroom. I fiddled with my phone while I waited. Nothing held my attention and something Jason had said was nagging at me, though I couldn't place it.

"You ready?"

"Yeah man, let's head out."

We rode the elevator down one floor and exited to find the pool deck slammed with people dancing and partying. The opening act for Full Throttle was on the stage and I was no fan of Iron Heart.

"You wanna go into St. Maarten? I heard they have good beaches ..."

Jason shook his head. "Nah, I'm not in the mood, but I skipped breakfast so let's grab a bite."

I'd already eaten but joined him in a cafe one deck down from the pool. My eyebrows rose as Jason proceeded to order two cheeseburgers, fries, and onion rings, along with a root beer float.

"Dude, where are you gonna put all of that food?"

He rolled his eyes. "Told you I skipped breakfast."

"Yeah, that reminds me, where were you this morning? Benny T and I got to the theater around seven. We started unpacking his kit but when no one else showed up we went to eat. I sent you a text ..." I glanced over at Jason and blinked.

His expression was weird like he was shocked-no, nervous. He was blinking and looking everywhere but at me and his fingers were drumming a light tattoo on the tabletop.

"Something wrong, man?"

Jason jumped and shook his head. "What? Nah, just hungry, wish they'd hurry up with that chow-"

"So what were you doing this morning? I got back to the room and you were gone ..."

I caught a glimpse of the squirrelly look again but he shrugged and it was gone, replaced by a smirk.

"Better question is, where were you last night?"

I ignored his arched eyebrows and leer so he laughed and gave up. "Fine, keep the deets to yourself. I'm assuming you're back with Tina?"

I nodded.

"That's great man, she's a cool chick and it don't hurt that her old man is frickin' Chad Crawford!"

I wasn't touching that with a ten-foot pole so I changed the subject. "Yep, so what'd you do this morning? Did you go to the theater?"

"Yeah man, I uh, must have got there just after y'all left. Started messing with Cliff's bass when the string popped, then I had to go to the med office for a band-aid when the damn thing wouldn't stop bleeding ..."

"Huh. That must have been when Warner showed up because he wasn't there when Benny and I were- did you see him?"

Jason looked down at the table and fiddled with the wrapper for his straw. For a minute, I thought he wouldn't answer but then he straightened and started looking around the restaurant. In fact, he looked everywhere but at me. I frowned. Something was off with my friend.

"Jase?" I tapped his arm to get his attention. "Did you see Warner while you were changing the strings?"

He jerked like I'd pinched him and then glanced at me. His eyes were narrowed. "Uh, yeah, yeah I guess so, but just for a minute. Why?"

I snorted. "I don't know, just asking. But ..." my eyes widened as it hit me. "Man, you were probably the last person to see him, well apart from his killer."

Jason's glance cut to me and then quickly went in the direction of the kitchen. "Huh, probably right-man, where is that- ah, here she comes!"

He leaned back as the server placed loaded plates in front of him. He thanked her and then rubbed his hands together. "Pass the ketchup, will ya?"

I handed him the bottle and then watched as he dived in and devoured the first burger.

"Damn dude, might want to chew."

He snorted. "Told you I was starving." He chomped on a handful of fries. "They really thinkin' Chad killed Warner?"

I shrugged and traced a pattern in the condensation forming on my glass of water. "Seems stupid if you know him, but they're going off of Chad punching him the other day and then last night ... hell, I thought he was gonna kill the dude."

Jason nodded. "Yeah, and if he had ..." he shrugged. "Guy deserved it. He was a piece of crap."

"Geez Jason, I know he busted your bass but, c'mon man, nobody deserves to be murdered."

Jason snorted and shoveled more food into his mouth. He swallowed and then took a break long enough to ask. "So, if Chad didn't do it, who do you think did?"

I blew out a breath and debated confessing what Tina had roped me into. I braced myself for a ribbing. "Well, we have a list of suspects, or I should say Tina does-"

"Wait, a list of suspects? Who are you, Dick Tracy?"

I smirked. "Hardly. But Tina feels like the security team isn't competent and she isn't content to wait on the FBI ..."

Jason paled. "The FBI? They comin' here?"

I frowned but shook my head. "Supposed to be boarding when we get to San Juan. Which is why Tina wants to find the killer before then; she doesn't trust the security chief and ... can't say that I do, either."

"Why not?"

"Because of what I saw at the meet and greet."

Jason's brow furrowed. "Huh? What'd I miss?"

"Sorry man thought I told you." I quickly hit the highlights on seeing Warner, Penshaw, and Thornton backstage. "So, guess I just think it's pretty suspicious the guy is dead. I mean, I'd swear Penshaw roughed him up that night ..."

Jason frowned and talked around a mouthful of burger. "Probably drugs."

My brow furrowed. "What? Why do you say that?"

He shrugged and took a swig of root beer. "I don't know, just figure it is."

I scowled. "That's pretty random ..."

He shook his head. "Nah, not really." He finished off the plate of fries and pulled the onion rings closer. "Warner's been dealin' for years and he was real tight with the young dark–haired guy that tends bar near the pool."

"Dude, again totally random."

Jason rolled his eyes and dredged a ring through a mound of ketchup. "Nope. The guy offered to sell me GHB the other night."

"What? Warner did?"

He shook his head. "Nah, the bartender."

"Wow, that's some crazy shit." I frowned. "So, you thinkin' the bartender was gettin' drugs from Warner?"

Jason shrugged. "Don't know, but probably." He polished off the rest of his food and shoved the plate away. "Guy's been a dealer for years, gotta figure he'd sell 'em here, too."

I frowned and started to ask him how he was so sure Warner had been dealing drugs but Jason's phone chimed, drawing his attention.

"Whelp," he stood and stretched. "Gotta go. Meetin' Cole to watch a movie, you wanna come?"

I yawned and shook my head. "Nah, I need a nap, didn't get much sleep."

Jason smirked but refrained from commenting. "Suit yourself." He signed the receipt and tossed a tip onto the table. "Some vacation, huh?"

I hadn't lied about being tired, but when I got back to the room there was no way I could sleep; Jason was a good friend, but the guy was a slob.

I straightened the covers on his bed, piled all of the used towels in one spot, and then returned to the bedroom. I thought my work was done until I saw the scattered toothpicks; used at that!

I growled and used a tissue to sweep the offensive things into the trash can, no way did I think the housekeepers should have to deal with Jason's crud. I glanced around and felt reasonably satisfied with my work. Now I could rest easy.

I stripped down to my boxers and flopped onto the bed but sleep wouldn't come. I closed my eyes but the conversation with Jason popped back into my head, specifically how he'd said Warner was a drug dealer.

He'd mentioned it a couple of times and also suggested Warner had been dealing for years. I yawned and drifted off as I made a mental note to ask Tina if Warner had been a drug dealer.

I also wanted to know if Warner had lived in Savannah. How else would Jason have known about him?

At the Helm

Tina

FOR WHAT MUST HAVE been the tenth time in ten minutes, I jerked to a halt and sidestepped a gaggle of meandering tourists. I huffed and turned to speak to Ian only to huff again because he wasn't beside me. I rolled my eyes and turned around to see him caught up in a knot of sightseers. Hands on my hips, mouth pursed, I fumed until he managed to catch up and then grabbed his hand to pull him along.

"Tina! For cryin' out loud, where is the fire?"

I ignored him until we'd crossed a busy intersection. Once passed the port terminal, most of the crowd was turning left; common sense, and my lack of patience, said we should go another direction.

To our right, the busy street turned into what looked like nothing but a sea of official buildings and parking lots. The lack of shade alone had me vetoing that option.

"Straight ahead it is." I tugged on Ian's hand and set off. The direction I'd chosen was narrow, clearly a side street and, unfortunately, it was all uphill.

By the time we'd reached the top, my calves were burning and I was panting like I'd run a mile. I leaned against a pretty yellow stuccoed wall and tried to calm my racing heart while Ian took his sweet time joining me at the top.

Bent at the waist, hands on knees and head hanging down, Ian's tennis shoes announced his presence; I wished I'd had the forethought to wear sneakers! I'd have never worn my wedge sandals if somebody had told me how hilly San Juan was!

"Ready to call it a day?" Ian laughed. "Or maybe just slow the hell down!"

I drew a deep breath, released it slowly, and then stood up straight. "I'll admit that hill was too much at that pace, at least for a non-gym day!" I frowned. "But Ian, we need to hurry and find out what that note I found in Warner's room meant!"

I set off to my left, talking over my shoulder. "I think we can go this way and- hey!"

I jerked to a stop as Ian wrapped a hand around my arm. "What gives?"

He shook his head and sighed. "Would you just stop for a minute?" He nodded farther up the road. "Do you even know where you're headin'? Or what you plan to do when you get there?"

I opened my mouth, prepared to give him a blistering answer when my eyes widened; the truth was, I didn't have a plan. I'd been so focused on arriving in San Juan and finding out who or what KaliSeb was that I hadn't considered the best way to go about it.

I wasn't usually so scatterbrained, despite what my bestie might have said, but in my defense, both men in my life had put me on the defensive last night and my continued irritation was fueling my decisions.

I pursed my mouth and thought of a few things to say before I opted for something that wasn't guaranteed to start an argument. "Okay, what's your plan then?"

He cocked an eyebrow, and I realized my tone might have been just a tad bit aggressive. I mentally shrugged. He deserved it after taking Dad's side last night.

After searching Warner's room, I'd rushed up to the suite, texting Ian to meet me there. He'd been taking a nap and was resistant to accommodating me until I told him about my clues.

His text had set my teeth on edge. Okay, Nancy Drew.

While Ian was patronizing, my Dad took a different stance.

“What- are you out of your mind?” He turned and scowled at Ian. “And you’re encouraging her?”

“Uh, no Sir! Well, not really. I did talk to Jason, but ...”

Ian sent me a nervous glance and I stuck my tongue out.

“Traitor.”

"Someone killed Warner. The suspect list isn't long. Just help me –"

"List? You have a list?" Dad's lips pressed into a line. "Who is on this list?"

I bit my lip but decided to tell him. "Well, Jason, the security guy, Rob, and, uh Nikki-"

"Nikki!" Dad's face reddened. He gritted his teeth and then went to open his cabin door. "Hey Nik, got a minute?"

I scowled at Dad, but he ignored me and addressed Nikki as she entered the lounge. "Guess what, Babe. My daughter is playing detective and has you down as a prime suspect for murdering Warner!"

I braced for Nikki's anger, but she just rubbed her eyes and yawned. "That's logical." She shrugged. "No secret I couldn't stand the guy."

"What?" Dad huffed. "Are you both nuts? Are you still half asleep, Nik?"

She rolled her eyes and went to the mini fridge for a bottle of water. "No, and no." She chugged the water and then nodded at me. "I heard y'all talking while I was trying to nap. You're looking for the killer, thank you."

My dad tossed his hands into the air. "Don't encourage her, Nikki!"

She snorted. "Someone has to solve this, Chad, and the sooner the better!" Nikki ignored Dad's muttering about authorities and turned to me. "For the record when Warner was killed I was with Rob Thornton. We had a meeting with the cruise director that started at six. We didn't leave her office until we got the phone call about Richard."

I wrinkled my nose. Now I had even fewer suspects. Not that I'd wanted it to be Nikki, but ... I blew out a breath. "Thanks, Nikki. That lets me knock both you and Rob off of my list."

"I still say you shouldn't even have a list!"

I sighed and addressed Dad. “Look, they’ve got you locked up.” I waved a hand to encompass the room. “It’s gilded, I’ll grant you that, but it’s still a cage!”

“Tina, they’ll sort this all out when we get to San Juan.” He sighed. “I told you, the FBI will find the killer.”

He might have been right, but my experience with being accused of murder was that law enforcement took the easy road and ran with the obvious suspect, even if it was all circumstantial. In fairness, they were overworked, underpaid, and pushed to close cases; they didn't have time to play Columbo and figured it was on the DA to sort it all out.

I said as much to Dad but my words didn't really click.

"Punkin' that might be true but I have faith that the legal system will function the way it's supposed to -"

"Supposed to-you can't be serious." My mouth dropped open in surprise that someone like my dad could be so naive. "Dad, even if the DA., or more likely the Grand Jury does a good job and realizes there isn't enough evidence to go to trial ... have you thought about the publicity? You can't let- Dad, it'd be a PR nightmare!"

He didn't argue which told me I'd made my point. However, he was still not convinced we, or rather I, with help from Ian, should be poking around looking for a killer, and, when I told him about the empty capsules and wad of cash I'd found he was even more unconvinced.

"Drugs!" Dad threw up his hands and started pacing. "Now you really need to stay out of this. Drug dealers are dangerous, Punkin'!"

Ian added his two cents before I could rebut Dad. "Tina, this is getting in deep. Jason said Warner's been a dealer for years, he's got connections to who knows-"

"So you talked to Jason! What did you find out?" I started to ask how Jason knew about Warner's dealing, but Ian stopped me.

"You're not listening!" He glanced at Dad, who nodded approval.

"Oh fine! All boys together then!"

"This isn't a game." Ian tossed up his hands when I rolled my eyes. "You need to leave it to the-"

"Don't start that again!" I shook my head and gave up. I'd do it on my own. "Ian, what did you learn from Jason. Where was he when Warner was killed?"

I frowned as Ian told me what little he'd gleaned from his talk with the bass player. The cut on his temple was a bit ... I worried at my upper lip and thought back to my arrival in the theater. There hadn't been anyone there, front of house or directly backstage. When I'd heard the noise and traced it back to the equipment room the emergency exit door was closing and then I found Warner and Dad found me.

We'd assumed it had been the killer leaving through the emergency exit. Jason couldn't have done it; he was in the infirmary. I'd wondered about Jason claiming Warner had been a long-time dealer but it didn't much matter since he had an alibi.

That put me back to my previous theory; Warner's death had something to do with the drugs I'd found. I had Ian tell Dad about seeing Rob and Security Chief

Penshaw in the equipment room the night of the meet and greet.

"Now you're thinking Rob Thornton killed him?" He heaved a sigh. "That's just nonsense, Punkin'-" He dragged a hand through his hair and then walked over and gave me a quick hug. "Sweetheart, I appreciate what you're trying to do, honestly, but let's just leave it to the ..."

His words trailed off as I stiffened and slid from his embrace. I looked at him and Ian. I hadn't managed to convince either of them, despite my theory having supporting evidence!

I'd let the matter drop, even made plans to tour Old San Juan with Ian as if it was just another day, but I was determined to at least figure out who or what that note meant before we left port.

"Earth to Tina ..."

I blinked as Ian waved his hand in front of my face. "Sorry, I was thinking."

"About lunch, I hope."

I started to fuss that there wasn't time, but the look on Ian's face made me bust out laughing. "Stop it, you are not going to starve to death!"

He patted his stomach. "You don't know, but my stomach does." He sniffed and pointed to our left. "That smells like something fried and awesome, let's go!"

Equipped with what we'd been assured were the best empanadas in town, Ian and I followed the pointing finger of the food truck owner and quickly found ourselves a shady spot in a quiet park.

Ian unpacked our empanadas, and handed me one, but not before taking a bite.

"Hey! Get your own!"

I wanted to be mad but the dimple I adored was peeping out and his blue eyes were sparkling with laughter. I huffed and shook my head at his nonsense before scooting over and laying out our side dish of black bean salsa stuffed avocados.

I reached for the bag and got my own empanadas and then took a bite as I watched Ian from the corner of my eye. I'd noticed the other night that he'd lost weight since we'd been together. Not that he'd been fat before, but the Ian I'd known was no gym rat; this older version clearly worked out.

The concert t-shirts he favored hugged his flat stomach and clung to well-developed biceps. Blue jeans were a constant in his life, so I was a bit shocked to see him in cargo shorts even if it was almost ninety in the shade.

He caught me looking and winked. "See something you like?"

I rolled my eyes, same old Ian; full of himself. I wrinkled my nose at him and dug through the bag for a spoon.

I savored a large bite of avocado before speaking to him. "S'that how you spent your time in L.A.? Learnin' how to sweet talk women?"

Unrepentant, he quirked an eyebrow and talked around a mouthful of pastry. "Only the sexy ones!"

I huffed out a laugh and nudged him with my elbow. "You're a mess."

"And you're as smokin' as ever." He wagged his eyebrows. "I meant to tell you, I'm diggin' the natural hair color, though you always rocked the crazy colors, too." His gaze roamed over me. "You've been dressed pretty tame on this cruise," he chuckled. "No Daisy Dukes and stacked heels today?"

I winced at the reminder of past me and her exhibitionist ways. Self-conscious, I tugged at the hem of my much more modest shorts and shrugged. When we'd been together, I'd had a thing for vintage clothes, bright hair, and pushing conventional boundaries.

A normal day's dress could have been anything from a Sixties-era minidress and go-go boots to a lace dress and Doc Martins. I still loved my vintage clothes, but I was older now. I said as much to Ian, and he laughed.

"Because you're so old!" He smirked. "You're just a baby."

I rolled my eyes at the familiar teasing; he was only four years older!

"Well, I toned my look down because I'm a business-woman. I need to look professional."

He grinned. "You, professional? Professional party girl, maybe!"

I flashed him a tight smile and concentrated on finishing my meal. He'd been teasing of course, but the jibe hit home. In his memory, that's what I was, a party girl, known at all of the local bars; a girl rarely seen sober after eight on any given evening and always up for a good time. The ocean was just visible through gaps in the shops but the breeze blowing off of it was glorious. I tipped my head back and closed my eyes as I sighed and realized we were at the 'regret for rushing into bed when we haven't talked' part of our relationship.

During my morning of "what the heck have I done" self lectures, I'd glossed over the fact that Ian and I had barely spoken before our stroll in the moonlight. We'd chatted and bantered but the conversation hadn't drifted into personal categories until he'd told me about his father and the whole mess with Judith.

I'd told myself we'd get to my sorry tale at a later date ... looked like it'd been marked on my calendar for today and nobody had bothered to notify me.

I blew out a breath and straightened. I met Ian's gaze and shrugged. "I've stopped drinking, actually."

His eyebrows rose. "You're serious?"

I nodded.

He blinked. "Wow, Tina that's great." He leaned over and kissed my cheek. "Why didn't you tell me?"

"When did I have time?" I smirked and bumped his shoulder with mine. "We've kinda put the cart before the horse."

Ian nodded and looked around as he polished off his lunch. "Well, we've got all day and nothing to-No!"

I pressed my lips into a firm line as Ian steam-rolled over the objection I'd been getting ready to make.

He grinned. "That note said three-thirty! It's the only thing we actually deciphered. If we go looking into it ..., there's plenty of time." He stood and offered me his hand. "Come on, let's explore and you can tell me all of your deep, dark secrets."

I laughed. He had no idea how accurate his jest actually was. I let him pull me to my feet without comment and tossed the empty bags into a trash can before letting him guide me back onto the main sidewalk. We walked along in silence as I tried to get my thoughts in order. With Warner dead and my relationship with my dad mended dredging it up just felt like beating a dead horse. Still, Ian deserved to know what had influenced such a big chunk of my life thus far.

I was just about to speak when Ian swung my arm and chuckled.

"No offense, but I never thought you'd ..." he shrugged. "I don't know, tame your wild child."

I didn't take offense at his incredulous tone. When we'd been together, I had been a heavy drinker. It'd been a large part of our reasons for breaking up; Ian had been given an opportunity in L.A. and didn't want me to come. I could remember that final night like it was yesterday. I'd dragged him away from working on a new song to enjoy an impromptu picnic on Tybee Island.

He'd told me he was going to L.A. after we ate and when I'd started talking about what preparations I'd need to make before I could leave he'd gently suggested he would be busy and had to get serious about his career. He'd said it'd be better if I waited until he was settled. We'd both known that day wasn't going to come.

I let my mind linger on the painful memories and what might have been for a few minutes, but the therapist Ivy had insisted I see had been right; I couldn't change my past, only learn from the mistakes. And I was learning. I'd been sober for over three months and I had goals and plans; I was on my way to being a responsible adult and part-owner of a thriving café.

I looked over at Ian and smiled. He was so handsome, so talented, so perfect for me in so many ways and I'd let him get away or maybe, we'd both been too young.

"What's the smile for? Something on my face?"

I shook my head and launched into my sordid little tale. I started with how I'd been after he left Savannah. How I'd spent those hours was a blur of music, men, and booze. But Ivy had stepped in or rather dragged me out of the No Quarter Saloon, and shaken sense into me. If not for her and the planning, and then the opening of the Cosmic Café ... it was possible I'd have drunk myself to death or done something equally stupid.

"Wow, I ...," he squeezed my hand and mumbled. "I'm sorry, I never thought-"

"This was never your fault, Ian. Most of the blame, well at least the cause of my drinking and general rebelliousness started with Warner."

"What?" Ian stopped and tugged me out of the line of pedestrian traffic. "What does Richard Warner have to do with you drinking too much?"

I drew a deep breath and exhaled slowly. Could I do this? I'd told the story once and, like then, I felt the need to keep moving.

"Let's walk to the point and see the Castillo San Felippe del Morro. I hear the views from there shouldn't be missed, and I think they filmed the Pirates of the Caribbean movies there."

We walked along the cobblestones at a slow but steady pace and, by the time we'd arrived at the historical site I'd reached the end of my tale.

"So, you see, Dad had a really good reason for attacking Warner-but he didn't kill him, I know he could-"

"Why not?" Ian stopped and looked down at me. A muscle ticked in his cheek and his lips were pressed into a firm line.

My eyes widened. Hands on hips, I stared at him. "Why not? Are you seriously-"

"You should have-" He snorted and dragged a hand through his hair. "Now I see why Jason said Warner needed killing, I'd have liked to kill the bastard, too."

I bit my lip and looked out over the fort walls and tried to accept what Ian was and wasn't saying. The view of the bay was incredible and breathtaking. Gulls swirled and dived against a backdrop of brilliant blue sky, and, in the distance, a yacht made its slow and steady way into port.

"Tina?"

I glanced at Ian and then back out to sea as I struggled to find my voice. "Um, ..." I huffed out a laugh. "I don't know how to respond to that." I turned and met his gaze. His eyes were swimming with tears and all I could think to do was hug him.

After a few minutes, Ian mumbled into my hair. "I think I'm supposed to be comforting you."

I laughed and leaned back in the circle of his arms. "Well, I appreciate the sentiment but I'm okay." He started to interrupt, and I rushed on. "No, really. I'd made peace with what happened that night-"

"But the drinking. You said it was still a problem until your friend made you get help."

I sighed and motioned for him to walk with me. A glance at my phone showed it was nearing two o'clock and I still hadn't deciphered the note.

"Ivy ..., it helped to talk to the therapist. Until then, I had thought my anger was with Warner, but she helped me to see that my drinking was to escape the condemnation I had heaped upon myself-"

"What? Why would you blame yourself?"

I shrugged. "Because I should have known better? I don't know, I just did." I grimaced. "I also held a lot of anger towards my dad."

"Because he didn't protect you?"

I shook my head. "No, not really. Well, a little maybe? Mostly because when I tried to tell him, he blew me off and continued being friends with the jerk, and I ..." I shrugged.

"I wasn't mature enough to understand that his addictions numbed him and ...oh, let's not talk about the past anymore. Dad and I have resolved our issues and you and I-well, we're good now? You understand why I didn't tell you about my dad?"

Ian nodded. "Of course, you didn't owe me anything, then or now."

I cocked my head. "I was selfish, and for that, I am really sorry."

He stared at me for a long minute and then grinned and stuck out his hand. “Apology accepted.”

I rolled my eyes and laughed before pulling the note from my bag. It was time to stop dredging up the past and see about securing the future.

“You still harping on this?”

Ian plucked the note from me and turned the paper left and right as if that would make the cryptic words clearer. We were standing at the entrance to the historic site, impeding traffic so I grabbed Ian’s elbow and moved closer to the fortress wall, just behind the ticket taker.

I leaned over Ian’s shoulder. “Well? Did you figure it out?”

He snorted and handed the note back. “Kaliseb twenty-three B ... the only thing I understand is the time.”

I stomped my foot. “Oh, this is hopeless! What the heck did he mean-“

“Pardon, senorita, you are lost?”

I jumped and spun around to find the ticket taker smiling at me.

“Oh,” I chuckled. “Well yes and no.” I waved the paper at him. “A ... uh, a friend left this message for me only I don’t understand what he wants me to do, and it says to do it at three-thirty so ...”

He held out his hand. “If I may?”

“Sure, be my guest.”

I glanced at Ian, who shrugged, and then watched as the older man frowned and made hmmm noises. I was ready to give up and ask for the note back when he grinned.

"Ah hah!" His brown eyes twinkled as he handed the note back and then leaned over, using his index finger to point as he explained. "Your friend, he does not speak Spanish?"

My eyes widened. "Uh, no, I don't think he did er, does, why?"

He grinned. "Because I think this is meant to be Calle, not kali and Seb might be Sebastion …"

"Oh! Well, what does that mean?"

"It seems to be an address? The numbers, and the letter after it? I think it is an apartment on Calle de San Sebastion, calle means street …"

My mouth dropped open. "Oh my gosh …," I laughed and looked at Ian. "Did you hear that? It's an address!"

"He said it might be, we can't know-"

"Easy way to find out, let's get a taxi." I dug into my bag and pulled out a ten-dollar bill, pressing it into the older man's hand and ignoring his protests. "Please, accept it. You've done so much more than you know."

He shrugged and relented, so long as I would allow him to procure us a ride. No fool, I was happy to oblige and in under ten minutes, Ian and I were riding in air-conditioned comfort as the scenery zipped by.

I was so happy to have solved the riddle, I didn't even object when Ian told the driver to circle the block and then let us off on the corner. He paid the driver and then guided me into a cafe.

"Ian, it's almost three-thirty, we haven't got time-"

"Get a couple of drinks, I'm gonna get us a table outside."

My eyes widened as I realized his intentions. A few minutes later I carried two icy mango smoothies outside and slid into the chair across from him. I had to hand it to him, we had a perfect view of the building we'd seen earlier from the car.

The address was a two-story building of red stucco. The ground floor was a dress shop. To the right of the shop's glass door was a wooden door painted bright blue. The number twenty-three was stenciled over the door frame. We sipped our drinks and stared.

When nothing happened I huffed and looked at Ian. "What now? Shouldn't we go-"

"Hold on, a taxi is slowing ..."

I jerked around just as the car drew to a stop. Seconds ticked by and then the door opened and a man carrying a briefcase stepped from the car. I sucked in a breath and grabbed Ian's arm.

"Oh my God, it's Security Chief Penshaw!"

Fair Weather

Ian

TINA AND I SAT on a bench outside of a conference room in a part of the ship accessible only by an escort. Tina yawned for the third time in as many minutes.

I slipped my arm around her and she rested her head on my shoulder. I sighed and let my head fall on top of hers. It'd been a long few days, hell the whole cruise had been a roller coaster ride of emotions, no wonder we were exhausted, and it wasn't over yet!

I wasn't keeping score, but the incidents that had sent my adrenaline spiking were adding up and my head was spinning. Tina getting assaulted, Warner being killed, Chad a murder suspect ... Rounding off the day with catching a murderer had done me in and it wasn't even dinner time.

The cherry on top was delivered via Judith ambushing us when we came back from San Juan. The security team was taking us to a debriefing room. We'd never stopped walking, but that didn't stop Judith from following behind and hurling snide remarks and invectives; I ignored everything except her parting salvo.

I drew a deep, shuddering breath and prayed I hadn't-

"Just text him, Ian." Tina lifted her head and met my gaze. "Better yet, *call* your dad. Judith was probably lying." Tina shrugged. "I mean, if your dad had suffered another heart attack your mom would have gotten in touch ..."

I nodded. "You're right. Of course, mom would have called or ..." I closed my eyes and tried to convince myself I'd not caused my father to relapse.

Running into Tina again had been a blessing above and beyond rekindling our relationship. Before the cruise, I had no concrete explanation for why I didn't like Judith Fogarty. Because all I had were feelings and words, my father steamrolled over my objections which was how the woman had come to be on the cruise.

I'd dodged a bullet in regards to Judith. She was a cruel, vindictive woman. When her jealousy flared, she showed her true colors and, thanks to Tina's quick thinking, I now had it on video; proof, if I needed it, to show my dad just how wrong she was for me. I sighed again and Tina nudged me in the ribs.

"Go on Ian, you aren't going to rest until you call your dad. Use the phone in my cabin and we'll let the management company sort the bill."

She was right, I wouldn't be at ease until I'd checked on him. I stood, ready to do as she'd suggested when the meeting broke up. Tina rose and grabbed my hand and we watched as Rob Thornton stepped out and closed the door.

My eyes widened. He'd been a sharp-dressed, slightly conceited wheeler and dealer type when I met him. Now, he looked to have aged ten years. His complexion was sallow, his expression haggard, with deep grooves bracketing both sides of his down-turned mouth. His eyes were red, and his shoulders slumped. His slickly styled hair was sticking up at odd angles as if he'd run his hands through it.

Our gazes met and Rob gave me a quick nod before he looked back at the floor and shuffled off down the hall.

"What was that all about?"

I looked at Tina and shrugged. "No idea. He looked like they put him through the wringer. Do you think he was involved with Penshaw?"

Tina shook her head. "Oh, I can't believe Rob would murder anyone! I've known him since I was a-"

The door opened again and three men in black suits and dark sunglasses exited. They chatted amongst themselves and paid no attention to us. I looked at Tina and smirked. She giggled in response.

"Feebs!" We both talked at once and then started laughing.

It was all so preposterous! Here we were, a musician and a chef, catching a killer before the FBI even got a foot on the ground and they never acknowledged it. They'd taken statements and then sent us out of the room to wait.

"Now that's a sound I love to hear!"

"Dad!"

I smiled as Tina launched herself into Chad's arms. They hugged and then came towards me. Chad shook my hand and started to express his thanks.

"Nah man, I was just along for the ride and to keep that one out of trouble. Your daughter is the detective."

Chad laughed. "Well, I'll still thank you both, and give you a bit more for watching out for Tina when I couldn't." He clapped his hands. "I don't know about y'all, but I could use a frozen fruity concoction right about now."

Chad smirked and shook his head. “You know, it sounds so much more manly when you just call it a drink!”

I snorted and followed father and daughter back to the passenger areas. Looked like we were finally going to start our vacation.

Storm on the Horizon

Tina

I PUSHED MY EMPTY plate away and groaned. "Oh, I ate far too much! Gonna have to hit the gym hard tomorrow!"

Nikki grinned. "No way, we're on vacation. Always put off until tomorrow what you might have done today!"

"Hear hear!" Benny T raised his glass to Nikki's.

Dad smiled and shook his head. "Now she shows us her work ethic. Guys, we just promoted her to acting band manager!"

Everyone laughed at Dad's teasing but I was also surprised. "Congratulations, Nikki, but what happened to Rob?"

Nikki looked at Dad and everyone grew quiet.

Dad cleared his throat. "Rob will be assisting Nikki for the rest of the cruise and effective immediately after, he'll be retiring and hopefully going into rehab."

I gasped. "So, he *was* involved with Warner."

Dad shook his head. "No, well he hasn't admitted to anything and there's no real proof, unlike Penshaw." He sipped his drink. "The agreement is that he retires and gets treatment in exchange for me not adding his involvement to my statements to the FBI and local authorities."

Ian frowned. "So, what did you tell the Feebs?"

"About Rob?"

Ian nodded.

"All they know is Warner was his supplier."

Ian's eyes widened. "So what I saw during the meet and greet was them fighting over the drugs."

Dad nodded. "Yeah, Rob told me privately that Warner was trying to double–cross him and Penshaw." He sighed. "They were partners and each one had a part to play."

I frowned. “Then why are you covering for Rob? I mean if he’s dealing drugs he should be punished-“

“He wasn’t dealing, Punkin. His involvement was for personal use and his role was merely to get Eclipse on the cruise line-up and to make sure Warner was included.”

I started to argue but Dad cut me off.

“I know, I know he’s technically guilty but if he gets clean I’m not carrying it any further.” He snorted. “Besides, there isn’t any hard evidence.”

I disagreed but bit my lip and let the matter drop. None of those involved were worth fracturing my relationship with Dad again.

Cliff leaned on the table and drew dad’s attention. “So, Rob’s part was getting us booked. What were that security guy and Warner supposed to do?”

“Well, Penshaw was head of security so he could make sure a blind eye was turned when the drugs were brought on board and Warner seems to have been the point man; he was gonna take the money into San Juan and bring back the blow-“

“Oh, that’s what Rob said that night!”

All eyes focused on Ian. He shrugged. “I heard the three of them talking as I was walking away, and Rob said something that sounded like Bro …” He snorted. “Thought that was an odd thing for a guy like Rob to say.”

After another round of laughter and the delivery of dessert for the gluttons, I got Dad's attention. I wanted closure and clarification.

"Penshaw killed Warner then?"

Dad nodded. "Yeah. He denies it, but thanks to your quick thinking, the authorities caught him and his dealer red-handed. He had the money Warner had brought-"

"But how? I turned in what I found in Warner's room."

Dad snorted. "Punkin, that was a wad of money for sure, but Rich had a briefcase with a half a million."

"Oh my gosh! That's a whole lotta reasons to kill."

Dad chuckled. "Yeah, especially when you plan to double cross your partners."

My eyes widened. "So that's why Penshaw killed him?"

"Looks like it. Warner was going to take the money. The San Juan police found out he'd rented a boat. They think Rich's intention was to take the money and head to one of the islands and enjoy the good life."

"Wow, what's that saying about living by the sword?"

Murmurs of agreement filtered around the table. It was a shame for anyone to lose their life, but Warner had been a vile man and I wasn't going to mourn him.

"Me either, Tina." Nikki shook her head. "He was a predator. I warned any woman I saw him playing up to." She snorted. "I never could figure out what they saw in him."

Cliff cleared his throat. "He lied to them."

I blinked and cocked my head as Dad asked Cliff what he meant.

Cliff followed his finger as he traced the rim of his water glass. I don't know if he did it all the time, but I know of two times when Warner pretended to be you."

"What?" Dad sat up straighter and leaned his elbows on the table. "How did he- are you kidding, Cliff?"

Cliff shook his head. "Nope. It was way back; we were just startin' out." He looked up and met Dad's eyes. "Seems like it wasn't long after y'all pulled that stunt and Warner lost his fingertip. You remember?"

Dad sighed. "Yep, not likely to forget that but what's it got to do with women? That was pure drunken male stupidity-and no, Punkin' I'm not gonna elaborate!"

I rolled my eyes, sat back, and closed my mouth as everyone laughed. Couldn't blame a kid for tryin'!

After everyone quieted, Cliff continued. "We were playin' the southern circuit and you and Alton went home for a few days. Me, Kev, and Warner stayed in the hotel. We were hangin' by the pool, everyone was pretty drunk, and on God knows what ... anyway, this girl was joking around with us, and you know how it is, those types of women?"

All the guys nodded.

"Well, she kept bugging us to meet you. She was really drunk so it was easy for Warner. He got her upstairs by claiming he was gonna introduce her to you, but you know what he did."

Ian and Benny made disgusted remarks while Dad swore under his breath and Nikki muttered about male pigs.

My eyes widened but I didn't comment. It didn't make me feel good to know other women had fallen victim to Warner. I would have been happy knowing I was the only member of that club.

I caught Dad watching me and forced a smile. I didn't have to say anything. It was obvious he'd figured out how uncomfortable the conversation was making me. He quickly changed the subject to the upcoming concert, and I let my mind wander.

According to the authorities, Penshaw killed Warner but with all the commotion, no one was talking about all of the other things. Penshaw had no reason to harass me or Dad. That left Warner as the culprit for at least some of it.

I worried at my bottom lip and mulled it all over. I felt like I was missing something-

"Something wrong?"

I jumped as Dad leaned over and squeezed my hand. I smiled and tried to put my unease into words.

"I don't know, maybe I'm just being silly ..."

"No, your confusion makes sense. Penshaw, Warner, Rob. None of them were responsible."

I huffed and looked around the table. All other conversations had stopped. I was about to speak when Ian butted in.

"If it wasn't them, who did all that stuff?"

Dad shrugged. "The FBI says it was mostly unrelated incidents. The light falling was just an accident caused by worn bolts and lax maintenance. The ship will be making restitution to Drew and the band's equipment will be replaced. The attack on you," His smile was sheepish. "It was like you said, Punkin; a fan looking to make a quick buck."

I nodded. The explanations were logical but ...

Ian snorted and drummed his fingers on the table. "Okay, but what about the other stuff? Who made that phone call? Who tied Tina's scarf into a noose? How did the FBI explain those things?"

Dad glanced at Ian. "Sorry kid, they are summing it all up as the scorned woman."

Ian shook his head and started his usual defense, though after what she'd said to him earlier it was a much weaker argument. I liked the idea and was perfectly willing to assign her the blame.

I just wished the FBI had been able to make her leave the ship. I shook off my concerns. I'd just keep out of Judith's way. I didn't think she'd hurt me, she was just hateful and a little embarrassing when she caused a public scene.

The talk turned to the concert again and my gaze drifted to the beautiful scenery. The sea was as smooth as glass, though I could see dark clouds forming in the distance. A server dropped a tray and my gaze was drawn back to the deck. I looked past the cleanup of broken china and caught sight of KC. She was hovering on the periphery of the dance floor. Her hands were clasped in front of her and she was shifting from foot to foot.

She looked lonely and uncomfortable so I rose and walked toward her. One of the opening acts had drawn a crowd and I didn't think she'd seen me.

"KC! How are you?"

She jumped and turned to look at me with wide eyes.

Tina! I didn't know you were here. The band is pretty good, huh?"

I nodded. "Yeah, everyone seems to be having a great time. I'm sorry for earlier but, you know how it is." I smiled. "What did you do today? Did you go on an excursion?"

She shook her head. "Nah, but I heard all about the excitement in San Juan! Congratulations, I'm glad you saved Da-, uh your dad."

I smiled. "Thanks. I'm just happy to have it all over. Now we can enjoy what's left of our trip" I jerked my head towards the table. "We're hanging out over there. You want to join us?"

Her eyes widened. "Oh gosh no, I don't want to intrude."

"You won't be, come on. You can meet my dad and boyfriend-"

"No. Thanks, but I was planning to attend the Full Throttle concert with someone." She sighed. "Looks like I've missed them. I should go. They might be waiting at the theater ..."

She looked over her shoulder and then started to back towards the stairs so I didn't press my invitation. "Okay, well have a good time. Maybe I'll see ya-hey!"

KC cocked an eyebrow.

"Are you busy tomorrow?"

She shook her head. "Not really, why?"

I grinned. "Because I have the perfect 'forgive me for being a thoughtless friend' gift."

She laughed. "You don't' have to- "

"I know I don't have to, but I want to!" I waggled my eyebrows and grinned. "You game for a day at the spa? We've never had any of our plans work out ..."

KC started to shake her head so I rushed on before she could say no. "My treat! Please say yes ..." I gave her my much-practiced puppy dog pitiful look and she laughed.

"Okay, you've twisted my arm."

"Excellent! Meet me at the spa. Nine o'clock? We can get all prettied up for the big gala dinner dance!"

Her happy expression faded when I mentioned the gala. "What's wrong?"

KC shrugged. "I, uh wasn't planning to attend. I don't have anything-"

"I do! I brought two dresses because I couldn't decide, and shoes too! Please, please say you'll come ..."

KC snorted. "Oh, all right, you've twisted my arm. Who can say no to a free day of pampering?"

"Yay!" I rushed over and gave her a quick hug. "I am so ready for this vacation to actually start!" I grinned. "We can get ready in my suite and share clothes and makeup ... I laughed. We'll be like sisters getting ready for the ball!"

I laughed again and backed away as KC continued towards the stairs. I glanced back and saw that she'd stopped halfway up. It looked like she was watching me. I lifted my hand to wave and then stopped as the lights from the dance floor illuminated her face.

Her lips were pressed into a flat line and her face was stiff and emotionless. I blinked, wondering what I'd done ...

The strobe lights pulsed and cast her face into shadows for a second. When it came back around KC was grinning and waving as she continued up the stairs. Huh, it must have been a trick of the light. I frowned and returned the wave.

A heavy gust of chilly air ruffled my hair and sent a shiver through me. I looked up. The sky was now an inky black, without a single star; looked like a storm was brewing.

Rocking the Boat

Tina

KC WAS WAITING OUTSIDE the Tranquility spa when I stepped off of the elevator.

"Hi! I'm so glad you came, thought you might change your mind ..."

A glimpse of the packed waiting area made my mood plummet, I should have made an appointment. Oh well, we could always lounge by the pool until they could fit us in.

KC shrugged. “Nah, sounds like fun.” Her bracelet jingled as she held up her hand. “Besides, I need to get my nails done. I busted a tip-off somehow and they look terrible.”

I glanced at her hand as I opened the door. KC hadn’t lied. Like many women, she’d removed the other tips when the one broke, leaving a pinkish stained mess on her real nails. I frowned, trying to remember what color hers had been. Seemed like they’d been bright red-

“I appreciate you working me in, this cruise has been a nightmare!”

I jerked to a stop just inside the spa doors as the snooty voice of Dr. Judith Fogarty reached my ears. I turned towards the reception area in time to see the young girl’s expression flash with sympathy.

She leaned across the desk and patted Judith’s arm. “Oh no! What’s happened?”

My lips pursed as Judith Fogarty commenced to denigrate me to everyone in the lobby. “... if the flirting wasn’t bad enough, this Tina Crawford has managed to turn my fiancé against me by telling tales that I’ve been harassing her.”

Mews of sympathy sounded from the girl behind the desk as well as several women in the immediate area.

I gritted my teeth and silently cursed Ian. He must have told her about the phone call and the FBI suspicions. I glanced at KC. Her green eyes looked like shards of jade.

"Who does she think she is, telling lies like that?" KC's hands were clenched into tight fists, and she was glaring daggers at Judith. "I'm gonna-"

Flattered as I was that KC was ready to take my side without knowing the facts of the situation, I put my hand out to stop her. I didn't need anyone defending my honor, such as it was. "Don't worry about it, she isn't worth it."

KC frowned at me and fiercely whispered. "No she isn't, but you can't let her get away with making crap like that up! She isn't even Ian's fiancé!"

My brow furrowed. I was pretty sure I had never told KC my boyfriend's name. I was running through the limited conversations we'd had when Judith's shrill voice distracted me.

"Oh, she just thinks the world should fall at her feet just because she is the daughter of some has-been rock star."

The derision in her voice was my final straw. The good doctor needed taken down a peg or three and the imp on my shoulder prodded me to be the delivery system.

I whipped out my phone and sent a text to Nikki before my better judgment could pipe up. Within minutes of hitting send, the phone beside the receptionist rang. Her eyes widened and I bit back a laugh as she sat up straight and nodded. "Yes Captain, right away, sir. We'll be waiting."

And that was my cue. Nose in the air in my best imitation of a prima donna, I grabbed KC's hand and strode to the desk.

"Excuse me." I nudged Judith aside without a backward glance. "I believe you've been waiting for my friend and me, I'm Tina Crawford."

The girl's eyes widened. She gulped and glanced between me and Judith. "Yes ma'am uh ...," She jumped from her chair and addressed the crowded waiting room. "Um, I'm sorry but the spa is closed for a private function, if you'd like to leave your name and treatment preferences we'll reschedule-"

"Please,"

The receptionist met my gaze. "I'll just clear the spa-"

"Oh, no need for that." I smiled at her and then at those waiting. "I'm sure no one here wishes to intrude upon our privacy or carry tales ..."

A few guilty expressions made a lie of my statement, but my next announcement would ensure that I, and by extension, my dad would be the heroes of any stories that made it to social media.

"As a thank you for letting us jump the line, give everyone here a treatment on my account." I ignored the gasps of delight from those waiting and the stammered replies from the receptionist, turning my gaze to Judith. "Oh! Doctor Fogarty I didn't realize you were there!"

I put my palm to my chest and poured saccharine into my Southern drawl. "Please forgive this has been rock star's daughter for cutting in front of you, it's so easy to get distracted when the world falls at your feet, don't you agree?"

Judith's face turned several alarming shades of red and her mouth opened and closed like a scalded goldfish. KC snorted and my lips twitched with the urge to laugh but I managed to maintain my haughty facade until we'd been shown to the herbal wrap room.

We laughed ourselves silly for a few minutes. I was wiping the tears from my eyes when KC grumbled that someone needed to teach the good doctor some manners.

"Nah, she's lost Ian. If she ever really had him." I shrugged and let my head rest against the wall of the sauna. "That's punishment enough, don't you think?"

I glanced over as KC didn't answer. Her expression put me in mind of the saying, *if looks could kill.* Gooseflesh dimpled my arms as KC muttered. "No, she needs to pay."

I blinked and started to reply when her face broke into a serene smile. "This is heaven. Thank you so much for this day. I've always wanted to go to a spa ..."

I smiled in agreement. I put the whole Judith situation from my mind and settled down for a day of indulgences with my new friend.

Tina

In the end, my plan to treat getting ready for the event like girls on prom night didn't happen. KC had opted to dress in her room and then meet me in the ballroom.

We'd had our nails done, French for me and cat's eye for KC, then the stylist had given both of us up-dos. My hair was finished first, so I had run on ahead and given KC the pin number to access our floor.

My eyes widened when I saw KC's hair; she'd gotten the same style and, though I'd never noticed it before, in dim light, we looked a lot alike.

We stood side by side and looked in the mirror. KC's hair was a few shades darker, more light brown where mine was definitely blond, but our eyes were similar shades of green and as for body type, my dress fit her like a glove.

"Wow, that looks great on you!" I'd given KC her choice of the cocktail dresses I'd brought. She'd chosen a side sheath dress in a blue that reminded me of the Georgia sky.

KC twirled and then frowned and looked in the mirror. She bit her lip and glanced at me as she plucked at the hemline. "You don't think it's too fancy?" Her gaze returned to the mirror. "I've never been to anything like this ..."

I wrapped my arm around her shoulders and gave her a half-hug, careful not to crush the dress. "Too fancy? No way, it's perfect!" I pulled the shoes from my carry-all. "You want to try these?"

KC's eyes widened. "Oh my gosh," she ran a finger over the tennis bracelet-styled strap of my stiletto sandals and shook her head. "Are those *diamonds*?"

I grinned. "Nah, but they look real! They're crystals, bigger than the ones on the toe strap and heel, but still, just crystals. Go on, see if they fit!"

KC looked doubtful but did as requested.

"Perfect! How do they feel?"

"Um, good I guess, bit high for me but I guess I'll just walk slow?"

I laughed. "Yep, you strut in shoes like that." I winked at her and pulled the other dress from the closet. "Channel your inner runway model."

"Ha, I don't think I have one of those ..."

I laid the garment bag on the bed and then got my jewelry box from a dresser drawer. I removed the blue topaz and diamond pendant I'd planned to pair with the dress. "Here, turn around and I'll-"

"No way!" Eyes huge and round, KC backed away. "I can't wear that, it must have cost a fortune!"

I shrugged and moved so that I could fasten it around KC's neck. "Maybe? Doesn't matter, you aren't going to lose it ..."

I looked over her shoulder at both of us reflected in the mirror. KC fingered the pendant and worried at her lower lip.

"I can't, it might come off and it must be special to you-"

"It has a safety clasp. Girl, I've worn this drunk as a skunk and it's never fallen off so you'll be fine and yeah, it's kinda special? Dad gave it to my mom when I was born, her eyes were that same shade of blue."

My gaze flitted back to the mirror in time to catch a strange look on KC's face; Like a cloud had crossed over the sun and sucked all of the joy from the day.

I frowned but she blinked and a radiant smile lit her face. It wasn't the first time I'd thought her moods changed like lightning but it was the first time I'd thought about how little I knew her. For an instant, I regretted letting her borrow the necklace.

A quick hug and peck on my cheek brought me out of my thoughts. I laughed. "What was that for?"

"Thank you, for all of this." She gestured at her outfit. "I've never, ever worn anything so ..., so fancy or expensive! This must be what a real princess feels like."

I smiled and looked at the remaining gown. It was longer than I usually wore, falling just below the knee, but the hem was a handkerchief so it didn't look dowdy. The purple silk was also a new color for me, which is why I'd brought the blue dress for backup.

The color was deep and rich, but, unfortunately, the silk had wrinkled badly.

"Hey KC," I zipped the garment bag and headed for the door. "I'm gonna leave you to do your make-up." She made a sad face and I lifted the bag. "My dress needs pressing so I need to run it to the laundry. They should have it ready by the time I shower and get my make-up on, don't you think?"

A huff made me look over my shoulder. KC was glaring in my direction. I cocked an eyebrow. "Problem?"

She huffed again. "Yeah! We were gonna do each other's make-up! Like sisters you said!" She stamped her foot and shoved my make-up bag off of the bed before plopping onto the mattress and crossing her arms over her chest. "Stupid dress!"

I frowned and tried to keep my expression neutral. I recalled the day we were supposed to go into St. Maarten. I'd been right to tell Ian she was clingy.

I kept my tone light to avoid any drama. "I know, but you always look great, you don't need my help and I won't be going at all if I don't get this dress steamed." I opened the door. "Help yourself to any of my cosmetics and, if you're gone when I get back I'll see you in the ballroom around eight, okay?"

I didn't wait for a reply. A glance at my phone showed I'd be lucky to get my dress back and be ready on time, I couldn't waste another minute on KC's temper tantrum.

The ladies in the laundry assured me they'd have my dress pressed and delivered in plenty of time so I left it in their capable hands and scurried back to my suite. I looked around, but KC had left.

I'd just stepped out of the shower when there was a knock on my bedroom door and Dad called out that he was hanging my gown on the back of the door and I needed to get a move on or we'd be late.

I rushed through my makeup, dabbed perfume on my pulse points, and then pulled my dress from the garment bag. It was a gauzy style so I didn't notice anything amiss until I'd pulled it over my hips.

"What the ..." I frowned and plucked at the fabric. A clump of silk came out in my hand. "Oh my God!"

I must have screamed because Dad was pounding on my door in seconds.

"Tina? What's going on? Let me in! Are you hur-"

"I'm fine, Dad." I opened the door. "But my dress isn't ..." I twirled and watched as dozens of tiny fabric scraps drifted to the floor.

"What in the world?" He frowned and crouched to get a closer look at my dress. "Look at this ..." He pulled at the skirt.

All along the hem, there were cuts, going up toward the bust. Some were shallow, some so deep they cut through the built-in bra.

Dad stood up and shook his head. “Need to call down to the laundry and raise some Cain.” He stomped towards the house phone on the end table in the living area, muttering. “Should hire people that know how to operate the machines-“

“No, Dad, wait!”

“What, why? They need to kno-“

“I don’t think this was their fault.” He set the phone back onto the receiver and walked back into my room.

“What makes you think that?”

I showed him the slashes in my dress and he whistled, long and low.

“Someone did that with what, scissors?”

I shrugged. “Maybe? Or a knife? I don’t know but what I do know is people are waiting on us and I need a dress so, let me change.”

He stepped out and I closed the door.

“Do you have another dress?”

I slid the destroyed garment off and grabbed a sundress. “I did ...” I slipped my black satin mules on, fastened the turtle pendant around my neck, and rushed out the door.

“You can’t go like that!”

I snorted and picked up my evening bag. “I know that!” I motioned for him to follow and boarded the elevator. “You go on to the ballroom.”

He frowned. “Where are you going?”

“There’s a boutique just off of the atrium on deck six. I’m hoping they will have something suitable. If so, I can just slip it on.” I pointed to my shoes. “I’m ready except for the dress, so I’ll meet y’all just as soon as -“

“I don’t know, Punkin, you aren’t supposed to go anywhere alone ...”

I rolled my eyes. The elevator jolted to a stop, and we exited. “Dad, Penshaw’s been arrested, there’s no danger-“

“Oh, right, then who slashed your dress?”

Well, he had me there. I shrugged. “I have no idea and no time to think about it. You can come along if you like but I’m going that way.”

I put action to words and heard Dad call out for me to be careful and he’d see me in the ballroom in ten minutes. I threw my hand up in a wave and continued walking to the dress shop.

The clerk was standing at the door when I walked up.

“We’re just about to close if you want to come back-“

“Oh please, I have to have a dress!” I slid passed her and moved to a rack of dresses. “I’ll be quick. Can you help me find a cocktail dress in a size four or six?”

Her mouth pressed into a thin line, but she did as I'd requested. A few minutes later I had four possible choices in the small dressing room.

"Any of those working for you?"

I discarded the first option for being too short. The second didn't fit right in the arms. I looked horrible in the yellow floral, which left a nude satin with a black lace overlay that fell just above my knees.

"Yeah ...," I looked in the mirror and twisted left and then right as I answered the clerk. The dress fit and black was always an acceptable color, but the neckline, oh my goodness.

I stifled a giggle. The dress had a circular collar, I vaguely recalled it being named a Peter Pan. Either way, I had never worn anything so modest in my life. Oh well, it'd have to do.

I pulled the curtain to the side and stepped out. "Can you take the tags off of this with me wearing it?"

"Of course! Let me get the scissors." I gathered my things and followed her to the checkout counter.

A quick snip and then she was totaling my bill. "So, you think the laundry damaged your dress?" She handed me the receipt and an ink pen.

"Hmm," I signed my name to charge the dress to our room. "More than damaged, it's been torn or cut."

Her eyes widened. "Oh wow! Why would somebody do that?"

"I have no ide-"

"What is it they say about karma?"

The clerk's eyes widened. I gritted my teeth and turned to see Judith Fogarty, wearing a hideous greige evening suit and a hateful smirk.

Making Waves

Ian

LAUGHTER ERUPTED AROUND OUR table as Chad finished a tale from his misspent youth. I smiled and chuckled in all the appropriate places, but my thoughts were far from the escapades of two teen-aged boys and a stolen school bus.

I looked around the ballroom, wondering who had damaged Tina's dress. My gaze fell on Judith Fogarty. God, she was such a bitter woman. Even from a distance,

I could tell her expression was puckered like someone who'd just sucked a lemon. Her disdain for her surroundings was clear, but what set up my hackles was the unwavering glare focused exclusively on Tina. In the ten minutes I'd been watching, Judith's gaze hadn't moved from Tina's back, and hatred was clearly written in her expression.

I didn't like Judith, but up until now, I would have said the acts of mischief and mayhem that Tina and Chad had experienced were beneath the doctor; she felt herself so far above us mere mortals that I couldn't picture her stooping so low as to steal Tina's scarf, much less fashioning it into a noose. Nor could I see Judith climbing the theater catwalk or knowing how to loosen the bolts on a par can. Nasty phone calls, even cutting Tina's dress in a fit of jealousy I could just about believe, but the rest?

I shook my head and took a sip of sweet tea. Maybe I was missing something or, perhaps the events weren't linked at all. It was possible that Judith had made the phone call and destroyed Tina's dress and Warner had done the rest ...

Tina's warm hand slid up my arm, drawing my thoughts toward far more pleasant things than Judith Fogarty or Richard Warner. I waggled my eyebrows at her and leaned in to whisper a proposition.

Her eyes widened and she sat back far enough to meet my eyes. "Naughty, Mr. Buchanan!"

I smirked. "And you love it."

She grinned and made her eyes widen to portray the picture of innocence. "I can neither confirm nor deny."

I snorted. "I have it on good authority-"

"Ready for tomorrow, Ian?"

I jumped as Chad sat down beside me. I prayed he hadn't heard my conversation with his daughter. "Uh, yes Sir, we've got things nailed down between Cliff, Benny T, and I but we never did get to run through the set with you ..."

Chad nodded. "Well, if you're staying the night with Tina, grab your gear and we can hit the highlights before we turn in," He arched an eyebrow. "Unless you had other plans tonight?"

Oh man, my face was hot and I couldn't hold his knowing gaze. Once again, he'd made me feel like a truant kid standing before the teacher. "No Sir, that is-" I scowled at Tina as she stifled a laugh. "I'll be there. What time?"

Chad looked at Tina and chuckled before meeting my gaze. "Nikki and I are gonna head out of here in about twenty minutes, see you back in the suite around ten-thirty?"

I nodded. "Sounds good."

A cheer went up around the room as the opening riff to a much loved southern rock song blasted through the mains.

"Great!" Chad stood and held his hand out to Tina. "Come on, Punkin' they're playin' our song!"

Nikki and I laughed as Chad and Tina took to the floor and launched into an enthusiastic version of swing dancing. Nikki nudged me in the ribs and yelled that we should give them a run for their money. I grinned and started to my feet when my phone vibrated in my pocket. I almost ignored it. My band was scattered around the ballroom, my girl was on the dance floor. Everyone I cared about was accounted for except ... I glanced at the screen and sighed; the last person I wanted to talk to.

I mouthed an apology to Nikki and sat down to text with my dad.

Hey Dad, what's up?

One simple question opened the floodgates. My phone lit up as one message after another popped onto my screen. I read the first couple and saw red.

Dad was on an epic rant about my defection from his employment plans. Since I'd said nothing about my decision to stick with my chosen career, I assumed Judith had been in his ear. My suspicions were confirmed, and my anger amped up to explosive levels when Dad started in about the loose woman I was cavorting with.

I gritted my teeth and waited until I'd reined in my temper before firing off one sentence.

Don't ever let me hear you talk about Tina like that again.

I tucked the phone back into my pocket, unconcerned with his response. I searched the ballroom for the interfering biddy who'd caused my current father issues but after walking around the perimeter without encountering her, I figured she'd put that big brain to use and got out while the gettin' was good. In my present mood, I couldn't have predicted what I'd have said or done.

My hunt for Judith had left me near the exit and we'd planned to leave after the current song, so I leaned against the wall and waited. Tina's giggle drifted across the dance floor as Chad twirled her around. She met my gaze and gave a little wave and then they were gone, lost amid a colorful background of couples grooving to the beat.

I was happy to see Tina and Chad enjoying each other's company but the irony wasn't lost on me; she'd mended her relationship with her father just as I was about to make decisions that would sever the cords of mine completely.

All at Sea

Tina

IAN AND DAD WERE busy with preparations for the final concert and I was at loose ends. I'd stayed up until after midnight listening to them rehearse so I had no desire to do anything strenuous; a day by the pool sounded just my speed and I'd sent two texts to KC, inviting her along, but she'd never replied.

I found two lounge chairs, just in case KC showed up, and then settled with a book I'd found at the gift shop. Though the mystery novel featuring a caterer who solved crimes usually held my attention, today all I could think about was my missing friend.

My mad dash to buy a dress had made me late for the gala. When I'd arrived, everyone had taken their seats and a comedian was entertaining while dinner was being served. I'd looked for KC as I followed the hostess to my table, but the room was crowded.

I sent her multiple texts throughout dinner and again just before the band kicked off but she'd never materialized or responded to my messages. It hadn't made sense. KC had been so excited to dress up ... her no–show last night had left me puzzled. Now, with the silence continuing, I was worried.

"Can I get you a drink, Miss?"

I jumped and glanced up at the server hovering beside my chair. "Oh! You startled me. Um ..., a virgin strawberry daiquiri would be great.." He started to walk off when I got an idea. "Hey, could you do me a favor?"

He retraced his steps. "Of course, how may I help?"

I smiled. "Well, a friend of mine was supposed to have met me for the gala last night and she never showed." I shrugged. "I've been texting her off and on all night and then again this morning with no response and now ..."

He nodded. "Would you like someone to do a welfare check?"

I blew out a breath I hadn't realized I was holding. "Yes! That would be awesome."

I gave him KC's name and room number and then went for a swim. My energy and interest lasted long enough to do about ten easy laps. Feeling virtuous for having done a little bit of exercise, I set about relaxing with a fruity drink and a good book.

I lounged, swam, sunned, and lunched in solitary splendor, topping the day off with a poolside nap. When I awoke, the sun was low and the crowd had thinned. I glanced at my phone. A couple of messages from Ian and my dad, but none from KC. I started to fret but a glance at the time had me scrambling to pack my things and get back to the suite; the concert started in two hours!

I was waiting for the elevator when I noticed the bartender pointing at me as he talked with another man in uniform. I frowned and started walking toward them but the crew member met me halfway.

"Ms. Crawford? I'm Ensign Beryl with the Bursars office. The steward passed your request for a room check on to our office."

My brow furrowed. I was pretty sure Bursars dealt with fees or something. I started to ask why his department was involved.

"Ma'am, can you tell me the name of your friend again?"

"Sure. It's KC Anderson."

The Ensign nodded and glanced at a paper he held in his hand. "And the first name is the letter K and C?" He glanced at me and I nodded. "Not C A S E Y? You're sure?"

I frowned. "Yes, I'm positive, she has a charm bracelet with those letters on it- look, what's this about?"

Ensign Beryl, again glanced at the paper in his hand and then looked at me. His gaze focused on my face for several minutes. Just as I began to think he wasn't going to answer my question he nodded.

"Ma'am, you're absolutely positive the woman you've been talking to on this ship is named KC Anderson and the cabin number she gave you was number forty-five, forty-one?"

I rolled my eyes. The woman I'd been talking to? What an odd way to phrase a friendship.

I huffed and hiked my bag strap higher onto my shoulder. "Look, I'm running late for the concert, yes to all of your questions, now, did you find her? Is she okay?"

Ensign Beryl drew a deep breath. "Ms. Crawford, I've been to cabin forty-five, forty-one and it isn't registered to anyone named Anderson, nor do the occupants of that cabin know anyone by that name."

I opened my mouth to protest but the Ensign rushed on before I could speak.

"I've also checked our passenger manifest." He pursed his lips. "Ms. Crawford, there is no one by that name registered as a passenger on this ship."

Batten Down the Hatches

Tina

THE ENSIGN'S WORDS WERE running through my head like a broken record as I rode the elevator to my deck. The man must have been mistaken. I wouldn't argue that I had a couple of screws loose but I wasn't so far gone that I had hallucinated a friend!

I fired off another text to KC, not that I thought she'd answer, and then rushed to my cabin to shower and change for the concert.

The suite was empty but a room service tray on the coffee table told me that Dad had already come and gone. The remains of what looked like grilled fish and a side salad reminded me that I'd not eaten since lunch, but stopping for dinner was out of the question.

My stomach growled, but I ignored my body's demands and headed to the bathroom; if I hurried, I could at least grab a danish and, a cup of tea.

I showered in record time and opted for my favorite blue jeans and a teal t-shirt. A couple of gold bangle bracelets, a pair of ballet flats, and I was ready to rock. I grabbed my phone off of the charger and checked for messages as I jogged to the elevator.

I wasn't surprised to find no word from KC but two messages from Ian did make my eyes widen; I'd figured he was too busy to wonder about me.

I let him know I was running late and slid my phone into my back pocket just as the elevator reached deck six. The crowd was moving as a slow herd towards the theater doors. I pushed my way through the throng and then sighed as the cafe came into sight. The place was packed, with lines running out the doors and down the hall.

The introduction for Ian's band reached my ears but I was starving. I whispered silent apologies to Bad Opera and took my place in line. The staff was efficient and the opening song was still playing as I showed my pass to the usher and was escorted to my front-row seat.

I smiled and nodded at my neighbors on the row and then sat down to eat my cherry danish and watch my very own sexy rock star. As Ian finished his solo and stepped back to the microphone to sing the last verse, his gaze met mine and he cocked an eyebrow. I assumed he was questioning my lateness so I grinned and silently toasted him with my hot tea.

He smirked and shook his head before slamming into the complicated guitar riffs of the next song. Jason and Ian were hamming it up, Cole was grinning like a fool ... the boys of Bad Opera were having the time of their lives and I couldn't have been happier for them.

The guys were doing the job of an opening act and the people around me were engaged. As Ian launched into the power chords of a well-known rock anthem the crowd roared and jumped to their feet and fairly soon we were all dancing in the aisles and enjoying the show. Four songs into their set, I noticed Ian looking to the wings and frowning. He did it several times and, by the end of the song he'd caught my eye and motioned towards the backstage area with his head.

We pantomimed back and forth until I was sure of what he meant and then I walked to the door marked personnel only.

My pass gained me entrance, but I wished it hadn't; backstage was chaos! Techs and stage crew were rushing around without direction, Cliff was pacing, Benny and Nikki were in an intense discussion, and my dad was nowhere to be seen.

I walked farther into the area and Nikki looked up and made eye contact.

"Oh, thank God! Where is your dad?"

All eyes turned toward me, and I felt like a deer caught in headlights. "Um ... getting ready to take the stage?"

Nikki's eyes widened and she shook her head. "That's just it, he should be, but some idiot ran into him and spilled red wine down his shirt ..." Nikki's gaze went to the hallway that led to the dressing rooms.

I frowned. What was the big deal? He was just down the hall. I said as much but Cliff interrupted.

"No, Chad didn't have another shirt, so he ran back to his suite, and I told him to get a tech to fetch it but he didn't want them having the code for the elevator or anyone going into the cabin in case you were there alone and now Bad Opera is going long and we were supposed to be on already and-"

"Cliff!" Nikki broke in and shut Cliff's panicky ramble down. "It'll all be fine, Cliff. Why don't you go back to the dressing room and practice the deep breathing and mantras we talked about?"

Cliff started in about Ian getting tired, but Nikki cut him off. "Ian will be fine, Cliff. He's a pro and we'll just change things up until Chad gets back, now Splif is gonna go with you ... that's right, deep breaths, in and out ..."

Nikki blew out a deep breath of her own as Cliff finally allowed himself to be led away by Splif Jenkins and another guy from the road crew.

"Whew, he gets so worked up." She shook her head and looked at me. "No idea where Chad is? You didn't see him in your suite?"

I shook my head. "Huh-uh, sorry." I bit my lip. "But, um, sounds like Dad went because of me so how about I go and look-"

"Would you?" Nikki's shoulders relaxed and she flashed a tight smile. "I'd go but-"

"Absolutely. You're needed here." I patted her arm and rushed toward the exit. "I'll be right back!"

Once out of the theater areas I could hear thunder and my promise to be quick looked to be a wild underestimation of the time needed to traverse the ship.

The humid air and distant clouds had finally produced the storm I'd anticipated, and rain was blowing sideways against the windows lining the hallway. The ship's crew were laying slip-proof mats and hanging signs that the outside decks were closed. Without access to all of the walkways, everyone not at the concert seemed to be concentrated in the atrium and half of them were queued at the elevators.

It took nearly half an hour for my turn at the elevator and, once on my deck, I sprinted to our cabin and burst through the door shouting for Dad.

I received no answer to my calls. The living room was empty except for the room service tray. Lightning flooded the room in spurts, casting strange shadows across the floors. The ship was starting to rock and a glance out the windows showed the sea was a moving canvas of white caps.

I looked around the living room and tiny galley but didn't venture out to the private garden and sun deck; there was no way he'd have been outside in the storm.

That left his room. I knocked. "Dad? You in there?" Hearing nothing, I turned the knob and looked inside. The lights were on in the bathroom and the stained t-shirt was soaking in a sink full of water. I shrugged. He must have changed and headed back to the theater. I turned off the lights and started to leave the suite when my phone chimed. It was Nikki, asking if I'd found Dad. I typed a quick reply of my findings and was putting my phone back into my pocket when I heard movement in my cabin.

I stiffened and took a few steps closer. My door was shut but a sliver of light showed under the threshold. I was positive I'd turned them all off ...

Had someone gained access to our deck? Was it housekeeping? The concierge? Dad? None of the options I came up with made any sense. No one should be in my cabin at this time of night and, if they had good intentions they'd have responded to my calls.

I was debating whether to barge in or get security when something crashed to the floor followed by a groan. Without thinking, I burst through the door. "What's going on in here-"

My breath caught as I took in the scene. The bedside lamp was on the floor and my dad was slumped against the headboard.

His complexion was ashen, his breaths were coming in fits and starts, and blood was dripping down the side of his head.

"Dad!" His eyes met mine and he started to speak as I rushed forward.

"Watch-"

"Well isn't this nice? Just one big happy family ..."

I jumped and turned around to see KC walk out of my bathroom holding a wet towel and a wicked-looking knife.

All Hands on Deck

Ian

I CHUGGED A BOTTLE of water, tossed it into the recycle, and then looked at Nikki. "Okay, tell me again, slowly."

I nodded my thanks to the tech that handed me a towel and started wiping my face and neck as Nikki Hardy filled me in on the missing Crawford family. I frowned and glanced at the clock hanging beside the stage director's desk.

"You're telling me Chad left to change his shirt over an hour ago and that Tina went looking for him at least twenty minutes ago?" I barely managed to restrain myself as Nikki nodded. "And you didn't think to, I don't know, CALL SECURITY? Send someone to find them?"

My temper was hanging by a thread.

"I was going to call security but since they arrested the chief they are short-staffed and also, I didn't want to overreact-"

My eyes about bulged from my head and I started to yell but Nikki held up her hand.

"Hold on, Ian. Hear me out!"

I drew a deep breath and nodded. "Make it quick."

"Look, I don't like this any more than you do, but Tina sent me a text saying Chad wasn't there and must be on his way back-where are you going? Ian!"

I stomped out the side door, not bothering to answer. I knew I was being difficult but I also didn't care. When Chad hadn't returned with his clean shirt I'd dismissed it for a few minutes but when Nikki asked me to play long I'd started getting a bad feeling. When they'd told us to wrap it up and Full Throttle was gonna jam until Chad came back the hair on the back of my neck stood on end; both Crawfords were MIA and alarm bells were clanging in my head.

I left Nikki with the responsibility of keeping the audience happy and headed for Tina's cabin. Away from the noise of the theater, I could hear the weather raising hell. Every now and then the ship would pitch and roll which just added another layer to my growing anxiety.

They'd closed the doors to the outside decks and everyone and their brother seemed to be milling around the atrium. The line at the elevators made me think Tina's delayed return might in part be the traffic congestion but her not answering any phone messages kept me from relaxing.

I paced in a small circle as the line to the elevators barely dwindled. After ten minutes I lost all patience and went to the reception desk. A brief explanation of my concerns got me an escort to the service elevator but halfway there the steward's radio squawked; clean up on deck eight.

The poor guy shuffled his feet and looked miserable and confused. "Look dude, point me in the right direction and we'll call it good."

He bit his lip then handed me his access card and high-tailed it to the sea sickness crisis.

I found the door he'd told me about and in minutes I was stepping into a side hallway on the penthouse deck. I started walking towards the Crawfords' suite when an elevator chimed. I increased my pace and rounded the corner in time to see Tina, Chad, and someone else stepping into the main elevator.

"Tina!"

I hurried to catch up but the doors closed before I could get there. I huffed and had a few choice words for the love of my life as I watched the numbers on the sign above the door. When the car stopped on Deck Seven I frowned. The theater entrance was one deck below where they'd stopped. I shook my head and rushed back to the service elevator.

My elevator exited outside the Alchemy Lounge, which meant the passenger elevators were to my right. The hallway leading to the atrium doubled as an art gallery. Halfway down, one wall turned to windows. The glass was foggy but, from what I could see, the wind was blowing the rain sideways and waves were easily breaking above twelve feet.

The ship pitched and I slammed against the window. My unease was fast rising to panic. I needed to get to Tina. I started to jog and in seconds I could see the coffee bar sign and gift shop. The passenger elevator Tina had used emptied at the other side of the gift shop. Deck Six was the way to the main areas of the theater. Why then had they chosen to go to Deck Seven? I was crossing the atrium when movement to my left caught my eye.

My eyes widened and I stopped to peer through the window. What fool would be out in that mess?

"Oh my God ..." My heart skipped a couple of beats. Tina. Tina was out in the storm with ... I squinted. The other person was female, but I couldn't make out who she was. They had Chad between them and ... I frowned.

Something was wrong with Chad Crawford. His shoulders were slumped and Tina and the person with her seemed to be helping him walk.

I banged on the glass but there was no way Tina was going to hear me over the torrent of rain and wind. I was about to burst through the door when the person next to Chad dropped his arm and turned towards Tina.

The breath rushed from my lungs; the woman Tina and Chad were with had a very large knife and she was waving it in Tina's face! My focus narrowed to three people standing in a torrential storm on a rain-slicked cruise ship deck.

I pulled my phone from my pocket, pulled up text messages, and hit the text to speech so I could keep my eyes on the scene outside.

The crazy person, who I was beginning to suspect was the chick Tina had befriended and then ticked off when she refused to go to St. Maarten, seemed to be yelling and punctuating her rant with waves and jabs of the knife. So far, she'd made no other threatening moves towards Tina or Chad.

I dictated what I saw into my phone and then hit send, praying Nikki would decipher the auto-corrections and send help. I swallowed past the lump in my throat as the knife-wielder grabbed Chad's arm and gestured at Tina with their knife holding hand.

Tina shook her head, another point of the knife by the crazy woman, and then Tina was putting Chad's other arm around her shoulder and the three were walking away from the window. My eyes widened. In seconds they'd be out of my sight.

I sent one more text to Nikki and then plunged into the raging storm.

Knock Seven Bells

Tina

"KC, HE NEEDS A doctor!"

KC glared at me and pointed forward with the knife. "He'll be fine, let's go."

Regardless of KC's demands, one look at my dad showed we wouldn't be going much farther. He was whiter than his t-shirt and his eyes were barely open. He was responding to the command to walk, but his feet barely left the deck; we were essentially dragging him.

I focused on putting one foot in front of the other as I tried to find a way out of the situation. My mind was reeling. KC was clearly unhinged and little things about her that I'd thought odd and then dismissed were now coming back to me.

Her moods had shifted like lightning. I'd first noticed it the day I met her. She'd been happy and laughing one minute but when I said I couldn't have dinner with her she'd looked like someone had licked all of the red off of her lollipop.

That had happened several times and then again the day that Warner had been killed. Ian had tried to tell me something wasn't right, but I'd been so focused on saving Dad from a murder charge ... I sniffed and pushed a hunk of wet hair off of my face. This was all my fault!

I drew a deep breath and promised anything and everything to any part of the universe that might be listening if only we got out alive. A flash of lightning lit the sky and illuminated KC's face.

Her expression was wild, almost feral, and the knife she held was long and tapered to a point; my guess was she'd snatched a boning knife from the kitchen.

The ship rolled and KC lost her grip on Dad's arm. God forgive me, I held my breath and hoped she'd go overboard, but before I could even think of dragging Dad to safety she'd found her footing and wrapped her arm around Dad's waist. I crossed my fingers and hoped for another strong wave.

With the storm, it was a definite possibility. If we'd been on land, I'd have called it a gully washer. There were no ditches to overflow on a ship but all the same, the water ponding on the deck was up to our ankles until a wave hit and made the ship list. Then the water would rush over the side until the ship righted itself and the whole process started over.

The direction that KC was forcing us to take meant we were walking directly into the wind. The slog through the storm was made more difficult because I couldn't get much purchase in my smooth-soled flats. My foot went out from under me for the umpteenth time in as many minutes. I screamed as I landed on my knee.

"KC, I can't-"

"Get up! We have to go!" She started jumping up and down. The hand holding the knife was swinging in an arc. "Get up, get up, get-"

"Okay, okay! Calm down! Just, just put the knife down." I groaned and pushed myself upright. My knee was throbbing. Not wanting to risk another fall, I leaned against the wall and removed my shoes.

As I bent over I caught movement from the corner of my eye. Ian! I closed my eyes and sent a silent prayer of thanks to whatever guardian angel was on duty in the heavens, and then opened them and made eye contact with my savior.

Thanks to our earlier bit of charades it didn't take me long to understand that he'd called for help and that I should ... talk? I frowned and shook my head.

I didn't know what his crocodile hand signal meant but it didn't matter; KC was jabbing the air with her knife and tugging on Dad's arm. It was time to move again.

I straightened and took up my half of Dad's weight, careful to avoid looking in Ian's direction. The precaution was probably unnecessary.

KC was frowning and staring straight ahead but every so often she would look out to sea and then mutter under her breath. I frowned. I had no idea what she was doing or why.

All was clear a few minutes later when we rounded a corner and KC drew to a stop. We were under a set of stairs, the rain was only partially blocked by the treads but a bulkhead was blocking some of the wind. We were still buffeted by the strongest gusts but I could hear what she was saying.

My blood ran cold.

"Happy family, happy family, happy ..."

I suspected the girl was off of her rocker and seconds later my suspicions were confirmed when KC shouted at my dad.

"Get in there!" She pointed at the lifeboat suspended on the side of the ship. "Hurry, hurry, hurry-"

"KC, what are you-"

"Shut up!"

She waved the knife tip at Dad and it was within inches of his chest so I zipped my lip but when she started to tug him from my grasp I had to speak.

"KC, he's hurt!" I shook my head. "What are you thinking, anyway?

She jerked around and pinned me with her stare and I realized just how insane she was. Minutes before, her eyes had been wild and slightly unfocused. She'd been jibbering like a child.

I didn't know what had set her off, but like a switch had been flipped, her eyes were clear and hard as jade.

"What am I thinking?"

I shivered. Her tone was almost whimsical and her expression was animated. Her lips twitched into a smile and her eyebrows lifted and fell in rhythm with her words.

"What am I thinking?"

Her voice rose, ending with a shriek that made my hair stand on end.

"I am thinking that you should be a good sister and HELP ME with our dad!"

I licked my lips and slowly leaned back as KC punctuated her words with the knife. My breath caught and I thought she was going to ram the blade into my neck-

KC giggled and backed up against the railing, leaving me to support Dad. My arms shook. I was gonna drop him-I spotted a white box in front of the bulkhead marked storage. Keeping my eye on KC, I shuffled over and sat Dad on the box.

I jumped as KC's voice sounded from right behind me.

"You always were the spoiled one."

I backed up, trying to get her to follow and be out of stabbing range of me and Dad.

She stepped closer to the railing and stamped her foot. "I have to do all the work."

My eyes widened. Loon-eee-tunes. My new friend was a certifiable nut. And Ivy thought she held the record for letting bad people into her life! If it hadn't been so scary, I'd have laughed!

I shook my head and focused on what KC was saying. I frowned as she once again went on a rant about me being the bad sister.

"KC, how are we sisters?"

She rolled her eyes and cocked her head. "Oh, all right Miss Precise Definitions." She sniffed. "We're half-sisters. Happy now?"

She turned her head and ignored me. "Daddy, when we get to our new home can I have the biggest bedroom? You always let her have ..."

Movement from the hallway drew my attention. I squinted through the rain and sighed as Ian came into site. The game of charades started again, though only Ian had the use of his hands.

I shook my head, frowned, and winced, my way through a silent conversation that resulted in me assuming I was to keep KC distracted because help was on the way. Ian drew back into the shadows and I wracked my brain for a way to stall for time.

I tuned back into KC's one-sided chat with my dad and found the perfect way to buy the much-needed time. "KC, how are we sis-er half-sisters?"

She looked at me and snorted. "And you're supposed to be the smart one." She huffed. "My mom and your dad were an item." Her lips moved into a sneer. "Until your mom came along!"

I frowned. What she'd said was nonsense. My mother and father had known each other since their teens. I didn't bother to argue, however. Her mood seemed to be shifting and, oddly enough, I preferred a chipper, talkative, and slightly snarky knife-wielding lunatic over a sullen, pouty, and raging one.

I quickly steered the conversation to something I suspected would keep her happy. "KC, what were you saying about the biggest bedroom?"

My hunch was right. In a flash, her eyes were shining, and her speech pattern was bubbly and a little lyrical.

"Daddy said I could, so don't you try and change his mind!"

I held up my hand. "Oh, I wouldn't dare. You've earned it, right? You said you had to do all of the work."

She sniffed. "Well, I did. You didn't help at all." She wrinkled her nose and looked at my Dad. "I was the good one, huh Daddy. Without me, we'd never have-Daddy you aren't listening!"

My poor father was almost unconscious. His head lolled when KC nudged him with her elbow, and I darted forward to catch him.

"Leave him!" KC waved the knife at me and put her hand on Dad's shoulder, pulling him back until he rested against the bulkhead.

I bit my lip. "KC put the knife down, you're scaring me!"

"I'm scaring you?" She snorted. "I doubt that!"

I frowned. She made no sense but I wanted her to talk more and wave the knife less, so I kept talking.

"I am scared, look." I held up my hand. I didn't have to fake the tremble.

"Huh. That's a first." KC cocked her head to the side. "Gotta give you credit. All the things I did ... you never ran away."

What was she talking about? I replayed her words and my eyes widened. "That was you? The phone call? The light? My dress? The necklace- You almost killed me! KC, why?"

Her lower lip jutted out. "You were supposed to run away!"

"What? Run aw-where? We're on a ship!" I sent a mental eye roll to myself for trying to reason with a psychopath; she showed not a hint of remorse or shame for what she'd done.

She huffed and stamped her foot. "You should have gone home!" She pursed her lips and her voice got so soft I had to strain to hear as she muttered.

"Not supposed to come. Messing up my plans." She kicked the railing and met my gaze. "You just had to horn in and steal Daddy. You always do that!" She waved the knife, setting her charm bracelet tinkling. "You get everything. You even took my name!"

I frowned. "I what? We don't-" My gaze went to her bracelet, and I remembered the charm with her initials. I gulped. "KC? Do your initials stand for-"?

"Of course they do!" She huffed and rolled her eyes. "Your mom stole my name!" She started to bounce on the soles of her feet. “I’m Kristina Carol, me! It’s my name just because you’re older ... it’s not fair!”

Her words ended in a sob. I drew a deep breath and worried at my bottom lip as I tried to figure out a response that wouldn’t send her farther around the bend. “Uh, I’m sorry. It’s a ... sibling thing.”

Her expression started to get stormy and when she got riled, the knife started swinging. I needed to change the subject.

“KC, what were your plans?”

Her gaze jerked back to me, and she stared. For a second I thought she wasn’t even seeing me but then she blinked, and her expression cleared. Once again, she was childlike. A creepy child, but still ...

“Daddy and I are going to the island, that’s why he has to get into the boat!”

My brow furrowed. Did she mean the island Dad owned? But we were miles from there. It made no sense. On the other hand, considering the source...

Ian made a noise, drawing KC’s attention. “KC!” She frowned and looked into the shadows for another second before shrugging and turning back to me.

I forced a smile. “KC, what island are we going to? I think we’re a long way from home-“

“I know, that’s why we have to go tonight!” Her eyes were big, and her voice reflected her eagerness and excitement. “There are lots of islands all by themselves. I’ll take one of those.”

The twilight zone theme sprang into my head. “Uh, then what KC? How are you going to live?”

She rolled her eyes at me and huffed. “Daddy is going to build a house, silly.”

My eyebrows rose. “I see. That, um that’ll be nice. I hope you’ll be happy.”

She sighed. “You’re coming too ..., since you wouldn’t go away!” She glared at me and pointed the knife. “But you do all the work! I get to the be the spoiled one now!”

She started to get agitated so I quickly agreed. “I will, KC, I’ll do everything. Thank you for letting me come.”

Dad moaned and I glanced into the shadows where Ian was waiting for help to arrive. They were taking their sweet time, and I feared Dad didn’t have much left. I had to act.

I made my eyes widen and tried for an unconcerned tone. “KC, Dad doesn’t look so good. I’m not sure what’s wrong but-“

“He argued with me so I hit him with the lamp.”

My eyes widened on their own. “Oh my God! KC, you could have killed him!” I stepped closer. “We need to get him to a doctor before-“

“No!”

I froze as the knife tip came within inches of my face.

"He'll be fine." She scowled and looked up. "We're wasting time. Let's go."

Help was supposed to be coming. I didn't want to move again and I also didn't think Dad could stand much more. I tried again to reason with her.

"KC, we've got to get him some help!"

"We will, just as soon as we get home. Come on, we need to go." She glanced at Dad and huffed. Then she pointed at me. "He can't climb. You go first. Then you can pull him up while I push."

I bit my lip and shot a look to my left. No sign of the calvary. All I saw was Ian and he was shaking his head, clearly telling me not to get into the lifeboat.

I almost snorted. Like I needed to be told!

Still, KC was waving her knife and the smile was fading from her eyes. I need to do something, quickly.

"Uh, KC ..." I shifted my weight and my bruised knee shouted complaints. It also provided me with a possible way to save us or at least delay until someone arrived to do the saving.

"My knee ..." I faked a whimper and leaned over, massaging my knee. "I can't get up there." I caught KC's eye. "Can you go first and I'll push Dad up?"

The storm clouds started to build in her expression.

"That way you both can help me get up. Then we can go and be an um, a happy family. Okay?"

I must have said some magic words because her expression cleared and she grinned. "You really are the smart one!"

She looked up at the lifeboat and bit her lip. I shifted closer to Dad and checked his pulse as KC tried to work out a way to get into the lifeboat.

One hand was still clutching the knife, the ship was still rocking when waves hit, and the lifeboat was swinging in the wind. Getting into it seemed impossible to me but so long as it kept her occupied and away from Dad she was welcome to try.

I sat down beside Dad and put my arm around him. "Dad?" He moaned. His breaths were coming in shallow bursts and he struggled to lift his head up off of his chest.

I swallowed past the lump in my throat and shifted him so his head was resting on my shoulder. The change in position seemed to help. His breathing evened out a little but I was terrified; where were our rescuers?

I jumped as KC stepped closer to me. She prodded me with her foot until I looked up and met her gaze. My breath caught as she cocked her head and smiled.

"I think I've figured it out."

My eyes narrowed. I had no clue what she was talking about.

She rolled her eyes. "The lifeboat, silly!" Before I could stop her, she grabbed my hand and tugged me to my feet.

"KC, Dad needs-"

"What about me? Can I be the most important one for once?"

I held my breath as she glared at Dad and took a step closer to him. "KC!"

She stopped and looked at me.

I smiled. "Come on, uh, show me what you figured out, he'll be okay."

She giggled and skipped back to the railing, motioning for me to join her. I hesitated and looked past her to where Ian was crouched behind a support pillar. I could just see his head shaking in a firm negative.

I wanted to scream. Of course, I didn't want to get closer to the nutjob or the knife she was clutching. For that matter, I wasn't keen on being next to an inches thick metal railing in a violent storm but I was running out of options and I saw no signs that we were going to be rescued.

I bit my lip and joined KC at the railing.

"Look up there!"

My gaze followed the knife she was using as a pointer but I didn't see anything but the bottom of the lifeboat.

"What am I looking at?"

She clicked her tongue. "That lever. I think it lowers the-oh, get out of the way!" She pushed me so hard that I stumbled and landed against the bulkhead.

"Gotta do everything myself ..." KC was mumbling under her breath as she put her foot on the bottom of the railing and reached up, trying to grab the lever.

A gust of wind set the lifeboat swinging. "KC, stop! It's too dangerous."

She turned her head and scowled at me. "Don't be a worry wart, if I can just get a little higher ..." She used the hand holding the knife to brace herself as she raised her foot to the next rung of the railing.

A flash of lightning lit the sky and drew my eye to the raging sea. A huge wave was barreling towards us! "KC, get down you're going to-"

KC screamed as the wave broke and the ship rocked. The knife clattered to the deck as her hand slipped and her foot slid off of the railing. She screamed again and her arms windmilled as she tried to find her balance.

I leaped forward and attempted to grab her, but the ship rolled again and I crashed to the deck as KC went over the side.

Flotsam and Jetsam

Ian

TINA AND I SAT on the couch in their suite and waited for the doctor to finish with Chad. She'd laid her head on my shoulder and then fallen into a fitful doze. I rested my chin on the top of her head and then stiffened; it was such a deja vu moment.

We'd been in a similar position after catching Penshaw. I shook my head as I realized just one day had passed since we'd caught Warner's murderer. What a mess. The whole cruise had become one unbelievable event after another.

I sniffed and dragged a hand through my hair. I hadn't mentioned it to anyone but, after seeing and hearing Tina's friend, I was starting to wonder if Penshaw was telling the truth about Warner's murder; that chick was crazy, and I wouldn't have put anything past her.

Tina stirred and whimpered. I pushed all thoughts of murdering psychopaths aside and focused on the woman in my arms. I'd almost lost her.

I kissed the top of her head and stroked her hair until she settled back into a restless sleep. Watching her with the lunatic ... several times I'd started to rush in and tackle the knife from her hand but then Tina would get too close, and the risk was too high.

My gut was still in knots two hours later. When my darling girl recovered from the shock of it all we were gonna have a serious talk about safety. I snorted. Safety, situational awareness, hell, stranger danger; my hair stood on end at just the thought of Tina running around Savannah befriending every person she met.

Savannah. That was something I wasn't quite ready to think about. I'd told Tina I had moved back, and she'd just assumed I meant to the same area I'd lived before. Coward that I was, I hadn't contradicted that assumption. The truth was, I'd been living about a mile from my parent's place in Bullton County, over an hour from

Tina's home on River Street; at least I assumed she still had the loft.

I snorted. Lots of assumptions had been made between us. We'd picked up right where we'd left off two years ago, fallen into the familiar camaraderie and banter found in long-time couples. Only we weren't long time or a couple. Not officially anyway.

Nothing had been discussed, no plans had been made, we were just casual, carefree, and taking it one day at a time. I'd been fine with that until she'd befriended a lunatic and just about gotten herself killed.

I drew a deep breath and willed myself to relax. She was fine, Chad was fine, the crazy chick was even fine, lots of broken bones, but not dead. Heck, that was probably why I was still so anxious. Knowing my tender-hearted wife-now where had that come from? Some would say it was a Freudian slip.

I shrugged and ran the idea through my mind. The more I thought about it, the more I liked the idea. I loved her. I wanted her. I could have lost-

"I love you." I murmured into her hair.

Tina stiffened and raised her head to meet my gaze. "What?"

"I thought you were asleep."

She wrinkled her nose. "Yeah right, I may never sleep again. But what's that have to do with telling me you love me? Only gonna say it if you think I won't hear?"

"Maybe. Gotta problem with that?"

For several seconds we stared in silence and then Tina's lips twitched. Mine copied hers and before I knew it, we were both giggling like the overwrought and emotionally drained couple that we were. I wiped my eyes and intertwined our fingers. I looked down and absently realized how thin her fingers were. Long, thin, elegant hands: great guitar player equipment.

I said as much, and she laughed. "Have to take your word for it. I am no musician. Dad tried to teach me but mashing those strings hurts!"

I smirked. "You build calluses." I smoothed a lock of hair from her face, tucking it behind her ear, and then I dropped a kiss onto her neck.

She sighed. "Sure are affectionate all of a sudden."

I snorted. "As opposed to not being the rest of the time?"

She chuckled. "You know what I mean. What's wrong?"

I almost changed the subject by cracking a joke but what I was feeling was too raw to ignore. I sighed and ran my thumb over her palm as I struggled to find words.

"Tina, if something happens, and let's be real, lots of unbelievable things have happened around us lately!" She laughed and then I continued. "So if I bit the dust tomorrow, I don't want another second to go by without telling you how I feel."

She was very still and silent. I was starting to wonder if I'd misread things when she sat up and turned to face me.

"I love you, too." Her lips twisted into a rueful smile. "I never stopped really, but I don't-"

I frowned. I was happy about the "I love you too," but she threw in the but and that made me nervous. "Um, there's a but?"

She smiled and scrunched up her nose. "Kinda?"

"What's that supposed to mean?"

She shrugged. "Well, I don't know. It's just all happened so fast! I mean, I never thought I'd see you again, much less run into you on this cruise and we have different goals and lifestyles and I just worry that we might be rushing-"

"Tina!" I grinned as she blinked and her mouth snapped shut.

"Calm down. I just said that I love you. No pressure, nothing you need to do, just know that I adore you and you scared the hell out of me by playing with the psycho and I wanted you to know. That's all; for now."

She bit her lip and nodded. "Ok, good. I mean, later right? Later we can talk about things?"

"Yeah babe, later. Let's recover from this disaster of a vacation first."

She laughed and then cocked an eyebrow. "Playing with the psycho?"

I shrugged.

She worried at her bottom lip and gave me a side-eye. I braced myself for a scold but the door to Chad's cabin opened. The doctor entered the lounge and our banter was forgotten.

"Doctor, how is he?" Tina jumped up and met the physician halfway.

The doctor grasped her elbow and led her back to the couch and then took the chair beside us. He started to speak and then waited as Nikki left Chad's room and joined us.

"Doctor?"

He smiled. "First, Mr. Crawford is going to be fine, no lasting damage or significant injuries other than a concussion." He held up his hand as Tina and I broke into relieved chatter. "However, I would recommend he be admitted to the hospital once we dock and let them do a full work-up, just to be thorough."

Tina nodded. "Of course. Is he awake? Did you tell Dad this?"

Nikki snorted. "Yeah, he's half out of it but he found the strength to argue about it."

Tina rolled her eyes. "Sounds like him, like all men actually."

She scowled at me.

"Hey, what did I do?"

She shook her head and the doctor cleared his throat, drawing our attention.

"As I said, he does have a concussion. Apparently, he was in a car wreck and had a brain injury then as well?"

Tina nodded. "Yeah, it was over ten years ago, why?"

The doctor shrugged. "Well, he said he has very little memory of the incident which suggests traumatic brain injury and, coupled with the current injury ... he should have some scans when we dock."

The doctor rose and headed for the door. "I'll leave my nurse here and we'll monitor Mr. Crawford until we reach port."

Tina held out her hand. "Thank you so much, doctor, we're so grateful and we've certainly monopolized your services-"

He laughed. "Not at all, Ms. Crawford." He looked over at the nurse. "Asia and I were just saying how unusual this cruise has been. We routinely have passengers coming to the med bay with all manner of issues but, apart from that light falling and you and your father being attacked, we haven't seen a soul."

Tina and I chuckled but something he'd said was nagging at me.

"Doc!" All of us turned to see Chad standing in the doorway, well, leaning against the door jam. I forgot what I'd been thinking.

"Mr. Crawford, what are you doing out of bed?" The doctor and I moved toward Chad, intending to get him back into bed, but he held his hand up to stop us.

"Hold on, y'all. Believe me, I'm going to bed. But need to make some decisions about the concert first."

My eyes widened. Some professional I was. I hadn't even thought about the concert.

"Chad, I told you, we can worry about it later. Fans will understand that-"

"No, Nikki. Fans might understand but it doesn't make it right. They paid for this cruise to see Eclipse play."

"Mr. Crawford, there is no way you can perform before this cruise ends. Now sir, I really must insist you return-"

"Okay, Doc. What about when we get back? When can I play?"

The doctor shook his head. "I can't say! You'll need to see a neurologist and your general doctor and they'll run some tests and after all of that a decision can be-"

"Ah, hell no." Chad turned and looked at Nikki. "One week from now. Get us something booked in Savannah and put the word out: make-up concert: Free, you know the deal."

He shrugged. "Show must go on, folks."

Land Ho

Tina

A LIGHT BREEZE RUFFLED my hair as I sat on the private deck outside our suite. I hadn't left the cabin since we'd arrived last night. The idea of being in a crowd of strangers freaked me out. We'd be docking in a matter of hours, and I couldn't get off of the ship fast enough.

I snorted. From the beginning, I'd said it was gonna be the cruise from hell and I'd been right, only for the wrong reasons.

My head was spinning like a top and I couldn't seem to focus on anything for more than a few minutes. After Dad's declaration that the show would go on, he'd become a model patient. He'd rested as the nurse insisted and I'd only seen him for a few minutes since then.

Nikki was running around doing her job, plus whatever Warner had done, and she now had Rob Thornton's responsibilities. Ian was helping her, along with getting his own gear in order for disembarking, which left me with more alone time than I wished.

I yawned. I also couldn't sleep. When I closed my eyes I saw KC falling. I heard her scream. I saw her twisted body sprawled across the neon orange cover of the lifeboat hanging one floor down. They'd life-flighted her off of the ship. They suspected she'd never walk again and that broke my heart. Regardless of what she'd done, she was family ...

I rose from the lounge chair and started walking, letting my fingers drift along the railing as I stared out to sea. The shipping lanes were active. Freighters were running parallel to our ship while others seemed to be parked; probably awaiting a slot for unloading at the ports.

We'd passed Little Tybee Island and I caught a glimpse of the hammock Dad had bought. I loved living in Savannah. I loved the hustle and bustle, the eclectic scene of art, movies, and music, and I loved the tourists that flooded our town all year long. Or at least I used to. Now, after a few hours spent with an unhinged maniac, I wasn't so sure living with Dad on a private island was such a bad idea.

And then there was Ian. He loved me. After the meltdown and heartache of our break-up, I should have been over the moon at his declaration. So then, why was my stomach in knots every time I thought about him, me, and being home?

The ship's horn blew, making me jump. It also pushed all of my unsettling thoughts to the back of my mind. We were sailing past Fort Pulaski and I hadn't even packed!

I rushed inside and started gathering my things. Everything else could wait. For now, I'd just concentrate on getting off of the ship in one piece.

Landlubber

Ian

TINA WAS MUMBLING TO herself and frying green tomatoes. I swiped one and then dodged a slap with the spatula.

"You know the rules."

I grinned and leaned against the counter on the opposite side of the kitchen. "Help or get out of the way." I winked at her and polished off my treat. "I can't cook, so what do you want me to do?"

She cocked her head. "Everything is ready, except for these tomatoes. I just need to plate the first course ..." She craned her neck and looked through the doorway that led to her living room. "Is Dom here yet?"

I shook my head. "If that's your friend Ivy's boyfriend, the answer is no."

Tina sighed and transferred the last of the tomatoes to a draining rack. "Ivy!"

A pretty redhead appeared in the doorway. "Yeah, Tina? You want me to help?"

Tina shook her head. "Nah, it's all done, just waiting on Dom before I plate. Where is he?"

Ivy grimaced. "There was another break-in over on Jenson Street."

"Oooh, that's close to home! Is that why you brought the brat with you?"

Ivy scowled. "Sergeant Pepper is not a brat." She wrinkled her nose. "Well, not at present anyway, but yeah, I have an alarm but, if someone broke in and the door was opened-"

Tina snorted. "The demon cat would be on the loose and he'd terrorize the city."

My gaze went to the fluffy white cat perched on the back of the sofa, taking a bath. With his big blue eyes, the cat looked innocent, but Tina had warned me not to pet him. Apparently, the little monster would bite.

Chad was sitting on the couch, talking on the phone. I wondered if anyone had warned him?

Tina started washing dishes. "So what do the burglaries have to do with Dom?"

Ivy picked up a dish towel as she launched into some story about a spate of burglaries in the historic district and how Ivy's boyfriend's security company was working overtime installing systems for terrified residents.

"Hey ladies, can I help?"

I rolled my eyes as Nikki came in and Tina put her to work while Ivy brought her up to speed on their crime spree conversation.

I'd had a cruise ship's worth of crime so I tuned them out and slid around Tina to access the freezer. She'd made some kind of frozen lemony stuff. It was a little overpowering in the sour department but the slushy texture was kind of addicting.

I scooped some out and headed for the living room.

"Ian!"

I whirled around and wondered if I was gonna get that lecture I'd avoided.

I relaxed as Tina smiled. "Will you take this to Dad?"

She grabbed a highball glass and moved to the freezer, adding half a glass full of the frozen stuff I was drinking.

I reached for the glass but Tina shook her head and popped the top on a can of ginger ale. She topped off the glass with the soda, added some of the green leaves I'd seen her chopping earlier, and then gave it all a stir.

"Here. Tell him we'll eat just as soon as Dom gets here."

I nodded. "Sure, but what is this?"

She frowned. "A mock-tail, same as you're drinking."

I shook my head. "Mine doesn't have all that other stuff in it ..."

Her eyes widened. "You've been drinking it straight from the freezer?"

Her reaction made *my* eyes widen. "Yeah ..., why?" I frowned and looked down at my glass. "Something wrong with it?"

She rolled her eyes and plucked the glass from my hand. "No, but didn't you think it was a bit ... sour?"

I shrugged. "You're the chef, I'm just the happy eater side of this relationship."

She laughed and fixed my drink the proper way. "Here's your Lemon and Pineapple Basil shrub. It has-"

"Ah-ah, just the eater, remember?"

She shooed me from the kitchen with a snap of her dish towel. I set Chad's drink on the coffee table and wandered over to the floor-to-ceiling windows that looked out over the Savannah River while he finished his call.

Tina's loft was part of the old cotton warehouses that lined River Street. The developers had kept most of the original structure exposed so the walls were old brick, though some areas had patches of stucco. It was like they'd started pulling down plaster walls and then got bored and stopped.

The ceilings were high, measuring against my six-foot-two frame, they were at least eighteen if not twenty feet. Thick wooden beams crossed the ceiling and the same honey-colored wood covered the floors.

The living room also held the dining area. The kitchen had two short walls at one end, leaving the space open and light. I turned back to the other great feature of her loft; the views.

Located at the lower end of River Street, her place had the best of both worlds. Open views of the river with a bit of the undeveloped areas of Hutchison Island combined with being the farthest distance from the bars and restaurants that comprised most of the lower shop spaces on the street. Realtors would market the million-dollar views and that was about what the place would sell for. I shook my head at how stupid I'd been to not have questioned things when Tina and I were involved the first time.

She drove a lime green convertible mini. Brand new when we'd started dating. I had been a little surprised that a chef just starting out would drive such a nice ride but she was young and single; I just figured she spent every dime she made. But then there were her clothes. I didn't know designer from a donut but one of Judith's insults mentioned Tina's preference for thousand-dollar shoes and something told me that hadn't been an exaggeration.

I snorted and glanced back at her dad. I would have never suspected her father was the world-famous Chad Crawford, but I should have figured she came from money. I wondered if she'd be happy with the constraints of a more modest income musician ...

Chad hung up and motioned for me to join him. I pointed at the drink I'd set on the table.

Chad nodded. "Thanks. What is it?"

I shrugged. "A mock-tail."

He laughed. "A what?"

"I don't know man, something your daughter cooked up." I held up my glass. "She said it's nonalcoholic, good for you, and I was to give it to you," I smirked. "I just follow orders."

Chad laughed. "Smart man." He took a sip and shrugged. "It's pretty good!" He looked at me and winked. "I find it works out best if I just do what the women in my life say."

He looked around the living room. "So, you living here?"

I sputtered and choked on my drink. "No sir, uh, no I gotta place over in-"

"Relax kid, she's a big girl." He cocked an eyebrow. "Kinda wish you were."

I frowned and he explained.

“I worry about her, especially after the making friends with psychos thing.” He shuddered. “I’d feel better knowing she was being looked after-“

“I don’t need a keeper old man.”

Chad and I swung around to see Tina, Ivy, and Nikki had finished in the kitchen. Chad stood and embraced Tina while Ivy answered the doorbell.

“Hey, Punkin’! Less of the old man stuff, thank you. Doctors say I’m fit as a fiddle.”

Nikki snorted. “Fact-checkers say that’s a lie.” Chad glared at her as Tina and I gave Chad a questioning look.

“I’m fine, really. They did say I was on the mend and nothing serious-“

“But they also said you shouldn’t be performing yet.”

Chad scoffed. “Show must-“

“Go on.” Nikki frowned at him. “We’ve heard that before.”

Tina sighed. “Just the one concert, right?”

Chad nodded and Tina glanced at Nikki. “Guess we’ll leave him alone about tomorrow so long as he agrees to at least a month of nothing but R & R afterward.”

Nikki and Tina shook hands and Chad looked at me. “What’d I tell you, kid, easier if you just go along with them ...”

“Spoken like a man in love.”

Chad and I turned to see a guy about my height had entered the room. He was dressed casually in shorts and a t-shirt but something about him screamed law enforcement. Ivy had said her boyfriend was in security so ...

I stuck out my hand. “Dom, right?”

He nodded and looked down at his shirt. “ Did I forget to remove my name badge?”

I snorted. “Nah, girls said you were coming.” I introduced him to Chad and Nikki while Ivy and Tina finished carrying the first course to the table.

“Y’all come get it while it’s hot!”

Chad rubbed his hands together and headed to the dining area. “Come on, boys. Something smells good!”

I took my seat between Tina and Nikki and studied the stack of fried green tomatoes and some kind of salad.

Tina leaned over. “What’s the matter?”

I shook my head. “Nothin, but how do I eat it?”

Laughter rang out and Tina rolled her eyes.

“It’s just crab salad between fried green tomatoes and that sauce on the side is remoulade. Just ...I don’t know, eat it!”

I grinned and pushed my fork down the side of the stack. The whole thing collapsed. “See? I’ve wrecked your creation.”

Across from me, I saw Dom nudge Ivy and mutter. “See? I’m not the only one ...”

I smirked and figured Ivy's guy and I would get along just fine. The conversation centered around the concert and other local happenings until Tina brought out dessert. We were indulging in Carolina Trifle when Dom asked about the cruise.

"So, Chad." Dom set his spoon down and leaned on his elbows. "Have you heard any more about the guy they arrested for the murder?"

Ivy elbowed her boyfriend. "Dom! What a thing to ask-"

"What? I'm interested!"

I bit back a laugh as Ivy rolled her eyes and mumbled. "Once a cop ..."

Chad laughed. "It's all right, Ivy." He looked at Dom. "What else is there to know? They arrested Penshaw ..." Chad frowned. "Though as far as I know, he hasn't budged from his insistence that he's innocent, of murder anyway."

Tina shook her head. "Don't they all say that, though?"

Dom nodded. "Most do, yes. But in this case ..."

Tina's brow furrowed. "What's so different about this?"

I laced my fingers with hers and gave a light squeeze. "Babe, I think there is some talk that it was the nutj-" Tina scowled and I quickly changed my choice of words; for some reason, she was very defensive of the lunatic. "Er KC."

Her eyes widened and she turned toward her dad. “The police think KC killed Warner?”

He shrugged. “There’s been some talk-“

“But why?” She shook her head. “KC had no reason-“

“Punkin’ she’s crazy!” He snorted. “And she did a lot of other things, so why stop at murder?”

Tina looked around the table. Everyone seemed to be agreeing with Chad’s assessment. Tina huffed and flopped back in her chair. “Well, I don’t think my sister killed anyone! She’s not well-“

“Not well!” I’d held my tongue the first couple of times Tina had defended the psychopath, but I’d be damned if I did it again. “Tina, she tried to kill you and your dad!”

She shook her head. “No, she wasn’t trying to do that, she just wanted us to be a family and got carried away-“

“Oh for the love of-are you hearing this?” I looked at Chad.

He raised his eyebrows and then winced. “Punkin, the woman-“

“Daughter, the word you are looking for is daughter. She’s my sister-”

“No, honey, she isn’t.” Chad held up his hand as Tina started to speak. “I know what the girl thinks, but I’m telling you she is not my kid.”

Tina scowled and Chad sighed. “Okay, remember when I told you about the woman that stalked the band?”

Tina's eyes widened. "Yeah? So what? That was years and years ago. What does that have to do with KC?"

Chad's mouth pursed. "Tina. I'm not suggesting KC is that woman, but I'm thinking it's her child."

"What? Why would you think that?"

Chad cocked his head. "I was half out of it, but I heard her claiming I was with her mom." He snorted. "I was not, I promise you-"

"How can you be so sure-"

"Seriously? Kristina Carol, what kind of man do you think I am?" He shook his head. "I know who I've slept with, thank you very much."

Tina squirmed in her seat and fidgeted with her spoon. "Sorry, Dad."

Chad patted her hand. "S'okay, musician stereotype. I've had women claim that a child is mine. Management handles it. A DNA test is offered, at our expense, and none have ever taken the offer. Make of that what you will." He sighed. "As I was saying, what if the mother KC was talking about was the woman that stalked me all those years ago?"

Dom cleared his throat. "I, uh was a little curious after Ivy told me what happened and ..." He glanced at his girlfriend and winced as if he were bracing for a slap.

"What did you do?"

Dom shrugged and avoided Ivy's gaze, focusing on Chad. "I ran the woman's name through the database, well I had a friend do it. Either way, I've got the particulars on Kristina Carol Anderson."

My eyes widened. "Wow, dude, pays to have friends! What'd you find out?"

"Well, if you want to hear it?" Dom cleared his throat and waited until had nodded before continuing.

"KC Anderson, or legal name, Kristina Carol, was the daughter of a woman named Cynthia Louise Anderson."

Tina looked at her dad. "Was that the name of the woman who was stalking y'all?"

Chad shrugged. "I don't know if I ever knew her name. We'd have to get with Rob." He nodded at Dom. "Go on, what else did you find out?"

"Cynthia Anderson gave birth to a baby girl, named Kristina Carol, on August 1st, 1994 and-"

"She's a year younger than me ..." Tina looked at Chad, who shook his head.

"I'm not gonna keep defending myself, Kristina, the girl is not my kid!"

Tina's eyes grew wide and she held up her hand. "Okay, okay, I believe you! But KC was so ... why would she think you were her father if you weren't?"

Chad sighed. "I told you, there were women who tried to get with band members. Remember what Cliff was saying about-"

"Oh my gosh, you don't think-" Tina bit her lip. "Dad, do you think Warner was KC's dad?"

Chad blinked. He started to shake his head and then he blew out a breath. "If you'd asked me that a few days ago I'd of said no, but now?" He shrugged. "Anything is possible. What else did you find out, Dom?"

Dom cleared his throat. "Well, there is no father listed on the birth certificate, and she kind of went off of the radar for about four years after the birth then things start going from bad to worse."

Tina frowned. "How so, Dom?"

"Eh, the little girl was in and out of foster homes. Seems Cynthia was a paranoid schizophrenic and when she'd go off of her meds she'd end up committed at Coastal General."

"Oh! Then they lived in this area."

Dom nodded at Ivy. "Yeah, multiple addresses in the Coastal Empire, and twice they moved across the line into South Carolina."

Tina sniffed. "That's no way for a child to grow up ..."

Everyone grew quiet for several minutes until Nikki cleared her throat.

"Um, where is this- um KC's mom, now?"

"Cynthia Anderson was committed for a brief spell in '09 and she somehow got hold of a razor blade and, well ..."

"Oh! How horrible! Poor KC. If her mom died, what happened to KC?"

Dom sighed. "She walked out of foster care shortly after her mom died and was undocumented for about three years. At nineteen, her employment records begin." He shrugged. "Nothing long-term. A bit of retail, warehouse work, restaurants. The longest stint has been this last job."

Tina's eyebrows rose. "So, she really was a cook?"

Dom nodded. "Yep, short order at a truck stop over by the Ports."

"She wanted to be me."

I frowned. "What?" I shook my head. "Why do you think that? Seemed to me that she wanted you out of the picture."

Tina's eyes were bright with unshed tears and all I wanted to do was change the subject, but Tina was intent on knowing why the crazy chick was, well ... crazy.

She shook her head. "KC was confused, I think."

"In what way?" Ivy asked.

Tina shrugged. "Well, the day I met her I told her I was a chef and she said she was a cook. Later, we met to go to the meet and greet-oh!" Tina turned to Chad. "Dad, I wonder if KC was the one that mangled your publicity still!"

He snorted. "Probably. Girl is nuts."

Tina shook her head. "No, well yeah, but ... it's understandable. She thought you were her father and I was her sister. I wonder if she watched me ..."

"What makes you think that?" Nikki asked.

Tina shrugged. "Just a feeling. KC would say things and, for instance, she had the same dress as me, just in a different color."

Nikki frowned. "That could be a coincidence though, right?"

Tina nodded. "Yeah, but when you add in other things ... I just think she'd been watching me for a while. She knew Dad and I didn't see each other. That's why she thought I wouldn't be on the cruise."

Nikki nodded. "I see your point." She shivered. "It's all pretty damn creepy and I am glad the girl won't be able to harm anyone else."

Tina's lip quivered and the tears threatened to spill from her eyes. "She didn't mean any harm, not really. She just wanted a family-" Her voice broke on a sob and she rose and started clearing the table.

I rolled my eyes and started to speak but Chad caught my gaze and shook his head. I recalled his earlier advice about dealing with women and closed my mouth.

Tina brushed aside offers of help, suggesting everyone move to the living room for coffee. I leaned against the door jam and watched her prepare the coffee as the conversation turned to tomorrow's concert in Forsyth Park. I took the tray from Tina and returned to the living room. I thought we'd exhausted the psycho girl conversation but Tina launched right back into it as she perched on the arm of the couch.

"Dad ..."

Chad looked up from his football conversation with Dom. "Yeah, Punkin'?"

She bit her lip. "Um, *do* you think Warner was KC's father?"

Chad sighed. "Honey, I don't-let's just put this all behind us and-"

"Put it behind us?" Tina huffed and started to pace. "What about KC? We're safe and our lives go back to normal and whatever happens to her- 'oh well, not our problem?' If she's Warner's daughter ..."

Tina had worked herself into an epic rant. She threw her hands in the air and made a disgusted sound. "That's-her whole life, nobody has given a damn ..."

She looked around the living room, seeking agreement? Consoling? I wasn't sure what she wanted and felt it safer to keep quiet and avoid eye contact. From beneath my lashes, I noticed everyone else had the same idea; except for Ivy.

Ivy stood and hugged Tina. "I agree. We shouldn't just abandon her."

"We? Ivy, you don't even know the woman!"

Ivy scowled at her boyfriend and I made a mental note to have Chad give the guy the how to deal with women lecture. It might help in the future but, for now, it looked like the poor guy was sleeping on the couch.

"What does that have to do with it, Dom?" Ivy rolled her eyes. "I swear, you men-"

"Okay, that's enough." Everyone turned to look at Chad.

"Let's not fight about this." Chad nodded at Tina. "I don't see how I am responsible, but I love you so, what do you want me to do?"

Tina frowned at him. "Not responsible?" She huffed. "Dad, if what Cliff said is true, you had to know Warner was a creep with women! Why didn't you-" She shook her head and looked down at the floor.

I got the feeling that Tina's anger wasn't coming from the situation with KC, at least not all of it. The look on Chad's face suggested he was cottoning on to my suspicions as well. I held my breath. A room full of people was definitely not the place for the confrontation I sensed was coming. The tension was palpable and everyone looked uncomfortable. I watched Tina and readied for the explosion.

Tina looked up and met Chad's gaze. "Why did you keep him around?"

Her voice was soft and childlike and my heart broke. I started to go to her but Chad beat me to it.

"Baby, all I can say is I'm sorry." He pulled her closer and kissed the top of her head. "It's no excuse, but I lived in an alcohol and drug-induced haze. I can honestly say that I had no idea Warner was a ..., a predator. If I had ..."

Tina pulled away and wiped her eyes. "I'm not blaming you."

Chad snorted and Tina shook her head. "I'm not! But I don't understand why you kept him around the band. Especially after you got clean. It was obvious he was a drunk and a sponge. What could he contribute that justified remaining friends?"

Chad sighed and returned to his seat. "Truth?" He glanced at Tina and she nodded.

"The truth is I felt like I owed him."

Nikki frowned and reached for Chad's hand. "Owed him? Why?"

Chad shrugged. "He lost his finger-tip because of me. We were drunk and doing stupid crap and I got the bright idea to blow up mailboxes ..."

"Wow, I never knew that." Tina shook her head. "But, if you were both drunk, it wasn't your fault, not entirely."

Chad sighed. "Maybe not, but if not for that." He glanced at me as he continued. "Rich was a hell of a picker, had he not lost that fingertip ... might have been him instead of Alton."

My eyes widened and I whistled. That explained a heck of a lot about Warner. I said as much, and Chad nodded.

"Yep. For a musician that injury was ... well, it's no excuse for his behavior but it's why I tolerated so much crap from him." He slapped his knee and stood up. "Enough of this pity party. We got a concert to play tomorrow and then, according to my girl and my kid, I'm on vacation."

Everyone stood and started gathering their things, ready to head out. I chatted with Ivy and Dom for a few minutes, staying a few feet back from the fluffy white menace she was holding, and then went to the kitchen to start cleaning up as Tina said goodbye to Nikki and her dad.

The door opened and Chad's voice rang out. "See you bright and early tomorrow, Ian!"

"Will do, man!" I continued loading the dishwasher, but I could hear Chad and Tina talking.

"Punkin', I'll see about a lawyer for KC and look into a DNA test for her against Warner: if she's his daughter, she has a right to his estate, and I paid him pretty well over the years."

The door closed and a few minutes later Tina came into the kitchen, set some dishes onto the counter, and then hugged me from behind.

"Love a man who does domestic work."

I grinned and rinsed my hands before turning around in her arms and nuzzling her neck. "We haven't discussed the pay scale ..."

She giggled and backed away, pulling me by the hand. "Let's take it out in trade."

Scuttlebutt

Tina

TRAFFIC WAS HEAVY AROUND the park and it wasn't much past eight. The long open fields at the south end of the park were already filling with concertgoers; Nikki had definitely done her job and gotten the word out. I drove down the alley behind the Cosmic Cafe, but someone had taken my parking spot. I ended up circling the block three times before giving up and parking in the mews behind Bacchanalia.

My friend Amy's shop was on the east side of the park and her shop had once been a large, private home. As a result, Bacchanalia Wine Emporium had a carriage house and private courtyard parking. I had an open invitation to use Amy's parking area but, being two blocks down from the Cafe, I didn't often take advantage. I parallel parked my Mini behind Amy's delivery van and headed for the cafe. My plan was to check in with Pete, and then secure a table outside and wait for Mr. and Mrs. Buchanan to arrive.

My attempts to broker peace between Ian and his father had the potential to backfire spectacularly. My stomach was in knots and, while I wasn't regretting extending the invitation to attend the concert to Ian's parents, I was rethinking the get to know them over breakfast but don't bring Ian part.

It had been an impulse. Ian hadn't intended to stay over but he'd fallen asleep while watching a movie. A blaring car alarm had jarred me awake. I'd been getting a glass of water when Ian's phone started to ring; it'd been his dad. Without thinking, I'd answered and ended up in an hour-long conversation with Charles Buchanan. He'd been wary of talking at first, grunting the barest of social niceties when I'd introduced myself and giving monosyllabic responses when I'd inquired about his health.

Talking to him was like pulling teeth and I had almost made an excuse and hung up but something had nudged me to keep talking. During a mind-numbing chat about the weather and local happenings, he mentioned an upcoming charity event of interest to his wife. He'd wanted to surprise her with tickets to the annual Diamond Head Island Beach Bash. The dinner dance and silent auction raised funds for the SeaTurtle Marinelife rehabilitation and education center and was the social event of the year; attendance was limited and tickets were coveted.

My mother had been a founding member of the organization and, after her death, I'd been asked to sit on the board. I was not above a bit of bribery, especially for a good cause, and to my mind, there was no greater cause than Ian's happiness. Though I rarely used it, being the daughter of Chad Crawford had always been my ace in the hole if I needed a door opened. I never dreamed using my mother's name could have the same effect; she was surely up in heaven laughing herself silly.

I still couldn't believe what I'd done. Spur of the moment stupidity, and this time I couldn't even claim inebriation; nope, it was all on me. The umbrellas were being set onto the sidewalk tables and several customers were already parked and waiting on To-Go orders when I reached the cafe. I waved at the servers and strode through the swinging door of the kitchen to find Pete raining hellfire down upon the head of an employee I didn't recognize.

I caught Pete's eye and then slipped into the office to wait. I was checking over the accounts and receipts from last week when Pete knocked.

"Come on in!"

Pete sighed and dropped into the chair across from me.

"Geez Pete, we haven't been open an hour and you already look like you've been through a war!"

He snorted and rolled his eyes. "It's the new kid. I've tried to cut him slack, but he's just not-"

"If he's causing you that much stress, cut him loose."

Pete chuckled. "Oh, that it was so easy!" He glanced out at the kitchen where the boy in question was slamming pots and pans around slopping water everywhere. "Lyle is the son of a woman I, uh ..."

I laughed. "Oh, Pete. Did you hire a girlfriend's kid?" His grimace answered my question. "Dude, I have no sympathy. You know better than to hire friends and family ... it rarely works out!"

Pete sighed and stood up. "I know, I know, but in my defense, his mom is smokin' hot."

Pete laughed and bounced out of the office as I tossed a pencil at him. When Ivy had decided to let me be a partner, we'd promoted Pete to my position as kitchen manager. I'd still act in that position on some things just as Ivy did, but hiring, and firing, were all on Pete.

I closed the computer down and headed outside to find a table and mentally prepared for my self-imposed peacemaker role. I'd lectured Pete on mixing business with pleasure but I didn't have much room to talk; I'd meddled in a family drama and odds were good I was going to get burned.

Tina

"So that was Ian's parents."

I nodded in answer to Ivy's question and continued checking the pallet of dry goods against the invoice.

Ivy huffed. "I can do that, you have-"

"It's fine, you need to finish prepping those salads or you'll miss the concert."

She rolled her eyes but didn't argue.

Ian's parents had been on time and we'd had a nice chat over breakfast. No one could ever accuse Charles Buchanan of being loquacious, but he'd been polite, even if he did let his wife Diane carry most of the conversation. We'd ordered breakfast and, once past the small talk, I'd opened the dialog by asking about Diane's nursery business.

That led to a discussion on growing and using herbs. There were several varieties of basil that I wanted in large quantities for the restaurant. I'd picked Diane's brain on the idea of setting up a community garden and also growing herbs for the cafe. We'd ended up pulling Ivy in and holding a mini business meeting. Ivy gave Diane a tour of the kitchen, leaving me in an uncomfortable silence with Charles Buchanan.

I looked out at the park, people watching and trying to not let him see how much his silent stare was bothering me. We continued like that for several minutes until Charles cleared his throat.

"You're different than I expected."

My eyebrows rose as I looked at him. "In a good way, I hope."

His face held no emotion. "Yes."

I bit back a laugh. Charles was blunter than me, which was saying a lot!

"Why did you invite us here today?"

I blinked. What was the proper response? I shuffled through a couple of social nicety reasons and then decided on the truth.

I smiled. "I know what it's like to be at odds with a parent and not speak for years."

His eyes widened. "You and your mother-"

"No, my dad. Before this cruise, we hadn't spoken in a decade."

"Indeed. May I ask the reason?"

He could, but I wasn't inclined to give him the details, not that I phrased it that way; Ivy would be proud of me. I tilted my head and shrugged. "We had a misunderstanding."

I could see by his expression that my answer was insufficient but I didn't care; this interview was about him and Ian.

Charles nodded. "I assume Ian has told you of our *misunderstanding*?"

I nodded.

He quirked an eyebrow. "You think I'm in the wrong."

I shook my head. "For wanting a good life for your son? No. But for never finding out how he's choosing to live that life before condemning it? Yes."

I thought I'd gone too far with my honesty. His face was stormy and I wondered if we'd need to call the EMS, but without warning, he chuckled.

I blinked and cocked an eyebrow. "Something I said?"

He laughed out loud at that. "You don't pull punches."

"Nope, sorry. Not in my DNA."

He smiled. "If my memory serves, your mother wasn't known to suffer fools, either."

My eyes widened and he laughed.

"That surprises you?"

I chuckled. "Yes. It's true about my mom. But I expected you to attribute my outspokenness to a degenerate rock star parent."

He blinked and sat back in his chair. "Dear me, what would make you think I'd say that?" He shook his head. "Ian, I suppose. He's probably told you I'm a monster."

I shook my head. "No, he hasn't said anything except how disappointed he's made you." I snorted. "It was your friendship with Judith Fogarty that made me think you'd feel that way."

Charles sat up straight. His eyes were wide. "Is she that bad, then?"

I laughed. "Oh man, she's worse."

I bit my lip and debated with myself for several seconds and then pulled out my phone. I showed Ian's father the short video I'd taken of Judith Fogarty telling Ian how he was going to cause the death of his father if he didn't fall in with the plans Judith was making for him.

Charles' mouth dropped open and then pressed into a firm line.

"That was ... unfortunate."

I snorted. "You think so? That really upset your son. Out in the middle of the ocean and she thought it was fine to tell him his behavior was affecting your health." I huffed and shook my head. "I'm sorry but, how did you ever think Ian could be in a relationship with that woman?"

He shrugged. "I don't know her that well. She's reasonably attractive, they both share a love of music and a similar background ..."

I shook my head. "Except Ian loves and respects all genres of music. Doctor Fogarty thinks classical is the only acceptable type to earn the title of music and she never hesitates to insult those that disagree with her."

I gave him a brief rundown on some of Fogarty's choicer comments about rock musicians.

Charles sighed. "I had no idea." He smirked. "I wonder what she'd think of my jazz collection?"

I laughed. "You philistine!"

He grinned and I saw where Ian got his adorable dimple. "I am a heretic with a pyre waiting."

We both laughed. I sat back and searched his face. He wasn't as harsh of a man as Ian had portrayed. He was just stubborn and prideful.

He cocked his head and raised an eyebrow. "What's that look for?"

My lips curved in a soft smile as my brow furrowed. "Have you really never heard Ian play? Rock and roll I mean."

Charles sighed. "No, much to my shame." He shook his head. "In my defense, he had so much promise. So much talent ..."

"That hasn't changed."

His eyebrows rose and he nodded. "Is that offer of front row seats still up for grabs?"

I grinned. "Play your cards right and I might get you backstage." I winked. "I got an *in* with the band."

Tina

For mid-June, the day was looking to be tolerable. Not a cloud in the sky, the sun was high, and the humidity was low, Perfect weather for an outdoor concert. I'd also managed to get my quasi-in-laws on the road to reconciliation with their son so, all in all, I was feeling pretty good about the day. Until I got roped into cat sitting.

After promising the Buchanans I'd add their names to the VIP list, they'd set out to do some sightseeing and I, like a dummy, went to see if Ivy needed help.

"We're good." Ivy continued checking the perishable delivery against the invoice. "Pete's got everything covered for the rest of the day and I've already helped them prep for dinner. You go on."

"Ok." I started to leave and then remembered something. "Hey, it's a free concert, no assigned seating or anything. But Nikki told me they're setting up an area down front for us. If I don't see you before the concert starts, just show your ID to whoever is checking ..."

Ivy nodded. I was almost out the door when she hollered.

"Hey, Tina!"

I turned and cocked an eyebrow.

She bit her lip and looked uneasy. That should have been my cue to cut and run, but I wasn't paying attention.

"Um, I wasn't supposed to work today ..."

"I know, which is why I offered to help." We'd had a prep cook call off and Saturdays were always busy, the concert in the park just doubled our usual crowds.

"Yeah, I appreciate that but, as I said, everything is done for tonight."

I rolled my eyes. "It's not good, so just spit it out."

Ivy huffed. "Rude!" She pointed at the office. "The thing is, I was walking Sergeant when Pete called about the staff situation and I came right over-"

"Oh no, anything but that-"

"All you have to do is walk him back to my house! Just give him some food and lock the door. If I do it, we'll be late for the-"

"All right, all right. But if I need stitches, you're paying my medical bills."

I went to the office and snapped the leash onto Sergeant's harness, ignoring his delusional mother's protests that he wasn't that bad.

"Come on, hell boy, let's see what havoc you can wreak on an unsuspecting city."

The shortest way to Ivy's townhome was through the park. The main walkways were a bit crowded, so I veered off to a side path to let the little monster sniff around. Walking the big ball of fluff always drew a crowd and people wanted to pet him. I'd need to carry a first aid kit to allow that.

I let Sergeant root around in the azaleas and then decided to walk over and give my VIP additions to Nikki before I forgot.

I scooped up the cat and climbed the steps to the amphitheater. I didn't see Ian or my dad, but Jason and Cole passed me carrying the drum kit, so the rest of the band was probably somewhere nearby.

Nikki, bless her heart, was surrounded by people all clamoring for her attention. She was juggling multiple clipboards and held the phone to her ear with her shoulder. I stood to the side and waited. She put out a couple of fires and then walked over to me, but, just as I started to tell her about Ian's parents and Ivy and Dom, someone rushed over in a panic.

I tuned the crisis out and absently watched Jason shuttling gear back and forth until Nikki gave a frustrated screech.

I cocked an eyebrow. "Problem, Nikki?"

She huffed and rolled her eyes. "Yeah, we've got a vendor needing something, and the clipboard with that info is ..." She growled. "I must have left that one in the equipment trailer ..."

She started to walk off of the stage when several crew members stopped her with questions. I caught her eye. "Hey Nik, I'll go. You said the equipment trailer?"

She nodded. "Yes, I think I left it on top of some of the guitar cases. Thank you!"

I waved and headed for the parking lot. Sergeant Pepper was squirming so I set him down when I reached the trailer. His leash was long enough to let him roam a bit while I hunted for the clipboard. Further inside, the trailer was in deep shadow, so I pulled out my phone for a flashlight. I'd just spotted the clipboard when a mountain of black cases came tumbling down and Sergeant Pepper ran past me like a bat out of hell.

"Oh, you little beast!" I grabbed his leash before he could escape and then turned to assess the damage his snoopy self-had caused.

Guitar cases and some of the canvas drum covers were scattered in a heap but thank goodness nothing seemed to have been damaged, or at least the cases were still closed.

I started to stack them back into some semblance of order when the case in my hand sprang open and something clattered to the floor.

"Shoot!" I bent down to see what had fallen out. "Probably a tuner ..." I muttered as I searched the metal floor using my flashlight. I was about to give up when the light shined on something red.

"Huh, that's odd." I'd picked up a piece of the guitar that'd been broken when Warner was killed. I shook my head at the incompetence of the investigators. They'd left a chunk of the murder weapon!

I shrugged and decided to set it back in the case. I was closing the lid when my gaze landed on something lying on the red velvet where the guitar neck would rest.

"What the ..." A closer look had me frowning. I used two fingers to pick up what looked like one of Jason Young's whisky-soaked toothpicks.

"Come on, Sergeant." I tugged on his leash, paying little attention to him as I pondered how Jason's toothpick could have fallen inside my dad's guitar case.

That it was lying around wasn't that surprising. Jason always seemed to have one of the nasty things in his mouth, but how it could have fallen inside the guitar case was a mystery; he'd have had no reason to be in that case.

I stepped out into the sunshine and stared at the offensive piece of wood. It'd been lying on the prop for the neck. If the guitar had been in the case when it fell from his mouth, the toothpick would have been on top but that wasn't possible because that guitar was in pieces.

Penshaw, or someone, at any rate, had bashed Warner over the head with it. There was no reason for anyone to open the case since the murder because the authorities had taken the broken guitar. Besides, the remaining piece of wood that had fallen out proved no one had opened the case since the murder.

For the toothpick to be in the location I'd found it, it would've had to have been dropped after the guitar was picked up ...

I held the toothpick up and frowned. "So, how did you get-"

A warm gush of air hit the back of my neck as someone sighed. "I wish you hadn't found that."

True Colors

Tina

I JUMPED AND SPUN around just as Jason, a toothpick firmly wedged between his lips, shoved me back into the trailer and slammed the door.

My eyes widened. Gears were turning and pieces were falling into place but at the same time, nothing made sense. Jason sighed and kicked the side of the trailer. "Now what am I gonna do?"

I wasn't sure if he intended me to answer so I kept my mouth closed and concentrated on getting myself and the little demon cat out of the confined space; one conversation with a lunatic in a lifetime was quite enough, thank you.

And, if my suspicions were correct and it'd been Jason Young, and not Penshaw or KC, that had killed Richard Warner, he was as crazy as KC.

All I had to go on was a whisky-soaked toothpick with teeth marks on the end but-I gasped as I remembered something Ian had said.

It was after the doctor had left and Dad had returned to bed. I'd managed to stub my toe and was hunting for a band-aid when Ian frowned and mentioned his confusion over the doctor claiming no passengers had come to his office when Jason had claimed to be at the med center getting a bandage at the time of Warner's murder.

We'd been beyond tired and they'd arrested Penshaw for Warner's murder so we'd just shrugged it off and went to bed. I shook my head at our blindness. Jason had also been the one to claim Warner was a long-time drug dealer.

I'd wondered how he would know that having just met the man, but again, he'd had an alibi for the time of the killing, or so he'd claimed.

"Come on, get going."

My head jerked up and I met Jason's gaze. He was pale and sweat was dripping from his nose. It was hot in the closed trailer, but I suspected nerves were contributing to his distress.

I bit my lip. "Um, what? Wher- where are we going?" I was pretty sure he'd killed Warner. Not just the things I'd found or remembered but because of the way he was acting. If he hadn't killed him, why was he acting so strangely over me finding one of his toothpicks?

I didn't get a chance to ponder because Jason lost his temper and shoved me. I crashed into the trailer door and it swung open. The rush of air was a welcome relief but a glance at the parking lot showed no immediate chance of rescue. I gave a mental middle finger to deja vu and, once again stalled for time by talking with a psycho. I decided to play dumb.

"Jason, what's going on? Why'd you shove me like that?" I edged towards the door and allowed slack in Sergeant Pepper's leash so he could exit the hot trailer.

"Don't. I know that you know, so just stop it."

I didn't have another plan, so I maintained my puzzled look. "I know that you - Dude, what are you smoking?"

I jumped as he kicked the side of the trailer. "Shut up!" He clenched and unclenched his hands and muttered. "What am I gonna do ..."

He didn't seem to be paying attention to me so I edged towards the door. I had one foot on the ground when he lurched around and grabbed my arm.

"Where are you going?" His fingers bit into my upper arm as he stepped down from the trailer and pulled me the rest of the way out.

I grimaced and tried to pull away. "Jason, you're hurting me!"

He snorted. "Like it matters." He shook his head. "Now shut up and let me think."

My eyes widened. He couldn't have made his intentions any clearer. I had to get away from him. Sergeant Pepper hissed and tugged on the leash, giving me an idea, but first, I needed to distract Jason.

"Dude, Ian will kick your ass for this." Jason jerked his head up.

"Let me go."

He snorted. "Not a chance, you know too much." Despite his words, he did release my arm.

I rubbed at my throbbing bicep and started calculating the possibility of grabbing the cat and running into the crowds gathering on the lawn but, just as I started to bend down Jason pulled a screwdriver from his pocket and pressed it against my throat.

I gulped and straightened very slowly. "Jason? Man, this isn't the way ... I'm sure you had a really good reason for doing whatever you did, self-defense even! But harming me isn't going to help-"

"Didn't I tell you to shut your mouth?" He kept the tool's point pressed just below my ear and used his other hand to nudge me to start walking.

Sergeant Pepper wasn't cooperating and for once, I loved the grumpy cat's stubbornness; it allowed me an excuse to drag my feet.

Jason growled. "Stupid cat, drop the leash."

I licked my lips. "I can't do that! He's an indoor cat, he'll get-"

"Pick him up then!"

I quickly complied since he punctuated his words with a prod from the screwdriver tip. Sergeant wasn't happy to be confined but I drew comfort from his fluffy little body. I snuggled him close, prayed he wouldn't bite me, and tried to figure a way out of my predicament.

Jason lowered the hand holding the screwdriver so that the tip was poking my ribs and nodded his head towards the road that ran parallel to the park. "Start walking."

I gulped. Of course, he wanted to go in a direction away from the crowds but that was the last thing I wanted to do. I needed time to think of a way out ...

I slowly started moving across the parking lot. "Jason, you're making a bad situation worse-no, hear me out!"

I sighed as the pressure from the screwdriver lessened, though he didn't stop walking, nor did he lower the tool.

"You wouldn't know this, but Warner was a predator and an all–around sleaze for years. I'm sure you didn't mean to kill him ... you just lost your temper. Temporary insanity-"

"Oh, I meant to kill the bastard."

My eyes widened. "But why?" I turned my head and met his gaze. "You barely knew him!"

Jason's jaw was set, and a nerve twitched in his cheek. His eyes. I shivered. His eyes were cold, hard, and devoid of emotion.

He snorted and came to a stop. "I've known Richard Warner my whole life." His voice was low, and his words were clipped. "He made my childhood a living hell-"

"What? How?" I shook my head. "I don't understand ..."

He glared at me. "Drugs! He supplied my mom with drugs! He fed her habit and kept her a junkie! Keep moving!"

I flinched as he pressed the tip of the screwdriver into my side. My flight or fight reflex was screaming at me. If he jammed the tool into me, would it hit something important? Could I still run before I bled to death?

I bit my lip and wondered if I'd finally lost my mind. My rational brain stepped in before I could test any theories and I returned to my plan of talking until I found a way out.

"I'm so sorry, Jason." I did feel bad for him, but I was also losing patience. I'd grown up with an addicted parent, it was no picnic, but it didn't justify murder; of Warner and especially not of me.

He jerked to a stop. "I don't need your pity! I had everything fixed and then he showed his face again ..."

I frowned. "What was fixed, Jason?"

He huffed. "My mother! I worked two jobs and played every gig I could find. I got enough money saved to get her into a private treatment facility."

His rage must have sapped his strength because all of a sudden his shoulders sagged, and his tone turned soft. He stared into the distance and muttered. "She was clean. Opening for Eclipse was my big break. I could finally focus on my career ..." He looked down at me as the fury once again took over. "Then he turned up. He was moving back to Savannah. I couldn't allow that. He'd get her hooked again, he couldn't risk her being sober."

I cocked my head. "What?" I could understand a dealer not wanting to lose a customer, but God knew there were plenty more to take Jason's mom's place. "Jason, how was your mom's sobriety a risk?"

He huffed and pulled my arm until I followed. "He was afraid she'd talk about the wreck." He shook his head. "The night before the cruise started. He came by the house. I heard him wheedling at mom, trying to get her to take the dope. She refused but it was only a matter of time."

I stopped and stared at him. "What wreck? I don't understand."

He glared at me. "The one that killed Kev Chase!"

I frowned. The wreck that had killed Eclipse's original drummer? That made no sense. Somehow I, or maybe Jason had lost the plot. "What does that have to do with Warner and your mom?"

He sighed and shook his head. "Because Tina, they were both in the car that night. Now move."

I huffed and ignored him. My temper was starting to override my fear. "Yes, so was my dad. He was driving. It was an accident-"

"No, it wasn't!" He wheeled around. The screwdriver pressed into my side as he leaned closer and sneered. "Warner was driving that night and he was drunk."

'No, my dad was-"

"No! It was Warner! He was driving."

I started to shake my head but stopped when Jason put pressure on the tool.

"Yes, he was! That's the whole point!" Jason looked at me and gritted his teeth. "The wreck killed Kev and knocked your dad out. Warner was hurt but he managed to get out of the car and, I don't know, he panicked."

"Jason, there was a trial, testimony-"

"From my mother!" He rolled his eyes. "She saw Warner pull your dad into the front seat and she testified that it was Chad and not Warner that was driving."

My eyes widened as I realized what he was saying. "Dad wasn't drunk. They ruled it an accident, caused by the snow ..."

"Now you're getting it!" He pushed me to start walking. "Warner would have gone to jail for vehicular homicide so he got my mom to lie for him-"

"Why would she do that?"

"Because she was dating Warner and then he kept her supplied with drugs ..."

I ducked my head and nuzzled Sergeant's soft fur as I absorbed what Jason was saying. Warner had turned Jason's mom into a junkie to keep himself out of jail. He'd let my dad think he'd killed his friend-

"If ever there was a 'he needed killing' defense ..."

Jason snorted. "Yeah, but it's not going to get that far. They've arrested that security guy. I get rid of you and everything can go back to normal ..."

I gasped as he jerked my arm and changed our direction so that we were headed towards a side street. "My car is down there."

Alarm bells started clanging in my head. If he got me to the car ... I had to act. I looked to my left.

The lawn was filled with people. Sounds of instruments being tuned mingled with the laughter and chatter of the crowds.

The sun was setting. With the heavy canopy of Live Oaks, the shadows were deepening. It'd be fully dark in an hour. I squinted.

We were less than fifty feet from two off-duty cops hired for security. A few feet beyond them I could just make out Nikki's bright orange hair and beside her were Ivy and Dom. That gave me an idea.

Sergeant Pepper had been remarkably tolerant of my holding him, but I knew the little monster could be provoked. A well-placed rub of his tummy would probably get him to hiss.

"Ouch, you brat!" My plan succeeded too well. Sergeant hissed and then bit me for good measure.

Jason scowled and jabbed at my ribs with the screwdriver. "Put that damn thing down and let's go!"

"Okay, okay, give me a second." I slipped the leash from the harness and set Sergeant down. With a silent prayer that he'd stay put, I let the leash dangle from my hand and stood up. Jason was nervously looking around and that was my opportunity.

I raised my hand and flicked the leather leash like a horsewhip. It hit its mark, cutting a slash across Jason's cheek.

Jason yelled; the screwdriver fell from his hand as he raised it to his wounded face. I grabbed Sergeant Pepper and started running toward the stage.

Jason was right behind me. I could hear his feet hitting the pavement. Any second, he'd be within touching distance. My gaze fell on the security team, and I screamed. "He's got a gun!"

People turned, someone started shrieking, and the cops sprang into action and tackled Jason ... I kept running.

Out of breath, beyond terrified, and struggling with a very angry cat, I reached Ivy and thrust the hissing beast into her arms as I collapsed onto the grass. "Next time, walk your own darn cat!"

Sink or Swim

Tina

I SAT NEXT TO Ian's father and waited for the concert to start. The arrest of Jason Young had delayed everything by about an hour, but things had finally settled enough that the guys could take the stage.

Dad and Ian had worried me to death. They'd fussed, fumed, and fretted as the EMTs checked me over and then declared the concert was canceled, regardless of my being perfectly fine. I was tired and a bit achy from the manhandling and tension, but Chad Crawford's stubborn genes resided in me. I'd argued with both men, and won by using my father's tactics; the show had to go on.

Ivy and Dom had run Sergeant Pepper home while the police did their thing and had returned just as Ian's parents walked up to the security cordon. Ian and my dad had already made their way backstage, and the final checks were being conducted.

The concert would start any minute and I hadn't told Ian what I'd done. I bit my lip and debated sending him a text or even running backstage and delivering the news in person. My mind ran through Ian's possible reactions should he spot his parents sitting beside me. He would be shocked and confused, but Ian was a professional, he should take it in stride ... I hoped.

Either way, it was too late to do anything about it now. I scooted to the edge of my seat as the house lights dimmed. As if from a distance, the long, sustained sound of a car horn filled the night. As it faded, Benny T began a steady rhythm with the kick drum. Cliff fell in with the bass line. The crowd was still, a unified feeling of anticipation hovered over us all as we waited for the familiar riff that marked the opening of Drivin Rain.

A roar went up as the lights came up in sync with Ian's guitar. Twice through the intro and then Dad's baritone echoed through the park announcing to the world, or at least the historic district, that Eclipse was in the house.

I bounced along with the beat, smiling as Ian and Cliff traded licks and Dad played to the audience. Caught up in the atmosphere, it wasn't until the third song that I turned to look at Ian's parents. Diane was enjoying the music. I doubted it'd take much coaxing to get her on her feet. Ian's dad was another matter.

Charles was sitting in his chair. Back straight, arms folded across his chest, lips pressed into a firm line ... my heart sank as it appeared my plans had failed; hearing Ian play had not softened his father's opinions. I tried to catch his eye, but Charles' gaze was glued to the stage, following every move that Ian made. Diane looked my way and bit her lip. She cut her gaze to Charles and winced, and I could tell she was thinking along the same lines as me.

I debated saying, or rather, shouting something to Charles. But what would I say? His body language suggested he was no closer to accepting Ian's chosen career than he'd been before. If seeing the joy on his son's face and hearing the melodies Ian wrung from wood, metal, and electricity didn't give Charles an appreciation for his son's talent and gift then nothing I might say could. I sighed and sat back to enjoy the show. No sense in borrowing trouble beforehand. I had no doubt my reckoning would come all too soon.

The rest of the night was a blast of dancing to great songs, and watching Ian and Dad entertaining the crowd;

they made a great team. I briefly pondered what would happen when Drew's arm healed. Eclipse had always been a four-piece band. They brought musicians in for certain parts when recording but, the core band was just Cliff, Dad, Drew, and now Benny T. Would they make a place for Ian?

Bad Opera was essentially defunct with Jason going to prison. Cole had always been a fill-in for Benny T. I nibbled on my bottom lip and wondered if Savannah could support a solo career for Ian or if he'd take to the road again? Would he return to L.A.? My stomach rolled at the thought of him leaving, but I couldn't make him stay. The question was, would I go with him if he did leave? Would he even ask?

My heart said yes. If Ian asked, I'd follow him to the ends of the Earth. I glanced down the row of chairs and watched Ivy dancing and having a good time. It was so rare to see her let her hair down. My best friend took life too seriously and I often didn't take it seriously enough: it made us a great pair.

I wanted to be a partner in the Cosmic Cafe, that was my goal and, even if Ivy somehow came up with the money that she needed another way ... the little inner voice that liked to lecture me was shaking her head. Her lip was jutted out, too. My voice of reason was gearing up to deliver an epic scold and I deserved it. No matter how much I loved Ian, I would be foolish to let my dreams go.

In the end, it was Ian's career and all I could do was be supportive while following my own chosen path.

"Hello, Savannah!"

My dad talking to the crowd cut my depressing thoughts off at the knees, for which I was grateful; I'd been working myself into a state of anxiety over things that hadn't happened!

"This city is a welcome sight any time but after our cruise from hell? Whew, it was a rough nine days, y'all!"

Laughter rippled across the lawn.

"You'd have to be living under a rock not to have heard about everything that went on while we were floating on the high seas. Drew sends his love and wants y'all to know that he's on the mend and hoping to be back with the band in a couple of months."

My eyes widened. So my assumptions about Ian's time with Eclipse ending soon weren't far off ...

"I miss Drew, he's been my best buddy for over forty years! But I have to say, I'm honored to play with this kid, and he's homegrown!" Dad pointed towards Ian. "No disrespect meant, by the way. When you get to be my age, they all start looking like kids!"

Someone in the audience yelled True Story and everyone laughed. When things settled, Dad continued.

"The man that has stepped into Drew Alton's shoes is Ian Buchanan. I have played with some of the finest musicians on the planet and this guy easily has a seat on that elite bus." Dad walked over to Ian and offered his hand. "It's a privilege to share the stage, man."

They shook hands and then Dad turned back to the audience. "Y'all give it up for the man of the hour!" The audience went wild, as Ian stepped to center stage.

I glanced at Charles Buchanan. He'd scooted to the edge of his seat and was staring intently at his son. I hadn't seen any sign that Ian knew his father was in the audience.

"Yo, Savannah!" Ian waited until the audience quieted. "Man, it's good to be home." His right hand fiddled with the knobs of his guitar as he looked out at the crowd. "Stepping in for Drew Alton ..." he snorted. "Somebody pinch me!"

More laughter erupted. When it petered out, Ian glanced to his right and my dad nodded. I frowned. What were they silently communicating about?

I didn't have to wait long to find out. Ian pulled the guitar strap over his head and handed it to a tech as he started to walk around the stage.

"Meeting the members of Eclipse was a lifelong dream. Playing with them feels surreal and writing a song with Chad Crawford?" He snorted. "Chad and I wrote this next piece while he was recovering from the concussion, so if it makes no sense, you know who to blame!"

The audience chuckled. “Seriously though, we’ve been through a lot over the last week or so and not all of it was bad.”

Ian’s gaze searched the front seats until he found me. He winked. “I reconnected with the love of my life on that cruise-“

The audience clapped. Ian smiled and nodded. “And Chad mended a relationship that had been rocky for years. Both of us walked away from that awful cruise with a happy ending and a new future. As musicians do, we expressed our feelings with music. This-”

His gaze returned to me and then moved one seat over. His eyes widened and his voice broke. He frowned at me and then cleared his throat and returned his attention to the crowd. “This song is called Broken Chords.”

The stage went dark. Charles leaned over and asked. “Is it over? What was that about a song?”

I stared at the stage. From my vantage point, I could see people moving around, though it was mostly shadows. I’d lost sight of Ian and Dad. I shook my head. “I don’t know what they’re doing, but-“

A single spotlight pierced the darkness. On the right-hand side of the stage stood a baby grand piano. Seated just behind and to the right of the piano was a string quartet. Before I could wonder at it being there, Ian took a seat on the bench. Eclipse had always been a guitar-driven band. In my memory, they'd never had keyboard parts, much less orchestration.

Charles looked at me. His brow was furrowed, and confusion was clear in his expression. I shrugged and shook my head; his guess was as good as mine.

I focused on Ian. He looked to the quartet, glanced over to Benny T and Cliff, and then with a nod to my dad, his hands fell onto the keys. A simple melody, tinkling, and sweet. Ian's hands danced feather-light and then he lifted his hands from the keys, paused, and let them fall back to the piano.

My breath caught as the melody turned darker, richer, and full of depth. His fingers flew up and down the keyboard in complicated chord progressions, the quartet struck up a counterpoint harmony, and a soaring classical piece washed over the stage. The song built to a crescendo ... and then a sound, reminding me of the pounding surf, roared over the instruments, slowly drowning out first the strings, and then Ian's piano.

A hush settled over the park. I felt like I was standing on the edge of a cliff, waiting, anticipating ... from the corner of my eye I saw Charles perched on the edge of his seat, mouth dropped open and eyes wide. The kick drum began a steady rhythm, one-two, double tap on the snare, one-two, double-tap ... Cliff dropped in with a bass line, the stage went dark.

All around me, people were murmuring in wonder and confusion. Another double-tap from Benny T and the stage lights popped on, revealing Dad and Ian center stage. Dad began playing the same melody that Ian had played on the piano. The music swelled, and the quartet came in, accompanying the band.

All the time, Ian had stood, head down, perfectly still, a man and his guitar. The melody came around again and in a flash, his arm rose, and then in a sweeping movement he launched into a riff of power chords and the audience erupted.

Goosebumps pricked my arms and I realized I'd been holding my breath. My eyes widened as Ian started to sing and I began to understand what their song, Broken Chords, was about.

"Family ... lovers ... friends ... tied by cords of love and hope."

I swallowed past a lump in my throat as Dad looked at me and harmonized with Ian.

"The fabric of life lies torn and bleeding when the cords break. Cast adrift, aimless ..., searchin' a frozen world for a ray of light, a drop of warmth ..."

My eyes met Ian's. He held my gaze.

"The cords are mended, my soul is patched by the warmth of your smile, the laughter in your eyes ..."

Tears overflowed and spilled down my cheeks as the song continued. I jumped as Charles wrapped his arm around my shoulders. Our eyes met and he smiled and mouthed, thank you.

On the Right Track

Ian

I SAT BACK IN my chair and stared at the people surrounding me. After a gig, I was always wired, and coming back down to the real world left me off-kilter until I'd decompressed. This concert had been no different except hours later, sitting in the Cosmic Cafe, everything still felt surreal. Tina had once again been in mortal danger and my head was reeling over the arrest of my oldest friend.

I still hadn't processed all of the facts, but knowing Jason's temper, and his years of misery over his mother's addictions, I could see how he'd have snapped. While I could understand what had driven him to kill Warner, his intention to get away with it by silencing Tina was something I'd never get over or forgive.

I reached over and intertwined our hands. She smiled and glanced at me, cocking an eyebrow. I winked and shook my head and she returned to her conversation with my mom. If the shock of Jason's actions had made my head spin, being on stage and seeing my parents sitting next to Tina had knocked the wind out of me. I had yet to learn how she'd convinced them to attend; maybe she was a witch. She'd certainly cast a spell over me and quite possibly over my dad.

After the show, she'd brought them backstage and my whole world had tipped on its axis; without a word, my dad had pulled me into a hug and whispered I'm proud of you. My dad was proud of me. I snorted and shook my head.

Stunned didn't begin to describe how I felt. Hours later, I was still dazed and just a bit confused. My gaze shifted to Chad and my dad. They were laughing about something. My eyes widened. They were discussing music theory and dad was inviting Chad to do a series of guest lectures-my God, would wonders never cease?

I smirked and looked at the woman who'd breezed back into my life, bringing the sun with her. She was talking with my mom about plants. From what I could gather, they'd made plans for Tina and Ivy to come out to the nursery and set up a farm to table something or other.

I yawned and stood up. If I was gonna let Tina stay and enjoy the evening I'd need to move around; the day was catching up to me. I wandered to the cafe window. The park was shrouded in shadows and most signs of the concert were gone. Everything was back to normal, and all was fast becoming right with my world or soon would be.

For four days, a box had been burning a hole in my pocket. As happy as I was to have my relationship with my parents restored, or at least on the right road, all I could think about was being alone with my girl and telling her how much she meant to me.

I jumped as Tina's arms wound around my waist and she laid her cheek against my back. The sound of chairs scraping the floor and calls of good night and meet again soon sounded from across the room.

"Everyone calling it a night, then?"

She tightened her arms and then stepped back. "Yep, it's been a heck of a day. I think we're all ready for bed."

I turned and waggled my eyebrows at her. She playfully slapped my arm. "Sleep, Ian Buchanan!"

I started to make a smart reply when my parents walked over. I smiled and accepted a kiss on the cheek from Mom, and then Dad offered his hand.

"Y'all be careful drivin back to the 'boro tonight."

Dad put his hand on the small of my mother's back. "Eh, your mom was sneaky. Apparently, we have a room at that B & B down the street."

I grinned and looked at Mom. She smirked. "Call it a staycation. It's been quite a while since we've been in Savannah."

I nodded. "Well, we can meet back here for breakfast if you want." I shrugged. "Maybe poke around town?"

Dad snorted and looked at Tina. "Seems the ladies have also made plans."

My eyebrows rose and I looked at Tina. She wrinkled her nose, unrepentant as ever.

"What is on our agenda then?"

She laughed. "Nothing more strenuous than a day at the beach house! Dad and Nikki invited us."

I nodded. "Sand, Surf, and loafing sounds good to me!"

We agreed to meet back at the Cosmic in the morning and my parents headed out. Chad and Nikki had already left so Tina locked up and we walked the two blocks to her car.

The ride back to River Street was quick. She parked the Mini in the alley behind the loft and we started across the cobblestones.

"I am ready for pajamas and a cup of hot tea, how about you?"

I grabbed her hand. "Yeah, but let's walk along the river for a minute."

She frowned but agreed.

Music streamed from a handful of bars still open. A few couples were strolling like us, but the river walk was mostly deserted. A warm breeze ruffled the trees and moonlight danced upon the water. I led her toward the rail, and we watched as a freighter made its slow and steady crawl to the port. I sighed and pulled her to stand in front of me, her back against my chest. I leaned over and rested my chin on her shoulder as I murmured. "Thanks."

She cocked her head and from the corner of my eye, I could see her lips forming a smile.

"You're welcome but what did I do?"

I snorted. "Waved a magic wand? Wiggled your nose? Cast a spell?"

She chuckled and turned in my arms. "What are you talking about?"

I met her gaze and smiled. "My dad said he was proud of me."

Her eyes welled with tears, and she pressed a light kiss to my lips. "I'm so glad."

"It's you. You're magic."

She rolled her eyes. "Hardly. He just needed a bit of prodding."

My eyebrows rose but I let it go. I'd find out how she got my father to the concert tomorrow. My mind was on other things.

All was right with the universe, and it was time I made sure it stayed that way. I reached into my pocket and pulled out a little black velvet box. I used my thumb to pop the lid.

Tina's eyes grew wide. "Is that, oh Ian, no ..."

And just like that, the stars went out.

Ship Shape

Tina

I BLEW OUT A breath and grabbed Ian's hand. "Let me explain, please!" He tugged his hand away and backed up.

"What's to explain? No, is pretty self-explanatory."

I sighed. "It .., I didn't mean it like that." I rolled my eyes. "You surprised me!"

He snorted. "See if I do that again!"

I huffed a laugh and stepped closer, wrapping my hand around his arm as I looked down at the ring lying in solitary splendor on a bed of white satin.

My head was spinning, and I had to wonder how a man with perfect rhythm could have such bad timing. I'd just lived one of the longest, most emotionally crazy days of my life, second only to the one I'd had on the ship. I was doing good to put my shoes on the right feet and walk in a straight line and my wonderful boyfriend decided to spring a proposal on me.

I shook my head and tried to get my head in the game. I ran a finger over the satin. "It's beautiful ..." I looked up and smiled. "Is it vintage?"

Ian cocked his head. His eyes narrowed a bit, and his smile was hesitant. "It is. Has papers and everything. Owned by some Roaring Twenties heiress or something." His gaze searched my face. "I - I thought you'd like it. If you don't that's okay, we can-"

"No! No, it's" Tears pricked my eyes as I chuckled. "It's beautiful and perfect, and - I love you ..."

Ian frowned. "But? I sense a but."

I swallowed and put space between us so I could gather my thoughts. How did you reject someone's proposal and not kill the relationship? I huffed. Where was the conditional rejection section of the couples manual when I needed it?

"Tina? What's going on?"

I sighed. “Nothing, it’s-“

“You did mean that no.”

His expression was wooden and the glow was gone from his blue eyes. I felt like a heartless beast, but ... “Not exactly.” I grabbed his hand. “Let’s walk, and put that gorgeous ring away before we get mugged!”

I waggled my eyebrows at that but Ian didn’t even crack a smile. I bit my lip and looked out at the river. “Okay, hear me out.” I glanced at his face in time to see his lips purse but he nodded.

I smiled. “Thanks. So, I love you.” I peeped at him from beneath my lashes. “That’s a given, please don’t ever doubt that.”

“Do you?”

I stopped walking and scowled at him. “See? That’s not hearing me out! That’s you letting emotions and insecurities-“

“Well, what am I supposed to think?”

I took a deep breath. I was getting mad and that wasn’t going to help anything. Somebody had to be the adult in the relationship and that appeared to now be me.

I leaned against the stone railing and waited until Ian had met my gaze. “Hi, nice to see you again, can we talk now?”

He huffed, then he smirked. “Being an ass?”

I held up two fingers. “Just a bit, a smidgen, a trifling, a ta-“

"Funny."

I grinned. "Well, I thought so." He was smiling. Reluctantly, but it was there and I'd take it.

"Seriously, I do love you and there is no one else I would want to spend my life with-"

"So why aren't you marrying me?"

My shoulders fell and I shrugged. "I don't know- I don't!" I ignored Ian's eye roll and plunged on, searching for words as I tried to decipher my own feelings. "I guess it's- how do you envision us being married?"

I crossed my arms over my chest and put the ball back into Ian's court.

He frowned. "Wha- well I don't know!" He scoffed. "I figured you'd want something on the beach, or that island your dad owns, though he doesn't have any buildings out there yet and no electricity, but if you want to hold a ceremony there ..."

I shook my head. "Ian, I didn't mean literally how we should get married! Men!" I rolled my eyes. "Look, day to day, week to week, month to month, year to year, how do you see us living. What's our future look like, Ian?"

His eyes widened and I silently cheered as my point struck home. "There. Now, do you see? We haven't talked about being married, we haven't talked about the future at all.

Ian wrapped me in a hug and rested his chin on the top of my head. "That's because you almost didn't have a future. Not once, but twice!"

His arms tightened until I squeaked. "Ian!" I wiggled and he relaxed his hold, though not by much. "Ian, is that why you're proposing? Because you got scared I'd-"

"Don't say it! And no, well, not entirely ... can't I just want to marry you?"

I smiled and bit back a laugh. He looked kinda pitiful that I was making him figure out his motives and feelings. I took pity on him. "Let's make a deal."

His eyes narrowed and he looked wary. "What kind of a deal?"

I smirked. "So suspicious!" I fished the jewelry box from his pocket and slid the stunning art deco ring onto the third finger of my left hand. "I'll marry you, but-"

"Oh, here we go with another but!"

I ignored his grumble because his eyes were once again twinkling and his dimple made an appearance. "But ... we have a long engagement and we discuss-"

"Okay, okay, no ceremony next week and yakking about feelings and futures, got it." He waggled his eyebrows. "Now can we get to the kissing part?"

He put actions to words before I could counter his nonsense and by the time we came up for air I'd forgotten what I was gonna say.

Ian sighed and hugged me close to his chest and lifted my hand. He dropped a light kiss onto the ring and then grinned. "Now you'll be safe."

My eyes widened and I bit back a laugh. Time enough to tell him his ring didn't have superpowers.

Hmmm, superpowers. I wondered who had robbed the comic store that had moved in next door to the Cosmic Café.

The End

Thank you for reading Broken Chords,

I hope you enjoyed spending time with Tina and the gang.

If so, I'd appreciate a review.

Join the Cozy Crew Club!

Meet Ivy's crazy Aunt Fey in a prequel available only to my newsletter subscribers!

Fey Goes to Jail

Fey Michaels, a cashier at an Oklahoma Indian Casino, lives by the motto, don't retrace the footsteps of your past, you might fall in!

She lives and loves freely, making the most of her one bite at the apple called life, but being the sole guardian for her ten-year-old niece, Ivy isn't always conducive to being a free spirit.

Knowing a child needs stability, Fey tries to settle and keep her feet on the ground, but hooking up with a Shaman, who thinks ten is the perfect age to begin exploring his personal brand of spiritualism, sets off a chain of events that puts Fey in the crosshairs of law enforcement and Ivy in mortal danger.

Fey and Ivy will have to think fast and keep their cool if they want to make it off of the Reservation alive.

www.rachellynneauthor.com

Also By

Rachel Lynne

The Cosmic Café Mystery Series

RING OF LIES

Join Ivy, Dom, Tina, and Sergeant Pepper in the adventure that started it all!

HOLLY JOLLY JABBED

A Christmas Novella in the Cosmic Café Universe
When someone gets their tinsel in a tangle ... the holly isn't so jolly!

New Series Coming Soon

THE HOLLY DAYE MYSTERY SERIES

Retired Sheriff's deputy, Holly Daye does a favor for a friend and ends up embarking on a new career as an events decorator.

Holly's artistic abilities gain her clients from all over the Lowcountry of South Carolina but it's her desire to help others, coupled with a cop's cynicism and a healthy dose of curiosity that lands her knee-deep in mysteries time and again.

Masquerades and Murder

(September 22, 2022)

Carolers and Corpses

(November 18, 2022)

Made in the USA
Columbia, SC
29 October 2024

44891671R00237